The Coffee House Murders

VICTOR MOSS

ISBN: 978-1-960399-26-7

Printed in the United States of America

This book is strictly a fictional account of the police officers and detectives of the Denver Police Department including descriptions of physical settings and the Department's rules and procedures. This book is strictly for entertainment. All characters are imaginary, and any similarity to actual persons is simply a coincidence.

The author is not aware of any criminal or corrupt cops as described in the book. Instead, the author has deep admiration for the hard work and dedication of the men and women who chose to serve and protect society even though their lives may be taken away from them in an instant.

To my wife, children and grandchildren, who have given me support and encouragement to keep writing.

Acknowledgments

I would like to thank my daughter, Katherine Stafford and my friends, Melanie Tappen and Keith Macari, for their advice and suggested corrections. I would also like to thank my sister and her husband, Mary and Duane Janssen, for their encouragement and their useful comments and suggestions.

Above all, I have enormous praise for my wife, Rita Moss, for her unwavering support and the many hours she spent reading and discussing each segment. Her suggestions and editing were truly invaluable.

About The Author

Victor Moss has been an attorney engaged in the private practice of law since 1974 in both Pueblo and Denver, Colorado. Prior to that time, he had been an assistant attorney general for the State of New Mexico and assistant city attorney for Pueblo, Colorado. His prior books are Beware the Wolves: A Soviet WWII Love Story, No Return Home, and The Soul Named Samantha.   He lives with his wife in Highlands Ranch, Colorado.

CHAPTER 1

Present day, Denver, Colorado.

MARCUS MILLER barged his way past a shocked assistant into Jeffrey Bowman's office, slamming the door behind him. His face, with seamed lips, was red with anger. He was enraged, sweat beading his brow. Stunned by the fury emanating from the man, Bowman jerked back, pressing himself deep into the back of his soft-leather desk chair. Never before, in the fourteen years that they were partners. Had there been a reason to fear Miller, but now terror gripped Bowman. Marcus banged on the desk with both of his broad fists, and Bowman's heart pounded, almost matching the rhythm of drumming. Bowman mirrored Marcus' heavy and hard breathing. He felt a sudden intense headache, an indication that his blood pressure had gone through the roof.

Marcus launched his body over the desk and shoved his large bearded face only inches from Bowman's. Bowman reflexively flinched away from the wild man. His chair rolled to the edge of the credenza standing below the office windows. He vaulted out of the chair and moved to the corner of the room as Marcus slid off the desk and came around it with his fist ready to strike. Bowman tried to get to the other corner, but Marcus swiftly blocked him. Bowman shut his eyes, waiting for the onslaught. After taking a couple of deep breaths, he said, "Marcus, for God's sake, what's wrong? What in hell pissed you off? Sit down. Let's talk!"

Marcus maintained his threatening stance. "What's wrong? What's wrong? You're selling our business right from under me, you SOB. Why do I have to hear that our coffee enterprise is up for sale? Why do I have to hear it from a broker? You bastard! Prick! You're going to ruin my income, my life."

"Calm down, Marcus," Bowman said meekly, his voice quavering as were his hands. "I only discussed the possibility of a sale with the broker. We're partners; how could I cut you out? I was going to talk to you about it." Bowman exhaled and took a couple of deep breaths while intently eyeing his partner. But Marcus's rage didn't seem to subside. Instead, to his chagrin, his partner's massive fingers clenched into a fist. Bowman knew that he was no match for the larger, younger partner. His insides shook, and his breathing shallowed. Eyeing the distance to the door for an escape, he realized Marcus would block him. Marcus towered with his legs apart, his jaw clenched, breathing like a bull ready to attack the matador. *The fact that he hadn't moved shows some restraint,* Bowman thought hopefully.

Bowman tried to calm him, "Hey, sit down. Let's discuss this. Why are you so worked up? It's a good thing if we sell the business. We get a good price, split it, and both of us are happy." He didn't dare add that a reason he wanted to get out of the partnership was that he had proof that Marcus was stealing him blind. Marcus doctored the books, keeping two sets, and over the last year or so, Bowman's share of the net profits was getting smaller each month. Also, he was tired of the business, especially the stress of buying coffee beans with the fragile third-world negotiations. Enough is enough. But now was not the time to accuse the furious man, who appeared ready to obliterate him- skimming from the business. Whatever words he spoke did not entirely calm his partner, but at least he listened. "Marcus, as I said, I just wanted to explore options with a broker. See what a market analysis would show. You've probably noticed that I have been burned out lately. I have other pressing obligations and have to get rid of assets."

Relieved that the more he talked, the more Marcus's demeanor seemed to cool. He was breathing hard but stayed silent for a minute as though debating his next move. Suddenly, a devilish look came into Miller's blazing eyes, his jaw stiffened, and his face turned brighter crimson. "Not my freaking problem that you're burned out or have other issues," he yelled. "You're not going to interfere with my income from this business. You and your prima donna wife are always flashing money around while I'm struggling. Always had to put up with you, but no more." Looking at Miller's rage-mottled face, Bowman's fear intensified. *He's mad enough to kill me!*

"Hey, hey, Marcus. Hold off." Bowman backed toward the corner as far as he could, almost tipping over a bust of Winston Churchill. "Let's not make a scene here," he pleaded. "Everyone will hear us. Sit down, and we'll talk about this." Bowman's hands were in front of him as if expecting a punch. "We used to talk about these things before. Please, Marcus, let's sit down. We can work this out. Who knows who can hear us in the next room? They may even be calling the cops, which would be very embarrassing." Marcus glanced briefly toward the closed door, realizing that he was indeed creating a scene. *I'll get him later,* he thought. He stopped his advance and stared with eyes stony with anger, deeply inhaling and exhaling, his wide chest heaving.

For an interminable moment, Miller stood silent, his face inches from Bowman's. Bowman could feel his breath and discern a faint smell of alcohol.

Suddenly, Miller backed off. Despite his anger, there is still an ounce of reason. That this is not the place for a confrontation. He could get into serious legal trouble and any gossip about their argument would, in fact, be bad for business.

He relaxed his fists, stepped back, turned to the door and started walking away. Abruptly, he turned around, facing Bowman. Marcus hissed, his voice raspy, "You're rich and don't need this business, but this is my only income, damn it. I won't let you do it. You hear me? I will never give you permission to sell the business. Go to hell. I'm the one who built it up from nothing. I'm the one who put my blood, sweat and tears into it. All you did was put money into it."

Bowman wanted to yell back and remind him that if it weren't for his money, there would be no business; there would be no income. They wouldn't be here today arguing. But he realized he was dealing with a madman and kept quiet. Marcus continued to glare at him with those penetrating gray eyes drilling a hole through his head. "You bastard, if you made up your mind to sell, I won't let you."

Now anger overriding his fear, Bowman blurted out with a shaky voice, "If you don't agree to sell, I'll bring a partition action in court and force a sale."

At that, Marcus once again approached Bowman, slamming both fists on the desk, "You're not going to sell this business. I'll see to that. Back off if you know what's good for your health."

"What are you going to do, kill me? Read the agreement, if anything happens to me, my wife has my fifty percent."

"We'll see about that." Jabbing his index finger at Bowman, he hissed, "I'm warning you, Bowman, you better back off of selling this business."

CHAPTER 2

IN A crisp blue suit, a starched white shirt, a solid silk red tie tied snugly around his thin neck and his short black hair meticulously combed in the latest style, Clint Hawk walked confidently through the door of the homicide unit of District Six of the Denver Police Department. It was his first day as a detective, and he wanted to impress. All eight people in the room looked up from their work, gaping at him as though he had fallen to earth from another planet. An attractive young woman, her blonde hair flowing down her slender shoulders, sat at the metal desk closest to the door. She smiled pleasantly at Hawk. "Hello, I'm Clint Hawk, and I've been assigned to this unit."

"Yes, hello," the woman said, her smile broadening. "I'm very pleased to meet you. We heard we're getting another detective, but I didn't expect anyone… ah…so young. My name is Marcie Turner and I'm the office geek, the only civilian in this room. I do the computer work, help with the research, study camera footage, stuff like that." Hawk returned the grin, his bright white teeth gleaming as he peered directly into her dazzling blue eyes, which reminded him of a brilliant cloudless day. Marcie's face flushed pink as she returned his gaze. "Here, let me introduce you to everyone."

Hawk looked around the large, rectangular olive-green room plastered with the bulletin and white boards filled with charts and photos. All eyes were still fixed on him. Of the seven at their desk, most were men, but there were two female detectives. The detectives seemed to be a motley crew. One had on jeans and a sweatshirt. One wore a dress shirt and a windbreaker; the rest had various colors of jackets and ties. The women were better dressed than the men; both were wearing pant suits. Overall, Hawk thought the look was *wear what you want.* He felt overdressed with his fine suit, but he didn't care. Dressing properly was his style. His mother always told him that people judged him by his clothes. However, he tugged on his tight collar and made a mental note to dress a little more comfortably.

Except for Marcie and one of the woman detectives, no one else appeared to be overly friendly, although they nodded with a smile. They surely overheard his conversation with Marcie, yet no one rose to meet him. *I get it,* he thought; *they are a club, they're used to each other and they don't appreciate changes.* "That's okay, Marcie, I don't want to take you away from your work, I'll get to know them soon enough." Nevertheless, Hawk gave them a wave and all waved back, then quickly stuck their heads back into their work.

Realizing that the reception for the new man was less than welcoming with no one offering to show him around, Marcie stood up and said, "Detective Hawk, you'll need to check in with Lieutenant Kent Bradford, he's in charge of this unit. The big boss, Captain MacGregor, is on vacation and you won't be able to meet her. The Lieutenant is probably expecting you. His office is through that door on the right, the one with all the windows. That way, the border collie can watch over his sheep." She chuckled, throwing her flowing silky hair back, appearing to be a fun-loving, care-free person. "I'll take you to him." Hawk returned the laugh as he followed Marcie, noting her hourglass figure and the slight wiggle in her step. She wore khaki beige pants and a light blue shirt that hugged her body. He was also quick to notice that she did not wear a wedding band. Marcie knocked on the door, and instantly, a gruff voice growled, "Come in."

"Lieutenant, this is the new detective, Clint Hawk." And with that introduction, she returned to her desk.

In a well-fitted tan suit jacket and a maroon button-down collar shirt accented by a silk-striped blue tie, Bradford cast a long measuring glare at Hawk as the rookie approached. The Lieutenant was a handsome sallow-skinned man with salt and pepper hair combed straight back with no part. He didn't rise to welcome him but motioned for Hawk to have a seat in front of his walnut-colored veneer desk. He allowed Hawk to sit in silence for a few minutes while he read over what looked like a report. Finally, with a knitted brow over his brown eyes, he thundered out in his deep, booming voice, exhibiting a wry smile. "So, you're the wunderkind that the Chief forced on me. Some kind of whiz kid with a master's in psychology from the University of Colorado. Making detective after only four years on the force. And what makes you think that you should already be in the homicide unit?"

Hawk felt as if he was in the hot seat in his high school principal's office. He realized that the Lieutenant was purposely trying to intimidate him. "I suppose, sir, that after I received a couple of commendations, the Denver Police Life Saving Medal and the Merit award, the chief appointed me to investigative duty and assigned me to the Sixth District and your unit. I realize this may not be a permanent promotion, and I serve at the pleasure of the chief and you."

"You got that right." Appearing displeased, he added, "This is not permanent. So, the chief likes you, huh? But it doesn't much matter here. You will do as I say or else, you're out of this unit. Understand?"

"Yes, sir. You will not receive any problems from me."

"Oh, you're a smooth talker, aren't you? Well, you better not give me any grief. Understand?"

"Yes, of course."

"Good. Now that you're here, who shall I team you up with? Since you're such a greenhorn and don't know squat about being a detective or solving a homicide, I'll give you the oldest here to teach you the ropes." The Lieutenant's full gray mustache seemed to twitch, and his eyes betrayed a devious inside joke of some kind. At that moment, Hawk realized that he would not be given anyone who could teach him much. *Sure, he will, with all the bad habits and old ways of doing things.* Hawk did not like it a bit, but he had no right to object, so he kept silent, wondering who his ancient partner would be. Bradford stood and went to the door. He was rather tall, about 6'4", four inches taller than Hawk, and considerably heavier with a bulging beer belly. Hawk opined that this was typical for so many fifty-something-year-old men. Hawk had sworn to himself that he'd do whatever was required to keep his gut flat. Sticking his head out the door, Bradford bellowed, "Wally, get in here."

Hawk heard a man grunt as the chair scraped across the tile floor. A minute later, an older man with a mostly white thinning head of hair and a large gut sauntered into the room. Clumsily, he slammed his elbow in the door jamb and swore. He wore a light brown plaid jacket that was unbuttoned but still looked too tight and black pleated pants. A greenish-blue tie hung loosely around his thick neck, a grease stain and yet another blotch decorated his light-yellow shirt. With labored breath, still rubbing his injured elbow, and without an invitation to do so, he sat down in one of the three chairs that faced the desk. "Yeah, Lieutenant, you wanted to see me? Hope it isn't what I think it is?" Hawk's assumption that Bradford would assign him a worn-out partner was correct. This only reinforced his suspicion that it was Bradford's intention to make him look bad from the beginning. *It's all part of his scheme to show the chief that I'm a loser.*

"This is our new man here, Clint Hawk. Hawk, this is Detective Wally Murphy. Wally, I'm going to reassign you as his partner, at least for a while."

"No. Please, Lieutenant." Wally turned his attention to Hawk and said, "Nothing personal, bud, I'm sure you'd be a great partner, but I don't want to break in anyone new." He then focused on Bradford, "I've been partnering with Jeffries for over five years and want to stay with him. I don't want to babysit a rookie, not this close to my pension."

"Sorry, Wally, but that's the way it's going to be."

"Who will Jeffries work with then?"

"He's going to work solo for a while. He seems to do better when he's alone," Bradford said. "He'll let you know if he needs your help." He looked hard at the disheveled detective, knowing that Murphy had been more of a hindrance than a help to Jeffries. It was Jeffries who had asked for a reassignment. Bradford turned toward Hawk and, with the back of his right hand, brushed his bushy gray mustache that covered part of his upper lip. "You see, boy, you've already caused me an administration problem."

"I was told that this unit needs an extra detective."

"Well, yeah, we do, but quite frankly, we need a seasoned detective. I don't know what in the hell the Chief is thinking?"

Hawk looked both men in the eyes, "I'll do the best that I can, and you won't regret me being here." Under his breath, Murphy mumbled something to the effect that he was already regretting it.

"Murphy, get over it and help Hawk in any way you can. Show him the empty desk across from you. I'm counting on you to keep him out of trouble. Oh yeah, make sure he follows the straight and narrow."

At that moment, a man of medium height, seemingly in a great rush, rapped on the door as he walked in. He appeared to be in his forties, wearing jeans, a black T-shirt, and a tan suit jacket. "What do you want, Jeffries? I'm busy here." Hawk noted the detective's shaved head reflected a shine from the overhead florescent bulbs. He made up for the lack of hair on top with a trim graying beard. He totally ignored both Hawk and Murphy and told Bradford that he had someone in interrogation and really had no time to question him any further since the guy wasn't about to admit anything. No one bothered to introduce Jeffries to Hawk. At that point, the Lieutenant dismissed Hawk and Murphy.

Hawk followed Murphy to his desk. "This is my area." With his stubby finger, he pointed to a desk covered with loose papers, disarranged files and three old Starbucks coffee cups. "No one touches anything on it without my permission, understand?" He next pointed to the desk immediately across from him. "That there is your desk. It hasn't been used for a while, although Detective Orlinski uses it occasionally. He complains that he doesn't have enough space on his. He writes more reports than any three detectives. A real bookworm. He also spends more time in the unit than anyone else, using the lame excuse that he's got a report to write. That just shows you that just because a man is busy doesn't necessarily mean he is efficient. I don't know why Bradford puts up with him." With that bit of gossip, Murphy turned toward the front of the room and yelled out, "Hey, Orlinski, get your crap off this man's desk." All heads in the room rotated toward him. One of the detectives shook her head and rolled her eyes.

Orlinski, a man with a round face and pug nose, his light brown hair receding, turned toward Murphy, "Get off my back, Wally! I'll do it when I'm ready! Just tell the new man to shove it aside." *Geez, friendly, aren't they?* Hawk thought to himself.

Before Hawk had a chance to sit down on the fake leather chair with its worn metal handles, Bradford stuck his head out the door as Jeffries left his office. "Hawk and Murphy, get in here."

"I've got a man for you to interrogate. It seems to be an open-and-shut case, but it would be nice if you can get a confession out of him. He's in Interrogation room 3."

"You bet, boss, I'll get right on it," Murphy said. "I'll show the rookie how to do it. What's the case?"

"He was hot-rodding on one of those scooters that you rent, a Lime or a Lyft or something like that. He weaved in and out between pedestrians on Larimer Street in RINO—River North Arts District in Denver—when an elderly woman walked out of The Market food hall and was struck by the scooter. She was shoved hard to the ground and smashed her head on the cement. A couple of hours ago, she died in the hospital."

"What does the rider say about it?" Hawk asked. Wally gave him an annoyed glance. He didn't like the rookie already asking questions.

"What do you think? He denies it, of course. But witness statements confirm that our man in custody fits the description perfectly. We're checking his phone app to confirm that he rented a scooter. Here's his file." Wally stretched out his hand to receive it, but Bradford handed it to Hawk. Murphy puffed out his checks and quietly exhaled. "I want Hawk to handle this." As Hawk took the file, Bradford winked at Wally with a grin. Hawk caught the wink and realized that he was being set up.

"Oh, all right, Lieutenant, let's see what he can do." Murphy was okay with that since he was also sure Hawk would botch it. The three walked out into the corridor and turned into a hall and into Interrogation room #3. They entered and stopped at a one-way window. The alleged perpetrator appeared young, in his early twenties, wearing a faded green and blue checkered lumberjack shirt buttoned all the way up to the chin. A trim black beard covered the lower part of his elongated face. He slouched in his chair, arms crossed over his chest. His hair was cut very short on the sides, barely visible, but at the top, his dark brown hair was combed neatly and stacked on top of his head at least two inches high. He wore reddish thick, framed rectangular glasses. His feet protruded under the table, displaying blue canvas shoes with white soles, no socks, faded jeans, the bottoms of which were rolled up, giving him a 1950s flavor. As they viewed him, he picked what appeared to be wax out of his right ear, looked at it and flicked it away.

"He's a hipster," Hawk commented.

"A what?" Murphy asked. "Heard the term, but I don't really know what that is."

"Hipsters are a fad that's been around a few years," explained Hawk. "Hipsters really seem to enjoy clothing that is a little off the norm, such as vintage. They love to listen to their own kind of music from folksy independent artists that few have ever heard of. They love gourmet food whenever they can get it; eat a lot of kale, pickles, or anything off a food truck. They drink a lot of fancy coffees and particularly cold brews, like Pabst Blue Ribbon beer and consider themselves smart, more intellectual than athletic. They try to beat their own drum, or at least they think they do. They are generally not criminal-minded. For example, I bet that fellow in there doesn't have a criminal record."

"Sounds like you've been around them," Bradford said. Hawk wanted to tell him these were just general observations he made while on patrol, but before he could open his mouth, Bradford said, "Look in the file, Hawk. See if he has a record, but I don't remember seeing one." Hawk thumbed through the manila folder and saw that his record was clean. "Okay, hotshot, get him to confess. He might be surprised to learn that he's facing a charge of criminal negligent homicide or vehicular homicide."

Before Hawk left the room, he asked Bradford if the suspect had been advised of his Miranda rights, particularly that he didn't have to say anything and that he had the right to a lawyer. "Jeffries assured me that he advised him."

CHAPTER 3

HAWK WAS shown the door to room No 3. He walked in knowing that Bradford and Murphy would be carefully watching him, probably hoping that he'd screw up and make a fool of himself. As soon as he walked into the room, the suspect sat up straight and blurted out, "As I told the other cop, I did nothing wrong, I didn't run into anyone and I don't have to answer any of your questions. I want to leave."

"Wait, man," Hawk said. "You're jumping the gun here. Let's get acquainted first. I'm detective Clint Hawk and you are John Simonson, right?"

"Jonathan, Jonathan, I don't like to be called John."

"Oh, sorry, Jonathan. I really don't expect much out of you, except denials. That's what most people on that side of the table do. So, there's no use talking to you about the case I came in with. I'd be just wasting my time, don't you think?"

"For sure. I'm not going to admit to anything since I did nothing wrong."

"That's understandable. But I'm supposed to spend some time with you. So, what do you want to talk about? The weather is nice today, don't you think?" Jonathan rolled his eyes and threw up his hands in disgust.

"Are you kidding me, man? Jonathan looked incredulous. "You want to talk about the weather when I'm stuck in this rat hole room."

"Fair enough, Jonathan. Hey, you were in the RINO district yesterday afternoon, right?"

"I'm not saying anything."

"No, no, I'm not asking about the case, I just want to know about RINO. It's an interesting place to visit. Lot of bars, restaurants, art galleries. Tell me why the young and the hip like to go there. I heard that basically the whole area was built by millennials and they love to hang out there. Fill me in, why do you like to hang out in that area?"

"It's just a cool place," Jonathan started to open up. "I see my friends there, we hang out. The bars and restaurants serve the kind of beer and food I like, not that unhealthy crap in fast food joints. You're right; most of the people are young and fun, fun to be around."

"You feel like you fit in and belong?"

"Yeah, it's great."

"I still think I'm young, even though I'm in my early thirties. Would I fit in?"

"Sure."

Behind the glass, Murphy glanced at Bradford, shook his head back and forth and commented, "What in the world is he doing? Boy, he's so green. It's a mistake letting him in there, he'll never get a confession out of the punk that way. You have to be hard with him, Lieutenant, let me go in there and I'll be the 'bad cop.'"

Bradford smiled. "It's unusual, but I'll let him go with it a few more minutes. Actually, I'm interested to see what he comes up with next."

Hawk continued, "I suppose I need to get rid of my suit to fit in over there, don't you think? For example, do you consider yourself to be a hipster? And should I dress like you do?"

"I guess I'm a hipster. But we all don't wear the same things. I have my own style, man. Everybody can tell it's me by what I wear."

"So, you're pretty recognizable?"

"I think so. I mean there are other hipsters in the area, but I have a flare."

"Like what is your flare?"

"See what I'm wearing now? I find the best vintage clothes, the real authentic ones that people always ask where I find them."

"Sounds like you're a man around town in RINO and that you hang out every day there. Do you live in the area or work there?"

"Oh yeah, man. I'm there every day. I work for a jeweler in RINO, but I can't afford the housing, guy. I live a half-mile away where it's cheaper. I'm a jewelry designer."

"Wow, that's great. I bet you're good. I need to get one of your creations for my girlfriend. Where is the Jeweler's place that you work for, is it on Larimer?"

"Yeah, *Jewels by Albright.* It's right smack in the middle of all the action."

"But you probably don't have much time to enjoy RINO during the day because you're working."

"Oh, I only work until 2:00 o'clock. I got all afternoon and evening to enjoy myself."

"So, do you go home after work and change?"

"Nah, I don't need to change. I just hurry home so that I feed my dog and take him for a walk."

"Any problems parking your car in RINO? I can never find any parking."

"I don't have a car. Don't need one. I usually walk or if I'm really in a hurry I just rent a scooter."

"Like yesterday afternoon?"

"Yeah. Wait a minute! I told you I'm not going to say anything about any incidents they thought I caused. You're trying to trick me."

"I'm just trying to help. To do so I need to get to know you better. I don't know if you know this, but the elderly lady that you ran into yesterday afternoon, the same time that you left work and hurried to get to your dog, well the poor lady died just a few hours ago." Hawk closely studied Jonathan's reaction to this information. Jonathan sucked in a deep breath through his nose, his nose whistled. His seamed lips quivered, and he turned his gaze away from Hawk.

"I'm not saying anything more to you, understand? Do I need a lawyer now?"

"That's fine Jonathan, but you can only help yourself in this situation if you fully cooperate. We know you were the one on the scooter that hit the lady. That's a no-brainer, Jonathan. We have witnesses that described you, your clothes, your hair. All we have to do is look at your credit card account to see that you rented the scooter yesterday afternoon. We can determine the exact time that you were on it. Why make it harder on yourself? You make our job easier by admitting to it and we'll put in a good word to the D.A. You make us go through all the hoops and we'll fight you hard. We'll make sure the prosecutor takes a hard-nosed approach and charges you with everything they got including the big one, getting the maximum time for homicide."

Hawk finished talking and stared hard and deep into Jonathan's eyes, his face stern on purpose. Jonathan began to squirm. He became agitated. Hawk could see his brain cells twirling. Clint knew he was making progress, but he needed to push him harder now. "Jonathan, get serious…get realistic. We know you ran that elderly lady down and you know that. You're going to face the music now, bud. Do you want a break from the DA and us? Here's a yellow pad and a pen. I want you to write down your name, address, date of birth and describe in detail what happened. Now we know you didn't mean to run into the woman. We understand that it was a negligent act, one that you didn't intend. Put that all down in your statement here. That'll help you with the judge." Hawk slid the tablet and pen across the table. Jonathan hesitated, looked at Hawk and then reluctantly lifted the pen, his hand shaking.

"Jonathan, believe me, it's the right thing to do. I'll promise to write a particularly good report in your favor showing your cooperation."

"All right, you win, man. What do you want me to write?"

"Write your name, address and date of birth. I can't tell you what to write other than what happened yesterday afternoon. Start with leaving your work, that you were in a hurry to walk your dog and then in your words describe what happened." Jonathan began writing as Hawk watched. After he finished writing a full page, Hawk read it over. "It looks good. Now sign it and I'll type it up so it will look neat and then you'll need to sign it again. I'll just add to it that the statement is of your free will, signed voluntarily and no one forced you to give it. Okay?"

"Okay. How long do I have to wait in this room? I got to get out."

"It won't take long. I'm a fast typist. Hang on just a bit longer."

Hawk took the hand-written sheet and walked out of the room. He was met by Murphy and Bradford. "A little unorthodox, but I guess it worked," Bradford said. Murphy didn't say a word but he didn't look happy. Bradford hated to compliment Hawk, but he was impressed, particularly with the part that he'd throw in that it was a voluntary confession. "Okay, Hawk, type it up then call an officer to take him after he signs the typed confession. And I want a full report of this interview on my desk by 8:00 A.M."

Hawk hurried to his computer and typed the words exactly as written by Jonathan in just a few minutes, saved it and tried to print the document. He tried several more times but was unable to print it out nor did he know where the printer was. He wanted to ask Murphy, but Murphy was gone. So, he saw an opportunity to ask Marcie for help. As he walked over to her desk, he felt the other detectives' eyes on him. from the detectives watching him, especially the good-looking brunette. "Hi Marcie, I'm having a problem printing a document."

"Ah, I'm not sure that computer is even hooked up to the network since no one has used that desk since I've been here."

"Well, may I email it to you and have you print it out for me? I'd really appreciate it."

"Of course, pleased to be of assistance." She gave him her email address and with a quickstep, he returned to his computer and sent her the email. In a couple of minutes, she handed him the typed confession ready to be signed.

"Thanks a bunch, I owe you one."

"Oh, I'll take you up on that."

Jonathan signed the confession and was escorted back to the holding cell by an officer. The hipster's head felt as though a hatchet had split it in half. *What had I done? He* thought. *That detective better comes through with his promise to help me get a light sentence.*

Returning to his desk, Hawk immediately began working on a report for Bradford. He was not one to procrastinate and almost neurotic about it. Orlinski still hadn't removed his papers so Hawk stacked them in a pile and slid them to a corner of the desk. Marcie made a point to walk over and volunteered to set his computer up so that it would be part of the network and print. Hawk readily agreed but before he had a chance to move, Marcie leaned over, her body touching him, her hair only a few inches away, and began punching keys. The scent of her lavender shampoo enveloped him. He felt a magnetic pull and remembered that there exists between people some sort of chemical reaction that attracts one to the other. And he certainly felt it as he enjoyed her nearness. But in a few seconds, as she finished, she straightened up. "There, Clint, you should be set to go," she said, looking at him with her sparking blue eyes. "Just call me anytime you need me."

Hawk's breathing was hard as he followed her intently with his dark eyes as she sashayed down the aisle back to her desk. *What am I doing? I can't be involved with an office romance. That's only going to screw me up. I need to concentrate on this job and do it well. Besides, there is probably a rule against an in-office romance.* His conflicting thoughts were abruptly interrupted by Bradford's booming voice calling him and Murphy to his office, "pronto!"

Murphy had just returned to his desk from a vending machine with a candy bar and must have noticed the brief interaction with Marcie. He said as they walked toward Bradford's office. "Hey that Marcie is sweet on you, stud," Hawk did not reply, but he realized he needed to keep it cool with Marcie.

"We have a 215 with a 140—carjacking and murder," Bradford announced. "Since you, Murphy, don't have much of a caseload and Hawk has none, you have more time to take it. Although, I know it's probably a huge mistake assigning it to both of you. Don't disappoint me."

CHAPTER 4

HAWK WAS anxious to get to the scene of the crime. Adrenaline surged within him. His first major case as a detective. Murphy, though, didn't seem in a hurry at all as they walked to the parking lot. To Hawk, his pace couldn't be any slower. Frustrated, he asked, "Shouldn't we be in a hurry to get to the scene of the crime?"

The senior detective's pace slowed. He paused and turned toward Hawk. "There's no rush. They'll wait. We're the detectives in charge after all." Hawk's irritation level reached a new peak. *A kick in his butt is what he needs.* "Yessiree, boy, this is real July weather. Sure is a little warm today, but they say it'll be cloudy tomorrow and cool off." *Come on Murphy. Get a move on it.*

Murphy took a long look at the radiant sky. "Well, my friend, that's my vehicle there, the dark blue one." Murphy pointed to a vehicle that was parked headfirst. All the other squad cars were backed into position for a quick response.

"It's an old Crown Victoria that should have been put out to pasture years ago. But there's never enough money for anything anymore. They keep promising me one of those Ford Interceptors, but I'll probably retire before I get one."

It's as though a floodgate was lifted, and Murphy wouldn't stop jabbering as they approached the tired-looking Ford. Murphy's excessive conversation gave Hawk a sign that the older man now accepted the fact that they'll be working together, and he needed to make do. It was quite a transformation from the seemingly unpleasant, resentful detective Murphy to the relaxed Murphy. Hawk tried to ask about the homicide just assigned them but Wally kept gabbing about the numerous creeps he put out of commission over his career of thirty years. "After a while, you get to know the criminals and you know how they think. I'm good at analyzing a situation at hand and figuring it out. Stay with me, kid, and you'll learn a lot."

He sat in the driver's seat. Hawk waited for him to start the engine. *Well, go, man.* His story about a certain child abuser that he put away years ago seemed to paralyze him from cranking up the motor and get going. "Wally, do you think we should go before evidence at the crime scene disappears?"

"Oh yeah. I guess sometimes I talk too much. We don't have far to go, but I can start by telling you some war stories that I've had over the years." *Great!* Hawk thought. *Will someone put me out of my misery?* Murphy backed out and drove to the exit. Without looking to make sure the coast was clear; he gunned the vehicle onto Washington Street. A Chevy Silverado traveling down the street barely avoided a collision. The driver fell on his horn, but that didn't faze Murphy at all. "Those punks drive like a bat out of hell, expecting everyone to give them room. If I weren't in such a hurry, I should have written him up, but I'm not a traffic cop. We do have the right to hand out tickets as detectives, you know. But I don't have a ticket book with me."

Shaken up, Hawk didn't answer. *Holy cow! That was close.* Wally kept on talking while waiting for the green light at the corner of Colfax Avenue. He explained how he won that parking spot in the police lot a few years ago. "They say it's because of the length of service, but I say it's because of how good I am. Yessiree boy, I sure can teach you a lot about being a detective." After a left on Colfax, he continued jabbering, swinging his round head around keeping his eye more on Hawk than the street. Hawk barely listened. He sat erect, seat belted, nerves still on edge, expecting Murphy to make another bonehead move and cause an accident. In reality, his driving wasn't too bad, but his carelessness when his mouth was in motion alarmed Hawk. "Too bad we don't have time for a cup of coffee. I sure could use something sweet to go with it. But I guess duty calls, right my lad?"

He shot a glance over to Hawk in the hope that Hawk would say, "That's fine, we've got time." Hawk glanced back, "Duty calls."

With not a cloud in the sky, the mid-afternoon July sun beat through the windshield. It didn't help that Murphy hit every red light. Murphy fiddled with the air conditioner controls, complaining that he was sitting in a sauna. Hawk eyed him and sure enough, sweat poured from his smooth forehead. He adjusted his collar several times, finally loosening his tie some more. Hawk didn't feel hot at all. He actually thought that the air conditioner was blowing a little too cold.

"It sure feels hot today. I bet it'll be a scorcher," Murphy said. *Here he goes again with the weather.* "It seems that every summer it gets hotter. Hawk, do you believe in global warming?"

"Yeah, I believe that. The question is can we do anything about it?"

"You're not one of those obsessives that think it's the cows farting that's doing it, do you?"

Hawk really didn't want to get into a deep discussion over climate change. Now was not the time for him and Wally to discuss such matters, at least not on the first call. After they turned left on Lafayette Street, he was relieved to see what looked like a crime scene loom ahead.

A large group of people all with their smart phones held high, gathered behind the yellow police tape. Murphy parked behind the throng and switched on his siren and the red and blue lights. Hawk had never seen a crowd of people jump almost in unison. Murphy laughed so hard that his corpulent face became even redder. "I love to do that," he said, still chuckling at his prank while some in the crowd swore and threw the middle finger at him and Hawk. "Out of the way, out of the way, official business," Murphy commanded, pointing to his shield attached to his belt. Unfortunately, only part of it showed underneath his belly that hung over his belt.

Studying the scene as he approached, Hawk observed two patrol officers, one by the victim who lay on the street under a blanket. The other spoke with two witnesses. He noticed the medical examiner and her assistant.

Hawk appreciated carrying only a shield, a pair of handcuffs and his Sig Sauer .380 holstered pistol on his belt. The patrol officers were weighted down at their waist with a radio, a pistol, a Mini Mag-Lite, a stun gun, expandable baton, nightstick, double magazine holders, and double cuff case with handcuffs. *Just a small but real perk of being a detective.*

"You finally here," said Corporal Hopkins, one of the two officers at the scene. "What did you do? Go out for coffee? The medical examiner has been here a while, checking out the body but she can't leave until you clear it."

"Well, we're here now," Murphy said. "You don't have to teach me how to do my job, Corporal. Anyhow, what does it look like? Who got shot? By the way, this is our new detective, Clint Hawk."

Hopkins nodded to Hawk. "Yeah, we've met in the police academy. Nice to see you again, Clint." Hawk nodded and said something similar but knew that Hopkins didn't much like him and the feeling was mutual. *He was always jealous of my success. He took the detective's exam twice and failed both times.* Hopkins continued, "It looks like a carjacking that went bad. The victim's ID lists him as Jeffrey Bowman. He apparently was the driver and was shot point-blank in the forehead. Body dumped out and the perp hauled off with the car."

"Any witnesses?" Hawk asked.

Hopkins took out his pad and read off two names. "Yeah, a Cynthia Reynolds heard the shot. She is standing there in the green T-shirt. Next to her and Officer Alvarado is Sam Mallard. They wanted to leave, but we told them they had to remain until the detectives arrived."

"Thank you, Officer Hopkins, we'll take it from here."

"You betcha, de-tec-tive Hawk." Hawk heard the sarcasm and expected as much.

"That was handled pretty well, Hawk," Murphy said. "I could not have done much better. But from now on, you let the old dog like me do the talking. Okay?"

Hawk muttered an okay. *If I need to, I'll ask questions whether he likes it or not.* Bowman's body lay on the asphalt. Hawk smelled the rank odor of blood. He watched as Murphy lifted the blanket from the upper torso. Blood covered his face and ran down onto his shirt and finally onto the pavement leaving a large dark pool. Wally introduced Hawk to the medical examiner, Dr. Janeel Thompson. Thompson appeared friendly, said "hello" and proceeded to explain her preliminary findings. "A single shot to his forehead caused instant death. Looks like a large caliber bullet. Will let you know after I take it out. If you gentlemen hurry and inspect the body and the scene we can remove it and I can get back to work."

"Oh, what else is new, Janeel," Wally said with a grin. "You're always in a hurry. You know me, I'm very thorough. Don't want to miss anything."

"I know, Wally, so please hurry? I need to get back. The case looks pretty simple. A guy was shot close-range in the forehead due to a carjacking, his body pulled out of the car and the car taken. What else do you need to know?"

"Now, now. We detectives have to be methodical, don't we, Hawk? Hawk, what are you doing? Crap, where are you going?"

Hawk looked back at Murphy as he began walking away from the body toward the witnesses. "I saw what I needed to see. I'm going to talk to the witnesses."

"Don't do that without me. Doggone it, Hawk, come back here." But Hawk yelled back something about the witnesses having waited long enough. "Doggone it. Okay, Janeel, I guess I'm through with the body. You can take it away. I better get to that young whippersnapper before he botches things up. Doggone it." Murphy turned and waddled over to join Hawk who was already talking to the witnesses.

Hawk had already written down the names, addresses and telephone numbers of the two witnesses and thanked them for waiting. Murphy approached muttering, "You should have waited for me."

Hawk introduced Detective Wally Murphy to the two witnesses and suggested that Murphy question Sam Mallard while he questions Cynthia Reynolds. Murphy was taken aback at the brashness of this new detective. *When did he take over and start bossing me around? I'm the senior detective here and a sergeant as well. Doggone it. But then, why should I care at my age? I'm so close to retirement that it makes no difference to me. He wants to run the show, let the fool make his own mistakes. It's no skin off my back.*

"Ms. Reynolds," Hawk said addressing the witness. "Let's step over to the other side of the street so that we don't bother Detective Murphy while he talks to Mr. Mallard." Cynthia Reynolds agreed and followed Hawk across the street, unable to take her eyes off the body that was now in a body bag and placed on a stretcher. She was a pleasant woman in her late fifties, short and overweight, with grayish-brown hair and smooth skin on her round face. She wore red shorts and an oversized faded green T-shirt and pink flip-flops. She appeared somewhat stunned with what she had seen transpire.

"It was horrible, simply horrible. I heard someone yelling, 'get out, get out!' I turned around to see what was going on and I saw this man in a hoodie pointing a gun at the driver's window of a car. The driver started opening the door when he shot him. Just like that. The shot sounded like a firecracker that went off in my head. I shrieked and stopped breathing. It was so scary, so I ran and took cover behind a parked car over there. But I saw him pull the poor man out of the car, jump in, and take off. I never saw a carjacking before. It was horrible. I'm still shaking all over. I have to go home and take a valium. I'm sure going to have nightmares over this. Horrible, I tell you."

"Were you able to see his face? Hawk asked.

"No, he didn't move his face once. It was always directed at the car window. Even when he pulled the dead man out, he didn't turn his head at all."

"Were you able to see the man's profile?"

"Not much at all. Like I said, he had a hoodie on. I remember he had heavy-framed sunglasses that wrapped around his eyes. Oh yeah, he had a bushy, kinky black beard."

"Could you tell whether he was white, black, Hispanic, Asian?"

"Not really. He wore black gloves and his face was well covered up with the hoodie, the glasses and the beard. I suppose if I had to guess, I'd say he was black."

"Was he tall or short?"

"Couldn't tell that either because he was so hunched over. Never did straighten up the whole time I watched him."

"Was he heavy or thin?"

"He was pretty thin, I'd say. But it happened so fast I really didn't notice."

"What color of clothes did he have on?"

"Everything was black. A black hoodie, pants and black running shoes."

"What kind of car was it?"

"I'm not good at cars. It was big and white in color. It was a luxury car, I know that. I think it was either a Mercedes or Lexus. Maybe a Cadillac or something like that, but I'm not sure. He sure did take off fast with it though."

"Let me ask you once again so that I can get it straight. You said that the victim was opening the door to get out when the shooter shot him, is that correct?"

"Yes. I swear I saw his door open before he was shot."

"How far did it open, how many inches?"

"I can't tell you that." Hawk kept his eyes on her waiting for more of a response. "Well, if I have to guess, I'd say about six inches."

"Where were you standing when you first heard him yell, 'get out?'"

"On the east side of the street, about halfway between the body there and where we are now," she said looking back to the spot where the body lay."

"Were there any other cars around here when it happened?"

"There were a few, but when they heard the shot, I think they all took off. Didn't want to get involved. You know what I mean? But I'm a good citizen."

"Yes, you are. And thank you for that and for your description here. It really helps us. Do you need a ride home?"

"No, I live just a block away in a condo with my two cats. My husband died about two years ago and I'm all alone."

"I'm sorry about your loss, ma'am. Here's my card and if you can think of anything else, please call me." Oh, by the way, did you see where the victim came from and what direction he was going?"

"Yes, he drove out of that driveway in back of the *Coffee Aroma* building and their coffee shop. He went just about ten yards or so before he had to stop because there was a stopped car in his lane. It's at that moment when the carjacker came out probably between these apartment buildings and carjacked and shot him."

"What happened to the stopped car in front?"

"It took off after the man was shot."

"You're very observant, Mrs. Reynolds. Do you remember anything of the stopped car that blocked the victim's car?"

"No, other than it was a black SUV of some sort. Actually, like the vehicles in the FBI shows on TV."

"Thank you for your help. If you think of anything else, you have my card, please call me." With that, Mrs. Reynolds waddled off, swaying from side to side as she walked.

As Hawk finished writing details in his notebook, Murphy sauntered over with a big cup of Coffee Aroma and a half-eaten piece of banana bread. "Are you through finally? I guess as a rookie you spent too much time with the witness. I don't know what you talked about all that time. I got through with my witness in just a minute or two. It's not the biggest case in the world. Just a carjacking gone bad. We'll find him after we find the car."

"It's also a murder case and we need to be as thorough as we can," Hawk said, hoping not to aggravate Murphy anymore.

"Look, I've seen these types of cases over the years. A carjacking takes place and unfortunately, the victim gets shot just because he was in the wrong place at the wrong time. He probably didn't want to get out, maybe put up a struggle and was shot."

"Is that what your witness said?"

"No, not exactly. He told me that everything happened so fast. He saw a stooped man run up to the car from, he thinks from behind that apartment building," indicating with his fat index finger the building adjacent to the vacant commercial building on the corner. The hooded man pointed a gun at the driver. Next, he heard a shot and the shooter pulled the man out and took off with the car like a bat out of hell. We'll find him, rookie, don't worry. Let's go back to the unit. I'll show you how I fill out a short, to the point, report."

The men went back to the car. As Wally walked, he drank his coffee and on occasion spilled some. *What a klutz,* Hawk thought as he slid into the seat and belted himself. Wally was still out of the car and kept jabbering something about how efficient his reports are. Hawk used the time to mull over what he saw and heard at the scene. He noticed his new partner stuff the rest of the pastry in his mouth then try to juggle the cup of coffee in one hand, open the door and pull out the keys. Once settled in and the car in motion, Hawk said, "I don't think the carjacking was the true intent. I think it was made to look like strictly a carjacking, but it was a premeditated murder by the shooter, assassin style, right between the eyes. He had an accomplice in a car blocking the victim from driving off."

Wally snapped his neck toward Hawk, his gray eyes bulging, "You're crazy, bud. It is a carjacking gone bad, that's all. Don't make a real rookie mistake by thinking it's more than what it appears. I know you're gung-ho and want to make a name for yourself, but facts are facts. I sure hope you don't tell the Lieutenant about this; he'll probably laugh you out of the office. Premeditated murder! That's wild, son."

"I don't think it's wild at all. There's more here than it appears. If you don't mind, I'd like to talk to the other witness myself."

"I don't really think you care what I mind. Sure, go for it. I'd only like to be there and see your face when you fall flat on it. But I think the Lieutenant will laugh you out of the office when you tell him otherwise than what it is."

"So, then before I do, I'd like your help to try to get some more facts. We need to see the victim's wife, if he has one, and find out as much as we can about the victim himself."

"Oh man, you're going ape on me. Listen bud, I thought I'd let you hang yourself on this and let you take the lead since that's what you want, but I don't agree. We can talk to the next of kin and tell them the bad news, but we need to concentrate on the punk who did the carjacking without making a federal case out of this."

"Wally, I know in my gut that there's more to it."

"Hey, you don't have much of a gut, bud," Wally said, patting his big stomach. "And you don't have enough experience to formulate a gut response." They were silent for a moment, then Wally blurted out, "Okay, I'll go along with you for a while and try to keep you focused on the obvious."

CHAPTER 5

MORE THAN ready to follow his gut, Hawk was quite pleasantly surprised that Murphy wouldn't interfere in checking a few things out. *I assume he'll let me take the lead and do what I think needs to be done. Maybe, he's not as bad to work with as I thought.* Hawk took another look at him as Wally lazily drove the car back to the station.

Hawk wondered what kind of a detective Murphy had been over the many years. *He must have been serious about the cases when he was young. He certainly didn't appear to be now. To him it's just routine, do what you must and solve the case if you can.* He wondered if that is now his motto. *He is fat and slow now, but he must have been more in shape and raring to go when he was young. He was probably divorced, maybe remarried, but most likely single. I bet he lives alone in some apartment close to the station. But then, I live alone too.*

"Wally, tell me a little about yourself since it seems we'll be partners, at least for a while."

"What's there to tell? I eat too much and drink too much beer. I've been married three times and as you've heard, it's hard to keep a wife with this kind of job, with the hours that we keep. But, that's not the main reason. I think the main reason is that my wives couldn't take the stress of my not coming home someday. They all feared that every day that I went out, I could be killed. I should have married another cop. That way both of us might be able to deal with the thought of the other dying on the job. Haven't seen much of any of them since we split."

"Any children?"

"Oh yeah, I've got two from the first and one from the second. None from the third marriage."

"You see them often, the kids I mean?"

Murphy blew out his breath and rubbed his fat hand over his eyes and then down the side of his chubby cheek. "That's a sore point with me. I'm not close to any of them. Somehow, over the years we drifted apart. Might get a phone call for my birthday or Christmas. Lasts only a couple of minutes and then they say they got to go. I'm not even sure where they live now. But I'll tell you what, when I retire, I'm going to do my own detective work and track them down. I've got to do my amends before I die."

Murphy continued to breathe heavily, his chest heaving. He rested his head on the headrest and remained quiet for several minutes. Hawk knew better than to ask any more questions. He looked physically upset and Hawk felt sorry for him, regretting asking him anything. Then, as though something snapped in Murphy's brain, he suddenly became animated. "Look there, see that café over there," pointing to what appeared to be a dive, "They serve the best breakfast burritos I've ever had. And as you can tell by my stomach, I know a good burrito when I eat one." He chuckled as though he said the funniest thing in the world. Hawk also laughed as Murphy glanced at him. Hawk realized that his laughter masked the pain that he felt for his estranged family. *I wonder what happened. It's more than the wives couldn't take the stress associated with his job. Three wives and three kids and none want to see him. He must have a big flaw in his domestic personality. There are plenty of cops with successful, happy marriages.*

Murphy once again turned his neck toward Hawk. "How about you, hotshot, are you married?"

"No, I'm not."

"Why not? Everyone should be married so they know what it's like."

"I guess I never met the one I wanted to spend the rest of my life with. Like you said, it's hard to find a woman who wants to live with a cop."

"I guess it's best to marry another cop." Changing the subject, Murphy said, "Well, let's go see the widow now. I received a text that the victim was married and her address is on Pennsylvania Avenue."

"Before we go, I want to find out as much about the victim, Bowman, before we see the widow. So, let's stop at the unit first so that perhaps Marcie can get the information for us. As a matter of fact, if I call her right now, do you think that Marcie would look up what she can about him? That should save us some time."

"You might as well call her. I'm sure she will. The way she looked at you, she'll do anything for you."

"Oh, yeah, sure. I don't believe that for a minute, but I'll call her. What's her number, anyway?" Murphy gave him Marcie's extension. Hawk tapped out the number and Marcie answered on the second ring. She seemed anxious to help him and said she'd get started on it right away.

"You know, sport, that she could've texted the info to you. I'm sure you figured that out, but you wanted to see her again, didn't you?" He laughed heartily, cocked his eyes at Hawk, slapping him in jest on the shoulder. "She's not bad looking, blonde hair, sparkling blue eyes."

Hawk was not amused. "Listen, Wally, I'd like to see the info firsthand. Besides, we shouldn't be talking about a co-worker like that. They really drilled the rules into me at the academy."

"Okay, okay, bud, if that's the way you want it. But I tell it like it is." At that, he drove into the lot and parked. Hawk was rather surprised that his driving wasn't that bad. No close calls this time and he followed the rules. As they entered the division office, Murphy headed to his desk. Out of the corner of his eye, Hawk noticed his new partner shaking his head and most likely rolling his eyes as he walked by desks of fellow detectives. Then he ducked into Bradford's office. *He'll have all kinds of stories to tell about me.*

Marcie immediately called Hawk over, a wide grin on her face, her white teeth glistening. Hawk once again noticed the loose wisps of blond hair touching her shoulder. "I've got the information you wanted."

"That was fast."

"Just call me speedy. Really, it wasn't too hard. Actually, that's part of my job to do research and I enjoy that part of it. Come look at the computer." Hawk walked around the desk and stood over Marcie. He could see the part in her soft hair, one side of her flowing hair falling over the front of her shoulder, the other side behind her back. She smelled good and he noticed he felt comfortable next to her, in her space. But he wasn't about to get involved with her other than as a co-worker working on cases together. "Jeffrey Bowman is a partner in the coffee shop business known as Coffee Aroma. They have stores in three states and do a big business in importing coffee beans, mostly from Costa Rica and selling them wholesale."

"What about his partners?"

"He's got one as the coffee business goes. From the Secretary of State website, I found that the company is an LLC with members being Bowman and one Marcus Miller. They were organized fourteen years ago. Checking other sources, I saw that the coffee business is not Bowman's primary income. He is also involved in many restaurants, much real estate all over Colorado under various LLCs. His wife, Julia Bowman, is on several of the properties and has holdings in her name as well."

"So, we're looking at someone who had bucks."

"Yes. Wouldn't it be nice?"

"Thank you, Marcie. This really helps."

"Sure, anytime. Whatever you need." Marcie noted a slight blush on Hawk's cheeks. "I mean, as far as the job goes." *Wow, that was stupid,* she immediately regretted saying that. *What got into me?*

"Yes, of course. I really appreciate your help. I better get Wally and go see the widow."

As he dashed to get Murphy, Lieutenant Bradford walked out of his office, Murphy tagging along. Hawk nodded to his boss and moved aside expecting him to walk past. Instead, he grabbed Hawk's arm. "So, what do we have there? A carjacking with a bad result, right? At least that's what Murphy thinks. The victim was shot because he didn't want to lose his car."

"Well, that's what it appears. The poor guy was shot in the head, almost execution-style. Lieutenant, I think there is more to it than it seems. A witness told me that the victim was opening his door before he was shot. I don't think that he wasn't cooperating with the carjacker. I'd like to follow up on a hunch if that's okay with you."

"Ah, the young detective and his hunches," Bradford chortled sarcastically. "You better be looking for the hijacked car and see what evidence you can get from that. I don't want any theories that are unsubstantiated. Wally says it was a carjacking for the sole purpose of getting that luxury car. Was the man killed as a result? Yes. Those are the facts. And, Detective, I want a preliminary report to that effect tomorrow. Once the vehicle is found, you can add whatever you discover to your report. Got that?"

"Sure, no problem. A simple carjacking is what it appears right now. But could you give me some slack to follow my gut before the report is due?"

"Geez, you just got here and already have your gut talking to you. You're going to waste our resources on a wild goose chase. Well, maybe it'll be a good lesson for you to see that you are spinning your wheels. Get it out of your system. But I want that report that it was a carjacking and the victim shot as a result by tomorrow morning. As far as following your gut, I'll give you twenty-four hours to see if you come up with anything different. Then move on."

Hawk was disappointed at the Lieutenant's attitude. He needed more than twenty-four hours to investigate the case thoroughly.

Bradford continued with a smirk on his face, "With more experience, you'll find out for yourself that it doesn't pay to go beyond what it appears. You and Wally have twenty-four hours to do what you think you need to do. Then you have to stop, and I'll give you something else to work on. In the meantime, find that damn car before it's chopped up."

"Yes sir. We already put out a BOLO—be on the lookout—bulletin on the car. Hopefully, it will be found soon. Murphy and I will head out to the widow and notify her of her husband's death right now."

"What?!" Bradford's face hardened, a sneer marring his mouth. "You hadn't done that yet?!" His voice had suddenly become even more booming than before. "That should have been done before now before she hears it on the news." Hawk felt stupid and guilty. He always wanted to do everything the right way. He knew he should've had it done by now. But he really wanted more information about the widow's husband so that, if necessary, he could ask the right questions before too much time had elapsed. He looked distressed, realizing he blew it, in the eyes of his lieutenant and felt the stare of every detective in the room.

"I understand and we'll take care of it right away. But could you give us at least three days to work on the carjacking case? It's a complicated case and needs to be worked properly."

"Hell, no! You have twenty-four hours."

Satisfied that he alarmed the rookie, Bradford's face softened and with a wry smile, he said, "Go play!" That comment angered Hawk even more. His feeling of guilt for not notifying the widow vanished, and he was now determined more than ever to prove Bradford wrong.

CHAPTER 6

THE BOWMAN house, in the Capitol Hill area, was a magnificent old mansion sporting a historic designation plaque attached to the side of the front of the house. The pleasant shady tree-lined street of Pennsylvania had cars lined along the street creating a parking problem. The corner house stood alone, defiant to the many changes that had taken place all around it. Instead of original rows of wealthy residents, the area was now mostly sprinkled with a few remaining mansions. Most of them were converted into apartments or boarding rooms sitting among two- or three-story apartment buildings and newer multistory skyscrapers full of condos and apartments.

Since he was a young teenager, Hawk had been fascinated with architecture. He admired buildings, their design, craftsmanship and the beauty that in his opinion was lacking today. He knew that the jagged stone Bowman Mansion was a revival of Romanesque style with its symmetrical facade. It was wrapped in gray stone with intricate round-topped arches over the window. "Nice digs," Murphy said. "I love this old neighborhood. I could never in my wildest dreams afford a house like this. Not even one of those apartments," pointing to a twelve-story structure directly across the street to the south of the mansion. How much do you think the Bowman house is worth today?"

"It's a great house, all right," Hawk said. "It's one of the few still standing and owned by a single family. I bet this house is probably worth five million."

Wally let out a whistle. "Like I said, I could never afford it."

"These mansions were built by the silver barons in the 1870s-1880s. Did you know, Wally, that that was their heyday? They became filthy rich from the silver they took out of the mountains. Then most of them lost everything in 1893 when the silver market crashed. That was the biggest disaster to hit Colorado, even worse than the Great Depression. So many were bankrupted forcing the silver magnates to sell their mansions. Over the years, some of the mansions were torn down to make way for progress," he said, raising his arm toward the several tall apartment or condo structures. "That's why you don't see as many of the 1880s homes in this area. There are still many middle-class homes around Denver, though, in less desirable areas where development didn't come as fast."

"Okay, Einstein, I got my history lesson for today, now let's go see the widow," Murphy said.

The two walked up four deeply indented stone front steps onto an oak-floored grand porch covered with an ornate portico. Hawk pushed on the round brass button and heard the doorbell chimes. Hawk looked around and noticed a security camera at one of the corners. It was an inexpensive model, one that is frequently sold as a dummy, not to record, but just to scare the burglars away. He commented to Murphy about not expecting an expensive home such as this with that kind of set up. "They should at least get a *Ring* doorbell hooked up to a monitor or a smart phone that would show who was at the door."

"To each his own," Murphy muttered. "Maybe there's no one home." He pressed the doorbell again. They almost turned to go back, when they heard footsteps approaching inside the house.

"What do you want?" A determined female voice called out. "Can't you see the 'No Soliciting' sign next to the door?"

"Ma'am, we're not soliciting," Murphy said, striking a different tone in his voice, now deep and authoritarian. "We're police detectives and need to speak to you." They heard the lock slide and the door opened just wide enough for the woman's face to show.

"Why would you want to talk to me? My husband takes care of all business affairs."

"No ma'am," Hawk said. "This is not business, but extremely personal. We need to come in and talk to you. Here's my shield," he said, removing it from his belt and bringing it up to her face.

She hesitated, debating what to do. "Well, all right then, come in." Julia Bowman swung the door wider and showed them in. But her face, although beautiful, was not welcoming. She left just enough room in the foyer for them to stand inside unable to shut the door behind them.

"What's this all about?" Her mood seemed indeed foul. "You're wasting my time. I have a board meeting with the symphony guild." Hawk noticed her graying black hair was neatly combed and she was dressed in an expensive blue designer suit with a skirt at the knee, pink frilly blouse and what appeared to be expensive Manolo Blanco Italian shoes, an identical pair to the ones Hawk's rich aunt in Texas bragged about. Mrs. Bowman was tall, slim, her erect posture imposing. *A former model, perhaps?*

"Is there any place we can sit down for a few minutes," Hawk asked. Mrs. Bowman looked completely irritated with them. She glanced at her Rolex watch; lips thinned and shook her head. It appeared that she was prepared to tell them to get out of her house and even threaten to call their superiors. She stared at them with annoyed dark eyes, then took a deep breath, exhaling forcibly. *She is really in a bad mood. And now we're going to make it worse.*

"All right. I'll give you two minutes. Follow me to the parlor."

Murphy and Hawk glanced at each other, noting her superior attitude. Murphy rolled his eyes and whispered, "Parlor?" Hawk guessed that she was in her mid-fifties and acting every bit as a grand dame in the spacious foyer with its splendid curved staircase leading to the upper floors. Standing guard within the round of the stairs stood a large brass statue of Neptune holding a trident in his hand. They turned into a room filled with antique furniture including a curved purple velvet sofa and two blue wingback chairs on each side of a marble-topped coffee table. The walls were filled with portraits of individuals of days gone by, perhaps former owners and their families. Behind the chairs stood a narrow table with a bouquet of fresh carnations and gladiolas. She sat down on one of the chairs, crossed her bare legs, and motioned for them to sit on the sofa.

"Now what is this all about? You're interfering with my busy afternoon. Please be brief." Murphy looked at Hawk and nodded for him to proceed. Hawk was startled because it was Murphy who said he would break the news since he had all this experience in dealing with grief. *Did this woman intimidate him?*

"Mrs. Bowman, I'll get right to the point since you are in a hurry. It's about your husband."

"What about my husband? Get on with it. Should I be calling our lawyer?"

"No, Mrs. Bowman. Your husband—" Hawk hesitated. He had to notify families numerous times as a patrol officer. He never felt that he was sensitive enough or that he came across as caring. To tell them that their loved one was killed tore him up inside. He imagined being the recipient of the worst possible news that everyone fears.

"Well, for crying out loud. What are you trying to say? I've had enough of this. If you can't tell me why you're here, then please leave. You people, Denver detectives, have wasted enough of our time with your false accusations a few months ago. I mean it, get out." *What is that about? The Bowmans were being investigated for something? Murphy will kick me if I ask more about it now. He'll say I'm totally insensitive. I'll need to check that out later.*

"Mrs. Bowman, we're so deeply sorry to inform you that your husband was shot in what was an apparent carjacking." Her aggressive attitude made it easier to throw out the words.

Mrs. Bowman's demeanor transformed immediately. She had dealt with the local police before when they investigated them and she thought, *here we go again, these cops are at it again.* But this was so different. "Shot! Oh my God! Where is he? Is he all right? Why didn't you tell me this right away? You could've told me that at the door. What hospital is he in?"

"No, unfortunately, he died at the scene. Again, we're so very sorry. Please accept our sincere condolences."

"It can't be. There must be a mistake." Her big dark eyes widened in shock and she grabbed her head sinking her long-manicured fingers into her meticulously styled hair. She stared unbelievingly at the detectives with her anthracite eyes stretched wide. Her breathing ceased as if frozen.

Finally, she blinked, shook her head and submissively in almost a whisper asked, "Where is he? I need to go see him."

"At the medical examiners' office, ma'am." Hawk watched as the arrogant, proud woman further deflated before his eyes. Her formerly erect shoulders sagged as she processed the horrific information. She cupped her face with her trembling hands as tears streamed down the sides of her face smearing her makeup. She took deep breaths and drained her lungs forcefully. Suddenly, she shrieked a blood-curdling wail that the big house seemed to echo.

"He was my life! He was everything to me! I won't be able to go on without him."

Murphy got up and walked over to her, placing his beefy arm around her thin shoulders speaking caringly, surprising Hawk as he showed his tender side. "I know it's difficult and horrible news to hear. But life will go on. Life must go on. If there is anything, we can do for you, just call us and we'll help in whatever way we can." She turned her head to glance at Murphy and tried to get ahold of herself. Murphy gazed back at her for several minutes. She took several deep breaths, wiped the tears from her face with the back of her hands and stared at the round face that seemed to be hurting as much as she was.

She glanced over at Hawk, who also appeared to be distressed as well, and asked, "Can you tell me what happened? Was it a quick death? Do you know who did it?"

Murphy left Julia Bowman's side and rejoined Hawk at the sofa. Since she focused on Hawk, he answered her. "It appears to be a quick death and he didn't suffer. The carjacker shot your husband in the forehead, pulled him out of the car and took off with it. We don't—"

"Oh my God! A bullet in the head. In the head of my love. How dreadful. Oh, what a nightmare." She began to sob once again. "I'll be right back. I need a tissue." She came back, rubbing her eyes with the tissue, and resumed her seat. "Go on, I'm sorry. Tell me everything."

"We don't have much more information than that," Hawk said. "It appears that it was a random carjacker. We'll do our best to find him. It's just a matter of time." He studied her as she seemed to settle down, breathing shallowly but quietly, as everything sunk in. She sat with her head bent down, her eyes fixated on her beige and blue pointed shoes. The men sat quietly for a few minutes leaving her with her thoughts. When she looked up, Hawk asked her if her husband had any enemies.

"Enemies! I thought you said it was a carjacking. It wasn't random, then?"

"We don't know, Mrs. Bowman. It appears to be a random carjacking, but we need to investigate all possibilities. My question about any enemies is procedural." Murphy scratched the back of his head, arching his left eyebrow at Hawk. It was obvious to Hawk who knew by Murphy's penetrating glare that he strongly felt that that wouldn't have been a question that Murphy would ask at the moment. "Just in case, it would be good to know if there is anyone that might want your husband dead."

Mrs. Bowman again lowered her head, cupping it in her trembling hands. The detectives sat silent giving her time to respond. In those few moments, Julia Bowman thought of the unpleasant conversation with her husband the night before, *Marcus went wild—slamming doors,* cursing. *That son of a bitch almost belted me. He threatened me. It was all because I asked a realtor to give us a market analysis. Said it wouldn't be good for my health if we sell. We need to sell as much as we can, Julia, including the coffee business. We're in really hot water."*

"From Marcus?"

"No, not so much from him. I better not tell you anything right now. If you knew the names of the people I'm involved with, and they knew about it, you'd be in danger."

"Oh God!"

"All I can tell you is that we need to raise as much money as we can. They want their money and the properties are not selling as fast as they want. They don't care, they want the money now."

"Who wants their money?"

"Please don't ask for your own safety. All I can tell you is that they're powerful, vicious people. Listen, Julia, don't trust anyone, not even the cops."

"Can't you do something about it?"

"I guess I could go to the feds and ask for protection. We'll have to change our identities and get lost somewhere."

"Oh God! What in the hell did you get us into?"

"Mrs. Bowman," Hawk said, quietly and as gently after waiting a few minutes for her to respond. "Is there anyone out there that you think might have gone after your husband?" Wally coughed loudly and gave Hawk a stern look. Hawk paid no attention. He felt that the wife knew something.

Mrs. Bowman lifted her head. *Don't trust anyone, not even the cops.* "Well, I don't know of anyone specific, no." She sat quietly for another moment, sniffling but obviously pondering the question. "No, I really can't think of anyone. He had been in business and I suppose he might have stepped on a few toes. We have a lot of rentals and there are always angry tenants, but no one to the extent that would want to kill him. Of course, recently something was really bothering him. He did mention that he had to sell some of the properties. But I don't know why it was so urgent. All I know is that he's been stressed out more than usual lately."

Hawk plowed through. "I really hate to ask, but would you mind providing us later with a list of tenants or anyone that you feel was overly angry with your husband? Not only tenants but perhaps business associates." She nodded as she blew her nose. "It is my understanding that he also owned some franchises and of course, a partner in the coffee business."

"Yes, but we were trying to sell all our assets and I suppose live off the proceeds. As a matter of fact, we had already sold all our interest in the franchises and restaurants. But the money went quickly for debts that he said he owed."

"Do you know what kind of debts?"

"No, he tried to shield me from his business transactions. Anyway, most of the property was in his name alone. When I asked him why I wasn't included like a few of our older properties, he told me it was for my own protection." Julia Bowman fell into deep thought. She lowered her head again and stared at a small statue of a horse on the coffee table. "He refused to tell me what he meant by that no matter how many times I pressed him."

Hawk asked, "Mrs. Bowman, do you still own the coffee business?"

"Yes, with a partner, Marcus Miller. But Jeffrey was hoping to sell the coffee business but my understanding, Marcus was dead set against it. So he didn't know how to approach him about the sale. It would be sticky."

Hawk pressed on. "Why would it be sticky, as you describe it?"

"Oh, I guess there were words and probably unserious threats over the sale of the business from Marcus. Do you think Marcus, is involved in all of this?"

"We have no idea," Wally said. "My partner is just trying to cover all bases at this time. We'll get out of your hair. Are you ready to go, Detective?"

But Julia wanted to add, "It's hard for me to believe that his partner of so many years could do such a thing as kill someone. But if he's desperate, who knows what that man would do."

Wally began clearing his throat, loudly displaying his continued disapproval of his brash partner. Hawk paid no attention to Wally's dissatisfaction. "I'm so sorry to ask these questions, but again, its procedure. Did your husband complain to you about the business or about his partner?"

Mrs. Bowman gazed at Hawk as though he came from outer space. Nevertheless, Hawk could see the cells in her mind revolving to come up with an answer, obviously struggling with whether to mention anything at all. Finally, Mrs. Bowman spoke. "Actually, my husband did complain lately about it. We discussed how much money we were plowing into the coffee business and we felt that someone was ripping us off. He was sure that it was his partner. He had changed recently after his divorce. He began throwing money around at women, as though he was a playboy. Jeffrey wanted out. I know that. But I can't believe that he would carjack a car and kill Jeffrey in that manner. He is just not the type to commit such a horrendous crime."

"Again, ma'am it's just a process we must go through to check all the possibilities and all suspects." Mrs. Bowman's voice began to crack, and her hands shook. *I better not ask any more questions. I probably pushed it too far.*

"Surely, you don't think I'm a suspect, do you?" Her voice became louder and irritated.

"Not at all, not at all," Murphy blurted out, giving Hawk the snake eye. "My young associate here is a little too enthusiastic as he only recently became a detective." Hawk felt like someone punched him in the gut. *That no good for nothing blow bag just undermined me and my authority. He's an idiot and a fool. I can't show my anger, at least not here, not now.* Hawk took some deep breaths while Murphy was trying to be as sweet and concerned over the widow's plight as he could. "We're so sorry that my partner asked those questions of you. He's young and he wants to cover all the bases. We'll leave you now to your grief. Here is my card, please call me if you need anything, anything at all. I'll be over as quickly as I can to help or just be a companion. Please call me, it will be no imposition. In the meantime, will you be all right? Is there anyone I could call for you so that they could join you? *Murphy's over-the-top*, Hawk thought, *almost like a sycophant that wants to curry favors. Is he hitting on her? I wonder. And what's this with the 'young' comments? He's a real jerk, that old geezer.*

Mrs. Bowman took his card and placed it on the marble-topped side table. Then she picked it up and read the name. "Thank you, Detective Murphy. I'll do that if I need any help. You've been so kind and understanding." She turned to Hawk, her jaw tightened and the tone in her voice changed. "Goodbye, Detective. Keep me informed." She turned her head toward Murphy making an attempt at a smile and said, "Now I have the sad task of calling my daughters and telling them that their father is—" She broke out into deep and violent sobs. Murphy began to approach her to comfort her, but she held out her arm, "Please leave now. I need to be alone."

CHAPTER 7

THE TWO detectives didn't say a word as Murphy drove back to the station. The late evening sun overheated the interior of the car. Murphy was sweating a river. Still pissed off at his partner, Hawk appreciated the silence. After a few minutes of silence, Murphy opened his mouth. "That was a fine, classy lady. I feel so sorry for her. I sure would like to get to know her better. Of course, not now, but sometime when it would be appropriate." He glanced over at Hawk who was still seething, looking straight ahead at Colfax Avenue. On the corner of Downing Street, his attention was diverted to two vagrants shouting at each other. "You were over the top with that woman, Hawk. You shouldn't have asked her about any enemies. Her husband was just shot, my God!   If it were so important to you, we could've come back and asked her after a week or so."

Hawk remained mute, staring at the pavement, his breath heavy.

"Are you mad at me or something? I was just trying to save you from seeming belligerent and insensitive to that fine woman."

"Don't you ever do that again. You sabotaged me, made me look like a fool and I don't appreciate it. The time to gather evidence and leads is as close to the time of the crime as possible. She gave us a lead, and I'm going to follow it."

"Is this what you learned from some book? Well, I'm sorry I hurt your feelings, but the lady just lost her husband and you're pumping her with questions. She even thought that you accused her of being a suspect. You have a lot to learn about human interaction, my young friend."

"That's another thing, I extremely resent your 'young' comments. Compared to you, I am young. But I don't want you to make me look incompetent by saying that when I'm interviewing. Got it?"

"Holy cow, man. Don't get your underwear tangled in a knot. You should take it as a compliment. I'd love someone to call me young."

Murphy backed the Crown Vic into the station lot. He parked the vehicle a little too close to the car adjacent leaving very little room to exit, especially for his corpulent body. In his attempt to escape the car, he hit his head on the upper part of the door frame and couldn't maneuver his right foot out of the well of the floor. He stumbled and grabbed the red-light bar on the patrol car next to him.

Hawk suppressed his laugh at the ungainly scene. He rushed over to help Murphy, forgetting his anger at the fool. "I'm okay, I'm okay," Murphy said as he straightened out. "I don't need another workmen's comp claim right before I retire." He laughed it off saying, "It's just one of those things. Do me a favor, Clint, don't tell anyone about how clumsy I was. I'm tired of being the butt of jokes in the room, okay?"

"Sure Wally, mum is the word," Hawk said, realizing that Murphy has his own self-esteem issues.

Hawk's watch showed 6:22 PM when the two detectives walked through the door of their division. No one there except Marcie who greeted them with a pleasant smile. "You were out late; did everything go well with the victim's wife?"

"Yeah, I guess it was okay," Murphy answered, even though Marcie specifically looked at Hawk.

She studied Hawk with mesmerizing eyes that Hawk couldn't help but gaze into. "Yes, Marcie, I believe it was a good interview. You're still here! When do you go home?"

"I should've left at 5:00, but I wanted to finish up something here that Orlinski asked me to check out." She hesitated briefly as Hawk began to walk away, then said, "Anyway, I thought that you might need me for some research. I know it's late, but I have some time tonight."

Hawk stopped and turned to face her. "I hate to hold you up. I doubt you'll get any overtime for this. You should go on home."

"No, it's okay." At that moment Murphy walked past Hawk after checking his computer. He muttered that they were young and can take it, but he needed his rest and walked out the door.

"Well, Clint, is there anything you need some help with? Anything I can look up?"

Hawk smiled, nodded in the affirmative and approached Marcie. "Okay, if you want to be a glutton for punishment then you've asked for it. I can think of a few things that I'd like to know. Are you sure you want to do this?"

"I'll tell you what. Let's put in some time and then how about getting something to eat? I love that English pub right on Thirteenth Street. Their bangers are great."

Oh, oh. That would be great, but I need to avoid this. I can't get involved with this girl no matter how much I'd love to. On the other hand, what would it hurt? I am hungry and will be even more so later. Just can't let it happen too often. She needs to realize that we're just co-workers. "Actually, that sounds good. I've eaten there when I was on patrol and I like the atmosphere. I marvel at how those liquor bottles are displayed upside down and shots are poured out of their spigot. It's really cool."

"Terrific, then let's get started. What do you want me to do?"

"Can you find any carjacking that's taken place in Denver Metro in the last six months, and then more specifically in Denver itself?"

"Right on it. It'll only take me a few minutes." She began punching the keyboard. Before Hawk reached his desk, took off his coat, and booted his computer, she called out that she had the information all ready for him. Hawk trotted to her workstation. "There has been one in Aurora, and one in Thornton. Except for the one today, there were none in the past six months in Denver itself."

"What about those in Aurora and Thornton? Who were the suspects?"

"Well, one was a Wilbur Prescott in Aurora. He was being chased by the police, crashed the car and forced a woman out of the car in front of him, and took off with her car. He was stopped a mile down Peoria Street.

"And the second one?"

"That was Jamal Gleason. He jumped into a vehicle while the owner was filling his tank. The key was in the ignition and Gleason drove off. Gas poured out onto the owner's pants and shoes before he could shut off the nozzle."

"Good work, Marcie. Could you please go back five years in the metro area to see if there was a carjacking where anyone was shot?" Hawk stayed by her this time watching her fingers glide easily over the keys.

"Only one carjacking where anyone was shot. The perp was chased down and after a gun battle, was shot by DPD."

"That's okay. Now we'll wait and see if the stolen vehicle today turns up somewhere." As if on cue, his cell ringtone played 'Bad to the Bone' by George Thorogood and the Destroyers. Marcie heard him say that that was great news and that he'll be right down. *Shoot, I hope we still get together tonight.*

"Marcie, you probably heard. They found the vehicle and I need to go inspect it before they tow it to CBI. I guess I'll take a rain check on the dinner."

"I'd like to go with you. May I?"

"Well, I don't know whether it's allowed."

"Oh sure, why wouldn't it be? After all, we work together. I'm coming with you." She grabbed her purse, pulled a key out of it to lock the door."

"I guess it'll be all right. By the way, can you get me a key to this office?"

"I'll ask the Lieutenant in the morning."

"Maybe he doesn't want to give me one yet. Probably expects me to mess up royally so that he'll have an excuse to get rid of me." Marcie dismissively waved her hand and proceeded to lock the door behind them. The upstairs was fairly quiet. But that was not the case on the first floor. Patrol officers led handcuffed suspects into the booking room and seated them next to the officers' desks. The scene reminded Hawk of his life just a few days ago.

"Since I don't have use of a police car, I guess we need to use my car. I need to talk to Bradford about getting the use of one after hours."

"Good luck with that," Marcie said with a doubtful smile. "He is a real miser when it comes to doling out vehicles to the detectives. You better use your own after hours."

Both headed to the lot and got into his silver 2012 Jeep Grand Cherokee sporting a ski rack. Marcie buckled up and placed her handbag between her ankles. She glanced over onto the back seat and spotted a tennis racket and a gym bag. "Hey, you're quite an athlete, aren't you? A ski rack on the roof, a tennis racket in the back seat and is that a golf bag in the back."

"I like to stay active, what about you?"

"I stay active also. I'm pretty good at tennis myself and I'm a runner. But my passion is rock climbing. Do you do that?"

"I've done it a few times, but I don't care for it too much."

"You probably don't do it enough. By the way, where are we going?"

"They found the vehicle in the Five Points area, Lawrence and 33rd."

"Not all that far away. That's strange, isn't it?"

" Why strange, Marcie?"

"I mean if I had shot someone and carjacked his car, I'd take it as far away as I could or hide it good or take it to a chop shop."

"Maybe the perp just needed some quick transportation. But, you're right, it is strange. There's more to it than meets the eye, that's for sure."

"What do you think it was, Clint?"

"I think it was an assassination covered up to look like a random carjacking."

"Really. That's far out there. What makes you say that?"

"Things just don't add up. For example, one of the witnesses told me that the victim was getting out of the car when he was shot, bullseye, on the forehead. It appears to me that Bowman was cooperating and there was no need for the carjacker to shoot him. The whole thing doesn't feel right to me."

"Well, then who do you think did it?"

"That's what we'll need to determine. By the way, we're driving in Five Points. I'm fascinated at the history here. For example, did you know that from the 1860s to the end of that century this was a classy neighborhood? You can still see some of the old homes scattered around."

"Really, a classy neighborhood, huh?"

"Well, at least it was a remarkably diverse neighborhood where governors, mayors, all kinds of city officials, successful businessmen resided alongside middle-class workers. Later it became known as the 'Harlem of the West' because of discrimination. It was one of the few areas in Denver where blacks could live. They had their own stores, banks, theaters, nightclubs, hotels."

"What is this discrimination you're talking about?"

"In those days, there were home sale laws in other neighborhoods that kept black people out. Then around the 1950s this area fell into disrepair but look at it now. It is becoming gentrified because of its proximity to downtown. Property values have skyrocketed. Just look at all these new condos and apartments springing up like mushrooms after rain."

"I know, Marcie said. "I feel sorry for the residents of this area who are forced out of the neighborhood because of the increasing home prices and rents. Some were born here; all their friends are here. Now they have to move out and seek cheaper areas, of which few, if any, are left in Denver."

"That's for sure. Well, here we are. Looks like that Cadillac is still in one piece."

CHAPTER 8

HAWK AND Marcie approached Corporal Manuel Delgado, a brief partner of Hawk in the patrol division. "Listen Clint, I don't know what you hope to see just by looking at the car. Most detectives wait until the lab people go over it and give a report."

"Thanks for waiting Manny, I owe you one. I'm working on something and I want to look at the car as you found it. Thanks for calling me. I'll be brief. By the way, this is Marcie. She's in our unit." He turned to Marcie and apologetically said, "Marcie, I don't know your last name."

"Oh, it's Turner. Marcie Madison Turner."

"Nice to meet you," said Delgado. "Tough assignment having to put up with Hawk. He'll drive you crazy." Both men chuckled.

"Oh, I don't mind, Corporal," Marcie answered, showing Delgado a full smile. "At least not yet."

"So, when did you find the car?" Hawk asked as he carefully looked over the outside of the vehicle.

"Just an hour ago. I was driving down Lawrence and remembered the BOLO on a silver Cadillac DTS sedan. The plates matched the carjacked vehicle."

"Good work, Manny. I'll put that in my preliminary report." Hawk walked completely around the vehicle while Delgado and Marcie stood off to the side, Marcie shielded her eyes from the bright red and blue lights of the patrol Ford Interceptor. The crowd that stood around the vehicle seemed to gather larger than the few that stood there when she and Hawk arrived. Most in the crowd had their cell phones in their hands ready to take videos, hoping for an exciting, or better yet, controversial shot.

Hawk approached the driver's door and with his handkerchief pulled on the door handle, opening the door out about six inches. He then swung the door wide open, bent over and studied the interior. It appeared that someone did a poor job of wiping splattered blood off the passenger side of the dashboard, windshield, window and door. He noticed what looked like a slug lodged in the frame of the windshield. *The bullet went right through the victim's skull.* Droplets of dried blood remained on the left side of the driver's seat. A stream of dried blood led from the seat onto the aluminum door sash.

All indications were that Bowman was attempting to exit the vehicle when he was shot. Otherwise, why would the carjacker pull him out and shoot him at the same time. There were a few droplets of blood on the side of the black carpet, but hard to see unless studied carefully. He noticed the key in the ignition. He looked at the console. The storage compartment was wide open and empty. He focused on the gear shift lever and noticed that the black leather was clean of blood. The seat was pushed up close to the steering wheel indicating a short individual that had last driven the car.

Marcie came up to Hawk while his head was still inside the vehicle. "Did you find anything helpful?"

"Just more evidence that confirms my theory." He straightened and walked past Marcie to where Delgado was standing with a disbelieving expression on his face thinking, *he's wasting my time and his. Just got a new gig and now he has to prove something.* "Manny, you can call them to tow it away now. By the way, how are Jenny and the kids?"

"Their fine. Jenny says you need to come over some time for dinner."

"That would be great. Oh, before I forget, make sure no one touches the steering wheel, the door handles, gear shift knob and turn signals. I'll call forensics tomorrow and explain what I want. Manny, again thanks for doing this for me. As I said, I owe you one."

Delgado appeared jovial and accommodating, but as he walked away, Clint noticed a note of contempt in Manny's voice when he said, "You got it, boss." *Maybe I shouldn't have given those standard instructions that an officer and especially the lab techs would already know. I should watch that—it sounded arrogant.*

"So, you think that was helpful? I mean, to look at the car as Manny found it?"

"I think so." Marcie looked at him waiting for an explanation as they drove away. He didn't say anymore, seeming deep in thought.

"Hey watch out, Clint, there's a man trying to cross the street."

"Oh, geez. Thanks for that. When I'm concentrating on a subject, I tend to shut the world off around me. I won't do that again." When they passed under a streetlight, Marcie saw that his face looked flush with embarrassment.

"So, what were you concentrating so deeply on anyway?"

"I was thinking that a carjacker, if he wanted the car for any other reason than just quick transportation, wouldn't have shot the victim inside the car. It's hard to get rid of a car if it has blood and brain parts scattered all over. Who would want to bother with that car?

"So, you still believe that the purpose was not to steal the car but something else?"

"Yes, definitely. Tomorrow, I'm going to try to interview Bowman's partner. You still hungry?"

"Starving. I thought you'd never ask."

"Great. Since we're in the neighborhood, how about trying Denver Central Market on Seventeenth and Larimer?" Hawk thought of the place recommended by the hipster with the scooter. "It's a food hall and I hear it's a fun place."

"Sure. Let's go."

CHAPTER 9

"SO, WHAT do you feel like tonight, Marcie?"

"Oh, I don't really care, Clint, I'm hungry enough to eat anything. Besides, I'm not picky with my food, are you?"

"Not really. Hey, there's an Italian place. How about some pasta?"

"Sure, it's comfort food after all and I'm all for as much comfort as I can get," Marcie said, laughing as she gently touched her hand to his forearm. Hawk felt the warmth of her touch and it pleased him.

They each ordered eggplant parmesan with a side of spaghetti with marinara sauce. Being of a chivalrous mind, Hawk pulled out his wallet intending to pay for both. At the same time, Marcie retrieved her credit card. "Dinner's on me, Marcie."

"Oh no, you don't. We'll each pay for our own. After all this is not a date, is it?" She broke into a wide, open smile as she waited for his response.

Maybe it's better that way. We need to keep professional about this without any strings attached. "All right if you insist. We'll each get our own, but I'm not used to having a lady pay for herself when she's with me. But since we're on official business and, as you say, this is not a date, it's probably for the best." Marcie continued to display that captivating smile of hers. Hawk found it impossible not to grin back.

They sat at a high long table across from each other at the two available seats as the food hall was packed. The young people who shared the table were engaged in some lively conversation that on occasion included great peals of laughter. Hawk heard bits and pieces of the conversation and it seemed to involve a peculiar boss of one of the girls.

"So, Clint, tell me about yourself. Are you originally from the Denver area?"

"No, I'm from Texas. Born and raised in Tyler. You know, that's where they grow all those roses. As a matter of fact, I worked in a greenhouse while in high school."

"So, how did you end up in Colorado?"

"School. I graduated from CSU with a BA in psychology and a MA from CU. Never went back to Texas except to visit my family. I love this state. What about you, Marcie?"

"I'm from San Jose, California. I came out here to get my engineering degree from the School of Mines in Golden." She took another bite out her eggplant. Hawk speared a piece for himself. "But after I graduated, I looked for a job with what I love to do and that is computer research."

"Really, that sounds boring to me."

"Well, it's how you look at it. Personally, I really enjoy it. That's why I took this job with the police department, at least for a while until I settle down as an engineer." As she spoke, she played with her pasta, twirling it around her spoon before it disappeared in her mouth. "Quite frankly, I don't think I'll make a good engineer."

"Why not? You seem to have a good head on your shoulders," *and a great-looking one to boot,* he thought, wolfing down a large forkful of spaghetti.

With a burst of full-hearted laughter, she joked, "You couldn't tell before, huh?"

Hawk said, "Of course I could. You impressed me from the start."

"Thanks, but to be truthful, and don't you ever tell my parents, even though I'm good in math, I really don't like working with numbers."

"Oh, that's the pits—working hard to get such a difficult degree and already know that you'll not enjoy it."

"I know. I feel like I wasted my time." Marcie took another bite of her eggplant, as did Hawk. "My dad is an engineer and pushed me into the field. He's really disappointed that I'm wasting my talents playing with computers for the police department."

"Oh, I'd certainly disagree. You're terrific at your job, one that with modern police practices is indispensable. Look at all the victims you're helping with those dainty fingers of yours." *Damn, why did I say that. I'm not supposed to comment on any body features.*

"Well, thank you Clint. You are very reassuring. I needed that confidence builder."

After they finished eating, Hawk drove her back to the police station so that she could pick up her car. He watched her get into her red Mini Cooper convertible and drive off. He felt good about the "non-date" and wanted to repeat it soon. He knew that he really liked being with her and wanted to see more of her.

CHAPTER 10

THE NEXT day, Hawk convinced a reluctant Wally Murphy to go with him to interview Marcus Miller, Bowman's business partner. He really didn't want Murphy to accompany him, but he thought the Lieutenant would be more willing to approve the "wild goose chase" as he put it, if Murphy was there as well.

As they headed to the coffee business, Murphy said in a resentful tone, "You know, bud, you're barking up the wrong tree. You didn't see the report yet, but forensics lifted several prints off the Caddie's steering wheel and the gear shift knob. They matched to a Leland Freeman who has a record as long as your arm for burglary, auto theft and possession of drugs. That's who we should be going after, not some wild scheme of yours."

Surprised that no one informed him of this important information sooner, Hawk answered, "In that case, I'm sure a BOLO is out for him and as soon as they find him, we'll interview him. Don't you think it's odd that forensics found his prints in the car? Wasn't the murderer wearing gloves?"

"You're just trying to make a federal case out of this. Criminals are not the smartest specimens on this earth. The guy's prints were in the car, he has a record of auto thefts, and that's all I need to make a case against him."

"Don't jump to conclusions yet, Wally. I tell you there is more to this case than meets the eye."

"Ah, you're just a greenhorn and I'm stuck with you. I could be back in the station having a cup of coffee and a pastry."

"I'll tell you what, Wally. If we have the time after the interview, coffee and doughnuts will be on me. We'll stop at Lamar's on Sixth Avenue."

"Now you're talking. Let's go see what Miller says then maybe you'll back off when you see that you're wasting your time." Hawk thought, *he'll come around with my assessment of the case, but would never admit it now.*

Bowman's and Miller's offices were located on the second floor of the Coffee Aroma retail business. The receptionist, a pleasant-looking Asian woman with long hair in her early fifties sat behind a tiled counter reading a book as the two detectives walked in. Startled, she sat up, smiled and asked, "May I help you? Do you gentlemen have an appointment?"

Wally pointed to his shield, half covered by his stomach, and said, "This is our appointment. We need to see Marcus Miller."

The woman put her book down, her smile faded. "Yes, of course, he just left but said that he'll be back in fifteen minutes. You're welcome to wait. Is this about Mr. Bowman's death?" Hawk nodded. "Isn't it horrible what happened to him? We're all in shock. But then we expected something like that could happen."

"Oh," Hawk said. "Why do you say that?"

She glanced around the small room, her voice almost a whisper, "Mr. Bowman was not very pleasant. Hard to work for and deal with. He felt superior to everyone else and no one here liked him, not even Mr. Miller, his partner…he even received death threats.

"Really," Hawk said. "From Marcus Miller?"

She hesitated and glanced toward the front door. "Well, I heard them having an argument just a couple of days ago. Something about selling the coffee business. Mr. Miller didn't want to sell, but I guess that's what Mr. Bowman wanted."

Hawk said, I really appreciate any help that you can give us. My name is Clint Hawk and my partner is Wally Murphy. And your name?"

"Oh, I'm Suzy Cho. I'm sorry, I probably said too much. Everyone says I talk too much. It's a nasty habit, isn't it?"

"Not at all, especially if you can help us solve Mr. Bowman's murder. Did you hear Marcus Miller threaten Bowman? Is that what you said?"

She glanced at the door. Again, in a low voice, she said, "I heard Mr. Miller say, 'Back off if you know what's good for your health.'"

Wally smirked, "And you think that was a threat to kill him?"

"Well, yeah, I'd say. He sounded mean enough that he could do it."

"Did they argue often?" Hawk inquired.

"All the time, but this last time was a real doozie."

Wally asked, "And how would you be able to overhear all this stuff?"

"Whoever remodeled this upstairs, did a poor job. The wall must be paper thin because I could hear Mr. Bowman at times. His office is on the other side of this wall. And I think that part of the sound comes in through this light fixture in the suspended ceiling over my head." Both detectives craned their neck to look up at the fixture. "He was a loud talker as is Mr. Miller."

"Did you hear anyone else threaten Mr. Bowman?" Hawk asked.

"On occasion. But actually, it was more a shouting match. Although, one time, I got delayed going home and two men walked in as though they owned the place and barged into Mr. Bowman's office. There was no argument, but I think I heard one of them say that they need the money now and he better come up with it or he'll be pushing daisies. I guess that was a threat, wasn't it?"

Wally exhaled loudly. "All right, I suppose you can give us a description of the men?"

"They were white, not too tall wore leather jackets, even though it was hot out."

Wally turned to Hawk. "That doesn't give us much to go on. Let's go."

Hawk persisted, "Ms. Cho, any outstanding features on their faces?"

"No, actually I didn't see their faces. I only caught a glimpse of them as they walked past me. You see, I had my back to them reaching down to get my purse."

"Any other threats that you heard?" Hawk asked, pleased that they ran across such a loquacious woman. *Must be very bored sitting out here all by herself.*

"Probably, not much to it, but there was this one disgruntled employee that told everyone here that he'll get even with Bowman. Said that 'he better enjoy his life while he can.' But no one took him seriously." Her eyes suddenly widened, "Do you think that someone like that could've done it?"

"You can never tell. Do you have his name?"

"It was Abel Johnson. He worked in the warehouse. That's all I know about him. You'll have to get other info from HR."

Wally's irritation became more noticeable. He kept huffing and puffing while Hawk kept asking questions. Finally, he blurted out, "Okay, Hawk. We need to go. We've spent too much time here already." He looked at the woman and said, "Ma'am, don't let my young, eager partner lead you to believe that someone here could've carjacked and killed Jeffrey Bowman. It was just a standard carjacking by some punk that probably did it many times before." He looked at Hawk, "Now can we go?"

Hawk fumed. He thought he was making great progress with this woman. She gave him several leads as to who had a grudge against Bowman. He was flabbergasted that Wally didn't see it that way. *That lazy bastard just interfered with my questioning. I can't believe it. Bastard!*

"All right, Wally, hang on," Hawk said, not looking at him. "We'll be out of here soon enough. "Ms. Cho, may I have your full name, address and phone number?" She gave it to him and he wrote in down in his small notepad. "It appears that Mr. Miller still hadn't come back."

"No. He's become like that lately. Says one thing, then he does something else."

"Well, in that case, could you show us Mr. Bowman's office?"

Murphy exclaimed, "Oh God, man! What do we need to see his office for?"

"Wally, it's standard procedure in a suspicious death in case there is a something there that might lead us to the killer."

"I don't think it's suspicious at all. You go, then. I'll sit down here on this soft chair and wait. But make it snappy."

Hawk followed the receptionist a short distance down a hall. She had the key and unlocked the door. Before she left, she whispered, "Your partner doesn't seem happy with you."

"Oh, we just have a difference of opinion."

"I hope no one here killed him. It'll be more pleasant now that Mr. Bowman is no longer…oh my gosh! What am I saying? Of course, it's awful that he's dead. I certainly don't want to leave you with the wrong impression."

"I understand."

In contrast to a rather plain reception room with its reception counter, four arm chairs, light oak end tables stacked with magazines, Bowman's office was elegantly furnished. His hand-crafted desk and matching credenza immediately caught Hawk's eye. He gravitated toward the desk and began looking through a disarrayed pile of sheets of paper and scratch pads. It appeared that Bowman was deep in math calculations as evidenced by columns of numbers, totaling hundreds of thousands of dollars. There were sheets with addresses, names of realtors and invoices from suppliers and statements of amounts due. He looked through the drawers and saw account books, flash drives, bank deposit pads, CD's and insurance policies. *All of this may be very important and needs to be analyzed. It should be considered a crime scene and cordoned off. I'll talk to Bradford about it.*

Hawk walked out of the room. He looked at Wally and chuckled when he saw his lazy partner sleeping, his head rolled back, his mouth gapping open, drool making its way down the side. Suzy glanced at Hawk and snickered. "Poor baby," she said. "You wore him out."

After waking Wally up, he thanked her and asked that she lock the door to the Bowman's office and let no one in until his Lieutenant decides what to do."

CHAPTER 11

THE TWO detectives headed back to their car. Wally was still grumbling about "the wild goose chase" that Hawk put him through. But he quickly got over it after Hawk reminded him that he promised him a Lamar's donut and his choice of coffee.

"Now, you're making sense, bud," Wally said. I love those donuts, hadn't had them for months."

Over coffee and donuts, Hawk asked Wally, "Don't you see that there were several people that threatened Bowman?"

With a big bite out of the custard-filled donut, Wally managed to say, "So what? If you had a little patience, my friend…you would soon discover that it was just some gang banger, maybe a homeless person and found an easy mark." He finally swallowed the mouthful and was about to stuff in another huge portion when he casually glanced at an attractive woman that walked in. "Looky there, buddy. That woman is hot."

"Yeah, a little too old for me."

"Not for me. Maybe I should try to get her phone number."

"Go for it, Wally."

"Well, yeah, but it'll be just like all the other times, I'll get a quick brush off. Anyway, what was I going to say to you?"

"I don't know, Wally? Probably try to make me look like a fool."

"Oh, I wouldn't do that to my new partner…but if the shoe fits…" He started to laugh. Hawk didn't think it was funny at all. After he was finished with his fit of merriment at Hawk's expense, he said, "The carjacking and murder in this case is so obvious. I humored you so far, but I don't want you to be like that dog that chases his own tail and never gets anywhere. Look at what's in front of your nose and leave it at that."

"But that's exactly what I'm doing. Don't you think that Marcus Miller needs to be questioned? He was the partner, obviously they were angry at each other, and who benefits most out of Bowman's death? It's Miller. You have to admit that, Wally. And what about all the other people that threatened Bowman? Shouldn't we follow up with them?"

"Look, the longer you work as a detective, you'll learn to prioritize your time. We're too busy to go chasing after everyone that might've given a victim a dirty look. People threaten each other all the time. Doesn't mean that they'd kill. So, do the right thing in this case and find the carjacker and see where that leads us."

"Wally, that's exactly what I'm doing. It could very well be that Miller is the carjacker or he hired someone to kill Bowman. Someone wanted to get rid of Bowman."

"Bullshit! You're going to make me work on something that's in your mind and not what the facts show. Anyway, I don't want to talk about it anymore." He moved closer to the table and finished off the donut. "Hey, how about those Rockies? I got tickets for this Saturday. You want to come along?"

"I'm sorry, Wally. I got plans. How about a rain check?" The last thing Hawk wanted to do is spend the time with the guy at a baseball game.

Wally seemed upset, "Okay, I'll hold you to that. Maybe I'll ask Orlinski if he wants to go."

On the way to the station, Wally began another one of his stories. "I was in court testifying in this murder trial and the defense attorney was a real jerk. He tried to brainwash the jury that I didn't do a thorough enough investigation and didn't look to no one else other than the defendant. Well, I successfully testified that it was a cut and dry case with what was obvious and the jury convicted the sonofabitch."

Hawk couldn't believe what he just heard. The man was lazy even when he was younger. Of course, in Hawk's mind, he should have looked at all the possibilities. "This this supposed to be a lesson there for me somewhere. What made it so clear cut?"

"The facts as they played out, pal. Just as in this case with the Bowman's."

Hawk's patience was running thin with the same song and dance from his partner. He decided that he'll talk to Bradford and tell him what Suzy Cho had told them about the threats, including one from Miller, the employee, and the two men in leather jackets. And ask permission to follow up on that, regardless of how Wally felt about it. Also, he needed to gather up all the papers and account books from Bowman's desk.

Lieutenant Bradford's reply was a resounding, "NO." Growling he said, "Damnit, man, I told you that once we find the carjacker, this case will be solved and closed. Understand, rookie!" Looking at his face as it turned red, Hawk decided to drop the subject. He is the boss and he has to follow orders after all. "Don't you have a couple of reports to write—the one about the hipster and your interview with Julia Bowman?"

"Yes, sir."

"Then go do them…and, I want to know what you're doing before you go galivanting."

Angry, Hawk worked on the reports and was through within the hour. He was still irate, taking deep breaths to calm down. As he did so, he glanced around the room. Several detectives were out—on cases, he supposed. *Lucky them.* He knew that Orlinski was interrogating someone and he wished he was doing it. Wally had left, said he had some personal errands to run. Marcie was busy at her computer. He wished that she'd come by and say "hi." Suddenly the door swung open and that brunette detective strode in. Perhaps the same age as Hawk, she was an attractive woman, with dark brown hair tied back in a bun, striking intense dark blue eyes, very fit and toned.

She glanced in Hawk's direction and smiled. Instead of being cool about it, he awkwardly titled his head as though he was reading. He still hadn't met her and she made no attempt to introduce herself. She seemed to be a mysterious, intriguing busy person that he'd like to meet. The woman sat down and he watched as she peered at her smart phone. After intently reading something, she hurriedly stood and flew out of the Unit.

He looked at his Tag Huer watch. Time was simply dragging on. *Ten more minutes to quitting time. Bradford better assigns me something tomorrow since I'm blocked from investigating any of the leads in the Bowman murder. I really can't understand why.*

Six more minutes and I can get out of here. Bradford walked out of the hallway that led to his office. He looked Hawk's way but didn't acknowledge him. He stopped and talked to Marcie for a few minutes before leaving. Just as Hawk was about to leave, Orlinski returned to his workstation, his face flushed. *Must've been a tough interrogation.* He saw him throw a pad down on his desk and walk out. Only Marcie was still at her desk. Hawk met her as she stood to leave. "Well, Detective, how did your second day go?"

"Frustrating and boring, actually. How was your day?"

"Busy as always. You want to grab some dinner?"

"Yeah, sure. Sounds good. How about that pub we planned on going yesterday?"

"Terrific."

CHAPTER 12

ON THE WAY to the restaurant, Marcie wanted to know what he worked on, just for small talk, Hawk assumed. He told her about what the receptionist at Bowman's and Miller's office said, about how many people disliked Jeffrey Bowman and threatened him. "All those that threatened him should be investigated. I mean, isn't that what a good detective is supposed to do?"

"I would think so."

"Well, evidently, Bradford and actually Wally, also, are so dead set that Bowman's death was just as a result of a simple carjacking and they don't want to think outside the box. I can't understand it."

"I see your frustration, but you'll get further ahead if you do what Bradford says."

Hawk turned his head toward Marcie. Smiling widely, he said in a soft tone, "I guess so."

Finding a parking spot, he pulled his Jeep into it. Pints pub was on Thirteenth Street, a block away from the Denver Art Museum. The place was packed and Hawk thought that they'd have to wait to be seated, but a friendly waitress showed them to a tall table, the last available one.

Clint and Marcie smiled at each other as they adjusted themselves in the tall chairs. A short young woman in her early twenties with both arms covered with colorful tattoos came up to the table. She asked for their drink order and both Clint and Marcie ordered beer brewed by the pub, the third oldest brewery in Denver. They also asked the waitress if they could place an order for the food. They were both starving and looked forward to one of the specialties of the house, bangers and mash.

"Clint, I'm so sorry you feel so frustrated already."

"Yeah. Thanks…it's not what I expected. It seems that my detective training is in the way. We were taught to follow all leads and not to jump to conclusions." With a sad expression, Hawk blew out a hard breath.

"Too bad that Captain Iona MacGregor is on vacation. I suppose you could've gone over Bradford's head and talked to her."

"When will she be back?"

"I think sometime next week. She's on an Alaskan train going from Anchorage to Fairbanks."

"I wish I were there," Hawk chuckled. "I'd love to do that someday."

"Me too." Marcie suddenly looked concerned, "But Clint, if you were to do something like going over Bradford's head, you might be kissing your career goodbye. I think that MacGregor is a little intimidated by Bradford and will tell you to follow his orders."

"Really?' Hawk looked surprised. "Why?"

"I really don't know. He has an overbearing personality, but then, so does MacGregor, I suppose. But he's loud and acts as though he's in charge and probably MacGregor lets him slide on things just to keep peace in the Unit." She hesitated, in thought. "Bradford seems to be getting more aggressive lately. I believe that he's upset about something." She hesitated again, watching Hawk's reaction. He looked at her thoughtfully, considering what she was telling him. "Don't get me wrong, Bradford follows MacGregor's orders, but seems to question a lot of them."

"Huh! That's interesting. So, what is Captain MacGregor like?"

"She's very busy. She's in charge of both the Homicide and the Robbery Units. You'll meet her soon enough. She'll like you. She is tough but fair. A stickler for people that look and act professional and follow the rules. You'll really impress her with the way you dress." They each took a sip of beer.

With a pensive look, she continued, "She's been on Wally for some time to look neater in appearance. But I don't think he really pays too much attention to anything anymore. He's close to retiring and that's all he cares about." She took another sip, this time a little larger. "I get the impression that he's always been a slob and a klutz. But, he's funny in his ways and keeps everyone entertained." She chuckled as she continued gazing at Hawk.

Hawk returned the laugh. "Oh, he's funny all right at times, but lazy as far as I'm concerned. But yet, he can be very serious and thoughtful. But I know that if I remain as his partner, he's going to drag me down and make me look bad as a detective. You know, Marcie, I have this feeling in my gut that that is exactly what Bradford wants—to ruin my career."

"Well. If that happens, that wouldn't be the worst thing that can happen to you, would it?"

That comment from Marcie shocked him. "What do you mean by that?"

"I mean the life of a policeman, even though he's a detective, is tough and dangerous. You never know if you would come home. Tough on a wife ...I mean a spouse, even more."

"But that's my dream to be a good detective and make a difference in this world. I can't think of anything else I would want to do." He glared at Marcie, not liking what he heard after all the work and studying he'd done just to achieve the rank of detective.

"Clint," she said softly, as she reached for his hand. "I don't mean to discourage you by any means. I just met you and wouldn't want anything to happen to you, that's all." She smiled. "Please forgive me if I upset you."

"Marcie, it's okay. Sorry that I overreacted. I just had a very exasperating day, that's all. Besides, if I were to quit the force, I would want to do it at my own pace and not be shoved out with my tail between my legs."

"Of course, Clint." She reached over the small table and gently placed her left hand on his right arm. Hawk enjoyed her soothing hand on his arm. He enjoyed the comforting feel it seemed to give him.

The bangers and mash were served. Marcie complained of the large portion as she and Hawk dug into the food. She studied Hawk for a minute. He still looked down. "Okay, maybe a good joke would cheer you up. Have you heard of the two guys that walked into a bar—"

Hawk looked at her and let out a boisterous laugh. "You weren't going to tell me a corny bar joke, were you? I'm not that desperate…actually, that did cheer me up. Thanks."

"I'm so glad because if that didn't work, I was prepared to do a cartwheel for you and that might not be that pretty."

Hawk continued to chuckle. "Actually, I'd like to see that, Marcie."

"Oh, no you don't. I tell you that would totally embarrass you."

"I'll take my chances." Marcie laughed along with Hawk.

The conversation stilled. A few minutes later, trying to make conversation as he took another swig of beer, Hawk asked, "Marcie, do you live far from here?"

"Not too far. I live in Glendale. You're welcome to come over for a nightcap, if you wish." She smiled broadly.

"Oh, thanks for that, but that wasn't why I asked. I just wondered what part of this metro area had your home. I'll take a raincheck on the nightcap. But don't forget to ask me again…it's just that I feel that I need to be alone tonight and just winddown. Besides Stella is waiting for me to come home.

" Stella?"

"Yes. She is a pretty blonde. Very sweet and smart." Hawk chuckled.

Marcie's mouth flew open. "I should've asked if you were seeing someone. Your file indicated that you're single."

"You looked into my file?"

"Um, oh. Sorry about that. I was very curious. I'm good with computers, you know."

Clint let out another hearty laugh. "Stella is not my girlfriend, she's a Labrador Retriever and when I'm away, my neighbor watches her. She adores the dog."

Trying not to show how relieved she was, Marcie said, "Oh. Well, in that case, the invitation for a nightcap stands anytime…unless you're worried about work fraternization?"

"Well, no. Kinda actually."

"Okay, then this is not a date, just two coworkers discussing cases over dinner." Marcie laughed, mischievously.

"Not a date, you say?" Hawk grinned. "I still insist on paying for this high-level meeting. You can get it next time."

Marcie's smile spread across her face. "Okay, it's a deal."

CHAPTER 13

AFTER DROPPING off Marcie at her car, Hawk made his way home. He was tired. The stress of the new job and the feeling that Bradford is out to get him wore him out. After taking his dog for a short walk, he plopped onto the bed and immediately fell asleep in his street clothes. A couple of hours later, he woke up, changed into his sleeping gear, brushed his teeth, and jumped back into bed.

Hawk was up early, dressed quickly, fed Stella and hurried outside the door. He wanted to be first in the Unit. Unfortunately, an automobile accident blocked all the lanes of travel and he was stuck. *Doggonit! I'm going to be way late now!* He banged his hand on the steering wheel out of frustration. *Damn! Damn! Damn! Bradford will have a field day with me now for coming in late.*

Sure enough, he was the last to arrive. Marcie gave him a wide smile as he entered. He returned the smile. Walking past her desk, his eyes locked on the dark blue eyes of the attractive brunette detective staring at him. She smiled pleasantly. It was an opportunity to introduce himself, but as he headed for her desk, Orlinski stopped him at his. "Rough night?"

"No, I got royally delayed by a traffic accident." *What's it to him, anyway?*

He was interrupted, again, when Wally shouted out, "Get over here, Hawk. I've got Bradford on the phone."

Um-oh. Wally probably told Bradford that I came in late. And now he'll be yelling at me. But that wasn't the case. Over Wally's phone speaker, Bradford commanded, "I want you two to head to Bowman's residence. Pronto. It appears the wife was killed during a burglary."

"Did you hear that, ace?" Wally said, as he wiped powdered sugar off his lips—a half-empty bag of cookies by his side. Instead of rushing out as ordered by Bradford, he flopped down into his chair, shaking his head in disbelief. He was breathing hard. "It can't be. Not poor Julia. Bowman. Oh, that's really crap. She was such a class act. What an unlucky set of circumstances. First her husband in a carjacking and now she in a burglary. Unbelievable."

"Wally, we better go." *Maybe I'll have another case to work on.*

Wally reluctantly stood and followed Hawk out the door.

Driving over to the mansion, Hawk commented, "This whole thing seems really strange, don't you think, Wally?"

Wally remained silent, seemingly deep in thought. Then a few moments later, he said, "Now listen, don't start with me again. You'll probably find some reason to say it wasn't a real burglary, won't you? And that it was some conspiracy to kill both Bowmans. The Lieutenant will have your hide if he disagrees. He likes a neat, quick solution, one that is obvious."

"Wally, until we get there and investigate the scene, I'm not jumping to any conclusions." Hawk glanced at his partner who appeared truly upset and couldn't understand why. Suddenly, Wally gunned the engine, lit the red and blue lights, hit the siren and sped wildly to the Bowman's house. Hawk didn't say a word but sat tense expecting a crash with the angry and aggressive way he was driving. Luckily, without incident, Wally screeched to a stop near the house.

Two police cruisers and two unmarked police cars sat in front of the place. They saw what they knew were forensics experts walking in. The medical examiner, Dr. Janeel Thompson, and her assistant, a skinny, nerdy type who didn't look old enough to shave, followed them into the house. Hawk recognized the two officers on the porch of the house, chatting casually with Lt Williams of the Fraud and

Financial Unit. *What in the hell is Williams doing here?* Hawk thought that was so unusual on a burglary or homicide call.

Williams gave Hawk a warm smile. "Nice to see you, Clint, it's been a while. I guess you're getting your feet wet fast here." As Hawk smiled back, Bradford came out of the house.

"Ah, you're finally here." He looked straight at Hawk. "You and Wally get in there and get to work. *Why is Bradford here? Maybe it's because it's a high-profile case? Very interesting.* Today Bradford wore tan pants and a blue blazer with brass anchor buttons. Hawk also wore tan pants and a blue blazer similar to Bradford's. "What did you guys do, call each other this morning and decide what to wear?" Williams chuckled. "You almost look like twins. Now remember, I said almost." And then he snickered, looking at Bradford's gut.

"We have a dead body here so show some respect, would you," Bradford chided. At first, Hawk thought that he sensed some animosity in Bradford for Williams, but then he noticed the beginning of a grin tip the corners of his mouth followed by a wink.

"Hey, lighten up, you know I was laughing at how both of you look," Williams said. "Of course, you're absolutely right. This is a solemn occasion. Do you mind if I join you?"

Bradford said, "No problem, Williams, let's go up."

"I'd like to know who found the victim?" Hawk asked.

"Yeah, okay." He turned to one of the officers. "DeSalvo who notified you of the crime?"

"Lieutenant, it was the housekeeper, Mrs. Alice Cordova. We received the call shortly after 9:00 this morning. She is in the kitchen waiting for the detectives."

"All right. Hawk and Murphy can talk to her later."

As they entered the house, Murphy asked DeSalvo, sighing, "Where is the body?"

"In the master bedroom, at the top of the stairs to your right. McAfee and Salardino are up there now protecting the scene. The medical examiner and her assistant are already up there."

Williams, Bradford, Hawk and Murphy walked up the wide highly polished dark walnut staircase with its wide handrail and a subdued red runner covering almost the width of the risers and threads. In the wide hallway at the top of the staircase, stood an elegant gilded table topped by a massive bronze Remington statue of a cowboy on a horse. Hawk thought it was probably one of a kind and worth many thousands of dollars. Above the table hung a large, magnificent oil painting depicting a cowboy on a bucking horse. The painting looked similar to the one he studied in his required art class. As the others walked into the bedroom, Hawk held back briefly to note that the painting was by Joe Beeler, a well-known western artist who had now passed away. *The burglar or burglars were not too interested in art objects. Those pieces alone would fetch tens of thousands of dollars.*

The bedroom reeked with a faint odor of a dead body. No matter how many corpses he had seen as an officer, he still felt nauseous. Everyone was bent over Julia Bowman's body except for his partner. Murphy stood away, looking out the bedroom window, his round shoulders stooped. He looked pathetic in his wrinkled beige suit jacket—two sizes too tight on him. Hawk felt sorry for him. He looked truly distraught. *In the few moments that he met* Julia *Bowman, he must have really fallen hard for her. Is that possible? Did he really think that he could hit it off with her? He's a fool to even think a lady like her would go for a poor overweight policeman. Oh well, love's flame burns eternal. I hope he'll find someone soon. He must be lonely and needs someone.*

"Are you all right, Wally?"

Wally sniffled, rubbed his fat fingers over his face and put on a fake grin. "Of course, why wouldn't I be? I was just checking out the back yard while everyone else was looking at the body. Do you know how she was killed yet?"

"I'm waiting for the two Lieutenants to stand aside before I'll take another look." *Although, why they are so interested in this case, I don't know.*

Hawk examined the room. It appeared that there was a struggle. A Tiffany lamp from the desk lay on the floor with its stain-glass shade cracked in several places. Three photos of probably her grandchildren were knocked off the dresser and a Chinese vase lay in jagged pieces on the floor. On the desk a knocked-over crystal decanter spilled its contents onto the rug. The struggle seemed to center around the bed, the desk and the dresser. On the opposite wall, not far from the unmade bed was a wood-burning fireplace. A poker stand stood at the side, containing a black brush and a brass scoop.

Hawk poked around the large master closet to see if anything was obviously missing. The jewelry compartment of a chest of drawers was wide open, mostly empty except for three diamond bracelets and two rings. He pulled on his nitrile gloves and examined each ring carefully. One ring he was sure was an emerald. The other he guessed to be tanzanite. Years before, he had taken an online gemology class just for the fun of it. *These semi-precious stones in heavy 14 karat gold settings are certainly worth some serious money.*

Next, he carefully pulled out the drawer underneath. It contained women's underwear and a watch box. He opened the box and saw a ladies' Patek Phillipe watch. He read about that brand of watches and knew that they were priced in the thousands of dollars. *That's strange, I would think the burglar would have checked all the drawers to see what else was of value and would have certainly taken all the jewelry, especially that watch. What kind of burglar was this?*

After the lieutenants went downstairs, Hawk examined the body. Her hair was soaked with blood, the pool of dark blood stained the colorful Persian rug which was almost large enough to cover the bamboo floor of the large bedroom. "Do you know how she died?" Hawk asked the medical examiner.

"Well, well, well. You're certainly busy at your new job, aren't you? Janeel said, smiling. Hawk smiled and raised his arms in agreement. "By the way this is Andrew, my trusty assistant." Andrew's complexion had a greenish tinge to it and the poor fellow looked as though he was about to puke. He gave Hawk a distressed wave. It was obvious that he hadn't been around dead bodies much. *Actually, no matter how many stiffs I had seen while on patrol, it's still hard on me to see someone dead this way. Look at Janeel, she's whistling to herself as she is examining the head. I don't know how these medical examiners do it.*

"Look at this, Detective Hawk," Janeel said. "You can see that a sharp object whacked her on the scalp. Don't know yet if she died instantly from that or whether she bled out?"

"Any idea what object was used to hit her?'

"No, but it looks like something sharp and pointed."

"Could it be a knife or a letter opener?"

"No, it was wider than that, at least half an inch or so with a pointed end." Hawk looked around the room to see if he could find something that the killer might have used. He walked over to the broken pieces of the Chinese vase. With his gloves still on him, he examined each piece. None of the pieces showed any evidence of blood nor were they large enough to inflict much damage. Next, he stopped at the Egyptian-style desk that stood at a corner of the bedroom. In back of it was a wooden chair carved with camels. *Such a beautiful piece of carving.*

Wally joined him. He heard the conversation with the medical examiner, but as yet, had not managed to view the body. He opened the decanter that was still upright and smelled the contents. Then he took a swig out of it. "That's gin," he told Hawk. He smelled the other liquid some of which spilled onto the tray on which the decanters sat and said, "That's scotch."

"Okay, that's good to know," Hawk said. But were those decanters used as a murder weapon? The stopper is sharp and pointed."

"I don't see any blood on them. Of course, the blood would have been wiped off. We should have the fingerprint boys check them out anyway. Can we go now? I'm through here."

"Wally, I have a question for you. Is there anything in this room that is missing? Something sharp and pointed?"

"How should I know what's missing from this room?" He asked in a very irritated tone. "It could be anything. What do you think that I'm clairvoyant?"

"Look at the fireplace. The fireplace had been used, maybe on a cool day in spring. You can still see the ashes. Now look at the tool stand next to the glass screen. There is a brush, a scoop or shovel, but there's no poker."   He turned to Janeel and asked her if a standard type fireplace poker could have caused the injury to the victim's head.

Janeel studied the wound more closely. "Yes, that could be a good possibility. Why do you think it was a poker?"

"Because one is missing from the room."

"Hey, good detective work. I'll check it out when I do the autopsy. Now, are you through with the body?"

"Did you see any defensive wounds on her, especially around her hands or arms?" Hawk asked. And could there be any foreign tissue under her nails?"   He bent over and studied the victim's hands as Janeel examined them.

"We always check under the vic's fingernails. It will be in the report."

"Thanks, Janeel. You're the greatest."

"In your case, flattery will get you everywhere."   She smiled and Hawk returned the smile. Before leaving the crime scene, Hawk examined each of the four windows to see if a burglar could have squeezed through them. Every window was shut tight. No evidence of a break-in.

CHAPTER 14

AS HAWK and Murphy came down the stairs, they witnessed Bradford and Williams in what appeared to be a heated discussion. Bradford had poked his index finger into Williams' chest. Upon seeing Hawk and Murphy, Williams motioned with his eyes in their direction and both clammed up. Hawk had overheard Williams tell Bradford that, "I tell you; I don't think it was him." *What's that all about?* Hawk thought. *Who's him?*

With a sheepish grin, Bradford quickly turned his attention to Hawk. "Well hotshot, what do you think? Not much to go on yet, is there?" Murphy again felt isolated and irritated that the Lieutenant addressed his young partner first.

"Probably not, but here's what I think." *Oh no, Hawk,* Murphy thought. *Don't put your big foot in your mouth.* Hawk continued, "I think that his original plan was to kill the victim in her sleep by possibly suffocating her with a pillow. Or if his intent was to burglarize the place, which I doubt, he didn't plan on killing the victim and must have startled her in his attempt to get to the master closet. That's, after all, where most burglars head for because in most houses that's where the jewelry is kept." Bradford and Williams listened to Hawk's analysis without interrupting, which surprised Murphy.

"At any rate, she got out of bed because she heard him or tried to escape as he tried to suffocate her. Once she was out of bed, he grabbed the poker, the nearest weapon. He might have had a gun, probably so, but a gun would make enough noise for the neighbors to hear. Besides, not using a gun and using something in the room would make it look like a burglary gone bad. He swung the poker and killed her. Julia Bowman went down immediately, and the medical examiner will tell us if she died instantly or bled out."

Hawk stopped for a second. He couldn't decide whether to push it any further since Bradford glared at him with an obvious displeasure. But since he didn't say anything, Hawk decided to plow on. "I've also asked the M.E. to pay particular attention to any defensive wounds or DNA under Bowman's fingernails   I don't think she'll find any because she was struck down before she had a chance to struggle. The burglar tried to make the scene look like a scuffle took place to show that she surprised him during the burglary, but I don't believe there was one. It's just too neat. I mean, there isn't a lot of damage. Only a few items were turned over." Murphy couldn't believe his ears. *Hawk came up with another fantasy based on nothing but his imagination. He couldn't believe that the Lieutenant hadn't yelled at him yet even though he sure looked pissed. How could Hawk just come up with that after spending a few minutes in the room?*

As he finished, Hawk noticed the brief eye contact between the Lieutenants. Williams turned to Bradford. "That's a bunch of bunk, although it shows some great imagination." He laughed a low, sluggish guffaw. "Detective Hawk, you'll never be able to prove any of it. But, it's not my department. I'm only here since I was close by, heard the call, and thought I might be of help."

He turned to Bradford and said, "Bradford, you've got one with great imagination, that's for sure. He should be a writer of novels." He began walking away and as he did, he said over his shoulder, "I'll let you figure this one out. It sure looks like a burglary that went bad, end of story."

"Bradford sneered. He felt like yelling at the brash detective but forced his anger to remain inside him. "Detective Hawk, you got all that out of just looking at the scene for a few minutes. Now you're suggesting that the intent of the burglar was to commit murder?" He shook his head. "You and your wild fantasy. You said the same thing about the carjacking, that it was what—an assassination?" Bradford laughed, belittling Hawk. "Murphy, surely you don't agree?" That question caught Murphy flatfooted. He took a second or two to answer. He believed that Hawk's theory was bogus, but he didn't want to throw his partner under the bus. While he mulled over his answer, Hawk spoke.

"Well, for one, what was the burglar after? Was it jewelry, the easiest and the most valuable items to steal? If so, why were there some gold rings, bracelets, and pendants still in the jewelry drawer? Some were obviously taken, but not all. He just wanted to give an impression that he was after the jewelry. Valuable statues and paintings were of no interest. The laptop, another prized item for thieves, still sat on the desk in the bedroom. All that computer and video equipment in the first-floor office is still intact."

Bradford asked, "Why didn't he take all the jewelry? It is certainly valuable as you say. I tell you why my young, ambitious novice." Bradford didn't erase his superior grin as he stared disparagingly at Hawk, "He was obviously interrupted and couldn't take it all." Bradford answered his own question. "I don't want to hear any more of your guesswork, detective." Showing more irritation with Hawk, he said, "I want a report from you describing ONLY what you saw and how the burglar got in. No speculations that you can't prove." Bradford seethed, his voice rising and his face flushing. "And I want to see you in my office later this afternoon. Do you understand?" Hawk nodded, his complexion turning red. *What's this about? Why is he so angry? Is he trying to hide something? I'm in trouble and I don't know why. I thought it was my job to analyze the scene of the crime.*

"Lieutenant, do we know yet how the burglar got in?" Murphy stunned by the Lieutenant's anger, tried to change the subject and appear relevant. He felt sorry for his new partner and he couldn't understand the Lieutenant's adamant stand. He did believe that Hawk was stretching it a bit, but, on the other hand, some of what he said made sense.

"Through that window in the parlor," Bradford said with his voice stern as he aggressively pointed his index finger to the north window. Get to work. I want your findings in the report as well. That should be an easy one for you, Murphy, and even you Hawk, as the window was unlocked. It rained last night, and I've been told that we found good shoe prints outside the window. And Hawk, if you think a poker was used, you better find it." He laughed to further belittle his detective.

After Bradford, Hawk said, "Let's not hold up the housekeeper. We should talk to her first."

"Clint, the Lieutenant wants us to check out the window. We better do it right away."

"And Wally we will. But as a courtesy, let's meet her and tell her we'll be with her shortly." They both trampled to the back of the house where Mrs. Cordova sat at the kitchen table reading her Samsung smart phone, her eyes soaked with tears. She was a sturdy looking middle-aged Latina. Her hair was dyed jet black and fixed into a bun held together with a turquoise ribbon. Upon seeing the detectives, she stood up to greet them.

Mrs. Cordova appeared extremely nervous and shaken. After Hawk and Murphy introduced themselves, she cried in a heavy Spanish accent, "Dios mio! My God, my God! This is a nightmare. Mrs. Bowman was such a good lady. I don't know what to do now. Do I work here still? Oh! I'll never forget what I saw! It was awful." Murphy took the lead and said, "Mrs. Cordova, is it?" She nodded. "You're the housekeeper here?" She nodded again. "Mrs. Cordova, we need to check something out first and then we'd like to talk to you. Can you wait for us to come back?"

"Yes, of course. Anything to help with the death of Mrs. Bowman," she tried to remain calm, but she couldn't hold it. Tears started pouring out as she wiped them away with a tissue. "Oh! I still can't believe what happened? Why would anyone want to do this to such a nice lady? She was always kind and generous with me and my family. We all loved her. Dios mio." She put her hands to her face and started to sob.

"Mrs. Cordova," Hawk said. "Would you like to be alone for a few moments? You're welcome to wait in the parlor if you'd be more comfortable."

"Thank you, but I'd rather wait in the kitchen. This is my place in this house. I'm sorry for my tears. I feel so sad for Mrs. Bowman. First Mr. Bowman and now Mrs. Bowman. What bad luck. I guess God wanted them both. Who would have imagined such a thing?" *It's also bad luck for her,* Murphy thought. *She just lost her job.*

"Very well, we'll be back soon." Hawk patted her shoulder.

"Let's look at the outside first," Hawk told Murphy. As they walked outside, Hawk again studied the camera supposedly covering the front porch; the one that he initially thought was a fake camera. It seemed not quite realistic. "As I told you before, I bet that's not a real camera. There's probably another fake camera over the back porch as well."

"Hawk, where are you getting all these notions? How could you possibly know that that is fake?"

"I made a point of studying outdoor cameras on the internet and at Best Buy."

"Okay, you may be right, but we better check that out for sure."

"Of course."

They walked around to the side of the house. The window was blocked by large juniper bushes. "That's not very smart having these bushes here," Murphy said. "Anyone can get back there unseen and do what they want."

Hawk nodded in agreement as they approached the window. Decorative river rock, bordered by a metal edger about three feet from the foundation, covered the side yard. Under the window it appeared that a bush had been dug up, the dirt smoothed over. Footprints underneath the window were plainly visible in the rain-softened ground. Mud scuffs smeared the brick wall. "See there," Murphy pointed, "that's where he climbed through the window."

"It looks like it." At that moment, a Crime Scene Investigator walked around the corner.

"Hello there, detectives, I'm Chet Watkins from the crime lab. I want to take photos of the scene and get a plaster cast of the shoe prints. The perp must have used gloves because we dusted the window frame and everything else around and didn't get much in prints. The few we found I think were probably those of the victim or the maid. We already have the victim's and we'll get the maid's fingerprints. We might have Mr. Bowman's on file." Chet looked at the footprints closer and said, "I'll bet you a dollar that those are a size thirteen with Adidas soles. It's an old shoe, sure has a lot of mileage on it. That was a big guy that went through that window— judging by the size of the shoe. We're lucky we had a thunderstorm last evening to soften up the ground."

"You sure know your shoes," Hawk said as he looked at the older, thin, and rangy man with a rugged unshaven angular face. He wore brown cargo pants and a tan safari-style short sleeve shirt with two large pockets stuffed with a pen and crumpled papers.

"I've been doing this job for a long time. I've seen and researched all types of shoes and their soles. And each one has its own character."

"That's remarkable," Hawk said. "That's something I should do; study shoe soles. Right, Murphy? That would certainly be handy info to know."

"Why bother? That's why we're around," Chet responded.

"I know that," Murphy said. "I have always relied on the good evidence CSI had provided me. That's what experience is all about."

The young detective realized that was a dig at him because Hawk's a rookie and has a lot to learn about how the system works. Murphy lagged behind as the trio headed back to the front door.

CHAPTER 15

JUANITA CORDOVA waited patiently for the detectives to return. She seemed confused as to why they had to take her fingerprints. She asked Hawk with concern, "Do you think that I did this?"

"No, no Mrs. Cordova," Hawk said. "Didn't they tell you that it's standard procedure to differentiate fingerprints from the person who did this?"

"Well, I don't like it. They treated me like a criminal and I'm not a criminal."

"We know that," Murphy said, touching her on her arm. "They should've explained it better to you. I'll talk to them, okay?" Mrs. Cordova nodded.

"Mrs. Cordova, it's standard procedure to ask you a few questions," Hawk said. "Is that all right with you?" See nodded, sniffling. "For the report, I need your name, address and telephone number."

"I already gave it to the first policeman that came after I called the police."

Hawk answered, "I understand, but would you repeat it for me, please." She complied, but somewhat annoyed.

Hawk continued, "At what time did you discover that there was something wrong with the house?"

"Well, I rang the doorbell several times and didn't hear anyone. So, I decided that Mrs. Bowman was gone, although it seemed odd, she would leave with her poor husband getting killed just yesterday. You know, she was a total wreck when I came to work yesterday. All her life was drained from her. So, this morning I used my key and went in. Everything seemed all right and I started vacuuming the house. O Dios mio, oh my God. It was terrible when I entered the bedroom. There was her body. I screamed." Mrs. Cordova's hands began to tremble. When she began to relive the scene, her dark eyes looked as though they might jump out of their sockets.

"Would you like to get yourself together before we proceed," Wally asked.

"Yes, please. I need to get my breath back."

After a few minutes, Hawk again asked the time that she discovered Mrs. Bowman. After she answered that it was around 9:00 o'clock in the morning, Hawk asked, "When was the last time you saw Mrs. Bowman yesterday?"

"I saw her yesterday evening when I left around 6:30. She was waiting for her daughter who lives several hours away, and she didn't want to stay alone so she asked me to stay. I know she hadn't eaten anything all day, so I fixed her some eggs and bacon. She didn't want to eat anything, but I stayed until she sat down at the table and started to eat. After that, I had to hurry home to feed my family and then babysit my son's kids."

"Do you generally cook her meals?" Murphy asked, seemingly pleased with his question.

"No. Just housekeeping and whatever the Bowmans asked me to do for them. Occasionally, they asked me to prepare a meal for them. I didn't mind doing that at all. They have always been so kind to me and my son, Hector. They tried to give him some handyman jobs around the house."

Murphy inquired further, "What are your regular hours and how long had you worked for her?" Hawk wrote all the answers down in his small top-spiraled notebook.

"I come in every day except Saturday and Sunday at 9:00 o'clock and usually leave at 4:00 o'clock. I've worked for the Bowmans for eight years. They are good people to work for. Oh God, I mean they *were* good people to work for." Mrs. Cordova quickly crossed herself and began to quietly sob. Evidently, she had a glimpse of the black body bag containing Mrs. Bowman as it was carried down the stairs.

Detective Murphy was ready to send her home and get out of the house himself when Hawk said, "Mrs. Cordova, I know this is extremely difficult for you, but are you up to a walk around the house to see if anything is missing?"

Hawk, Wally and Mrs. Cordova first stopped just inside the parlor. "Do you see anything missing in here?" Hawk asked. Please take your time and look at everything." In the meantime, Hawk took a quick look at the window through which the burglar allegedly entered.

Hawk examined the wood around the window, then the wall and the oak floor below it. He took a white handkerchief from his back pocket and wiped a portion of the oak floor. It was perfectly clean. "What are you doing cleaning the place," Murphy said, grinning broadly. "Mrs. Cordova must think that you think she isn't doing a good job cleaning the floor. Isn't that right, Mrs. Cordova?" Wally laughed, his eyes squinting.

"I don't know what that man is doing. But I just mopped the floor yesterday morning. It's supposed to be clean."

"Yes, it is clean as a whistle," Hawk said. "The burglar did not go through that window."

"Here you go again, jumping to conclusions. He might've taken his shoes off first before climbing in."

"Maybe, but very unlikely, my friend." Now turning his attention back to the housekeeper, Hawk asked her to accompany them to the rest of the rooms. Nothing was missing, including in the master bedroom.

The last area to check was the master closet. Mrs. Cordova looked at the open jewelry drawer and seemed surprised to see the jewelry. He couldn't tell whether she didn't know that the jewels were in the drawer or was faking her surprise. Maybe she didn't realize that some expensive jewelry still remained in the drawer. He couldn't imagine that as a housekeeper and alone in the house on a daily basis, she didn't have the curiosity to check what was in the closet.

"Do you know what was in the drawer?" Hawk asked her.

Juanita struggled to answer the question. He saw her mulling an answer over in her mind. If she answered that she recognized them, that would appear bad. She had no business going through the private drawers of her employers. After much hesitation, she finally answered, "Actually, yes. Mrs. Bowman showed them to me a few months ago. She bought a new sapphire ring for herself and when I admired it, she showed me her other jewelry."

Hawk, watching for facial twitches, and eye or hand movements, decided that she was lying. Why would Julia Bowman show her cleaning lady where her fine jewelry is stored? He pointed to a sapphire ring and asked, "Is that the ring that she showed you?"

"Yes, it is. But why didn't the burglar take all the jewelry?"

"That's a good question. Do you remember what other jewelry is missing?"

"No, not really. I don't remember each piece of jewelry that she showed me. There was too much to take it all in."

Appearing fidgety, Wally groused, "Are you through yet? Hawk we've been here an awfully long time. What else do you need?"

Hawk took down Mrs. Cordova's full name, address, telephone number and date of birth. "Mrs. Cordova you can go now."

"But where do I go to now? I just lost my job."

"I'm sure you know Mrs. Bowman's two daughters and how to get ahold of them. Before you call them, please wait an hour or so for the Police Department to notify them of this tragedy."

"Yes, yes, Mrs. Bowman left their information on a card by the kitchen phone." I'll give them a call. Maybe they'd want me to take care of the house until they decide what to do with it. Oh God! Why did this have to happen?" Her dark eyes welled up again.

"Mrs. Cordova," Hawk said, "It'll work out for you one way or another. Hopefully, the daughters, at least the one that lives here, will be by shortly. I recommend you stay here until she comes. By the way, you mentioned that you babysat your grandchildren last night. A son, you said?"

Mrs. Cordova hesitated again trying to figure out how she should answer this strange question. "Is it important who my son is?"

"Not really, just tying up loose ends."

"Well, it's my son Hector's kids. He is divorced and the kids have been driving him crazy lately. He just wanted some peace and quiet for the evening. He has full custody of the kids. Their mother is on drugs and we hadn't seen her in months."

"That must be difficult being a single father. Expensive too. I hope he has a good job."

"Well, he's in construction. With Denver booming, he's finally been working pretty steady after many weeks without work."

"What company does he work for?"

Mrs. Cordova's expressive face showed some alarm. "I really don't know. He doesn't tell me much."

"Can we go now?" Murphy said. "I need to grab some lunch."

CHAPTER 16

HAWK GAZED back at the historic house before sliding into the passenger seat of Murphy's assigned overused Crown Vic. He tried to get his restless mind off the unpleasant conversation with Bradford. Instead, he concentrated on the fantastic workmanship of the neighborhood architecture. Robert Lang, a famous architect during the Gilded Age designed a multitude of beautiful mansions in this area. Hawk forced himself to dwell on the beauty of the stonework, arches, columns and different shades of brick used in the houses. It didn't help, because his mind still reverted to Bradford, the suspicious conversation between him and Williams and the horror he saw in the house behind him. He knew that Murphy would talk about the scene, and probably criticize him for jumping to conclusions. But Hawk has a terrible habit of saying it as he sees it. *I needed to be less blunt and should've waited to hear what the Lieutenant had to say, especially in this new position. I bet Marcie is very diplomatic. Wow! Why did I think of Marcie now? I need to work on keeping thoughts of her out of my mind. Though, it sure would be nice to cuddle up on the couch with her. Hawk! Cut that out!*

"Well, you're sure deep in thought," Wally barked, corralling Clint's wandering mind. "I didn't want to say anything in front of the housekeeper but I'm getting a little perturbed that you think you know everything. Everybody else concluded that the window was the point of entry. Only you say it isn't. How did you come up with that? By wiping your handkerchief on the floor?"

"Where's the dirt, the mud from the outside, Wally?"

"Mud? Dirt?" He thought a moment, "he wiped it off his shoes on the bricks outside when he tried to enter through that window."

"Wally, how could anyone clean off that type of jagged sole and not leave mud evidence on the clean floor or on the wall beneath the window, for that matter?"

"Ah, forget it. I'm too hungry to think about it now. Any idea where we could go to lunch?"

"Actually, since we're in this area, there is a place I hadn't been to for quite a while. Ever been to Charlie Brown's Bar and Grill, Wally? It's in the Colburn Hotel and both have been around a long time. Charlie Brown's is one of the oldest restaurants in Denver and Colburn was opened in 1920s. Now it's mostly apartments. It's a great place to feel like you're back in time, way before either of us were born."

"Sure. Any place as long as we eat. I don't care that much about history, so you don't have to educate me about it. All I know is that I sure am hungry. I didn't have much of a breakfast and my stomach's been asking me if I had gone on strike." Murphy laughed heartily, again assuming that he made a real clever comment. "I mean, I need sustenance before I can discuss Mrs. Bowman's death with you and try to set you straight. After all, Bradford is right. It's straightforward. A burglar made his way into the house. I agree that she heard him, got up and he struck her. Then he took as much of the jewelry as he could and made his way out. Don't make it more complicated than you have to. By the way, where is this restaurant?"

"Not far. Go east to Emerson, turn left on Twelfth and it will be on the southeast corner of Twelfth and Grant." Hawk expected Murphy's pushback about Mrs. Bowman's murder. He wants everything to be neat and easy without much effort. *I just hope the Lieutenant will cut me some slack to work this through my way, but that won't happen. It's as though, he doesn't want to find who's guilty.*

The restaurant was, indeed, a bit of history in the historical Capitol Hill area. The rectangular bar in the center of the main room was definitely its focal point. It looked spectacular; sporting highly polished dark wood accentuated by impressive brass foot rails. Matching overhead rails hung below glass shelves which were filled with miniatures of people, beer barrels and old cars. The upper shelves displayed a variety of sailing ships and other interesting things. Murphy didn't seem interested in the décor or the historical value of the place. He rushed to a table that the hostess led them to, and studied the menu.

"I think you should buy," Wally blurted out. "But don't mind me. When I'm hungry, I get pretty mean. Where in the hell is the service? At least we got a menu. What do you suggest?"

"The gyro sandwich or the enchiladas are good, but I haven't been here in years."

"Okay. I'll take both," Wally said, patting his big stomach. He addressed his stomach. "It's coming soon. Hang in there." Then he giggled and said, "Well, where is a server? I better go and wake someone up." At that moment, a pleasant middle-aged man came up with a pad and pencil and asked what they'd like to drink.

"I want a tall glass of iced tea with sugar and lemon, but I'm ready to order." He placed two orders, the ones Hawk suggested. Both the waiter and Hawk thought only one of the meals was for Wally.

"So, which one of you gets the gyro sandwich?"

"I don't know what he wants," pointing to Hawk. "I want both and I want them ASAP."

The waiter looked a little stunned. He addressed Hawk, "What will you have, sir?"

"I'll also have a gyro sandwich and a glass of water."

The waiter left and Wally suddenly remembered. "Hey, he never asked me if I wanted fries with the sandwich."

Hawk had already noticed how irritable Wally got when he was hungry. He sat at the table without saying a word until the food arrived through another server, thankful that the service was reasonably fast.

"Wow, there is more food than I thought," Wally said. His eyes particularly lit up at the sight of a full plate of three large enchiladas. The gyro sandwich came with fries, and Wally grabbed three at a time and stuffed them in his mouth. "It's just too much food for even me. You better help me out with the enchiladas," as he began trying to transfer an enchilada onto Hawk's plate that was already occupied with the gyro sandwich wrapped in wax paper. Hawk refused the offer saying it would be too much for him.

"Listen, Clint," Wally said. *Oh, now that he has his mouth full of food, it's Clint, is it?* "I'm sorry that I'm so irritable. When I'm hungry I get that way. But more than that, the scene in the house, in the bedroom with Julia Bowman lying in a pool of blood on the floor really affected me. I don't know why, but I feel as though I lost a close relative. I really liked her, Clint. Let me confess something to you. Ever since I met that woman, I've been thinking about her all the time. I even dreamed about her last night. Strange, isn't it? Particularly, if I were to ask her the time of day, she wouldn't give it to me. Here I am an old retiring policeman and she being a wealthy lady. Clint, I am such a fool, but I fantasized about her. Crazy, isn't it?"

Wally's confession was too much to take in. Hawk didn't know how to respond. *That's probably the only time I have agreed with him since I met him yesterday.* "Wally, I don't blame you. She was an attractive woman and something about her struck a note with you. But I think you're right, you wouldn't have had a chance with her. She was nice to think about, but that was all. Now, let me pay for our meals and we better get back to the station."

"Okay, if you insist on paying this time, I'll get it next time. Can I trust you to not tell anyone about what I told you? I know that around the office, I'm kind of considered a clumsy, fat fool. So, I don't want to add to my reputation."

Hawk assured him and they headed back to the station. Wally kept silent and Hawk appreciated a little time to mull over the two murders. The drive to Washington Street was too short and he knew that he needed more time to put things together. He hoped that some of the forensics would be on his desk so that he could analyze the evidence.

96

CHAPTER 17

HAWK AND Wally walked into the detectives' room. Marcie met them with a heart-warming smile, pushing her hair back from her face. Hawk smiled back and for reasons unknown to him, he winked at her. She winked back. He liked that sexy wink but was afraid the rest of the afternoon would not go as well.

Most of the detectives were on their feet surrounding Lieutenant Bradford who pointed at a whiteboard covered with photos of the latest unsolved homicides. Hawk and Wally approached and saw photos of both Jeffrey and Julia Bowman. The other four victims, known gang members, had died in a gang war. No suspects were listed for them.

Pinned next to Jeffrey Bowman's photo was a mug shot of Leland Freeman as the alleged perpetrator. *What the hell? They already determined that Leland Freeman is the carjacker and murderer. Why didn't I know? I thought this was my case.*

Freeman's photo revealed a thinly built African American male in his early thirties with a full head of black hair. A trim short beard was his prominent facial feature.

"Well, you two finally made it in," Bradford said with a tinge of nastiness. "What did you do, have a three-martini lunch? Hawk resented his comments. Bradford knew that they stayed to further investigate the burglary long after the other officers left.

"Oh no, Lieutenant," Wally Murphy quickly responded. "We spent quite a bit of time in the Bowman house going over everything carefully. Then we grabbed a quick lunch in the area and now we're here."

"All right, all right. Let's get on with it." Bradford turned back to the board and placed his pointer on Freeman's face. He had a smug expression on his face as he focused on Hawk.

Hawk asked, "Why are you so sure that he's the one, Lieutenant?"

Bradford had a disgusted look, "Since we identified the prints as belonging to Freeman, Detectives Salazar and Ling found him and picked him up. Based on his record and his prints, it was obvious that he was the one who carjacked and killed Jeffrey Bowman. Since he had the address and the keys and garage door opener from the car, he most likely is the one that burglarized the house and killed Julia Bowman."

At that moment, Detective Stan Orlinski glanced at his computer and announced, "Lieutenant, this just came in. I followed up on your order to research the housekeeper and her family. Guess what? Mrs. Cordova's son, Hector Cordova, is a jailbird. He spent three years in Canon City for home burglary. Here's his mug. Bradford quickly hung Cordova's photo next to Mrs. Bowman as a possible second murder suspect. Hector was a heavy Hispanic male with black stubble on a clean-shaven head. A scorpion tattoo covered the left side of his neck.

Bradford looked straight at Hawk. "While you were lunching, Orlinski got the name of the housekeeper from the patrol officer. Things are not as complicated as you want to make them. What do you think of that now?" Not waiting for an answer, Bradford shoved his hands in his pant pockets and with much relish told Jeffries and Orlinski to pick up Cordova.

"Lieutenant, those are our cases. We'll pick him up and question him."

"No Hawk, I'm reassigning you to something else."

"You mean, we're off both cases?"

"Yes, Hawk. After we're through here I want both of you in my office."

Hawk's face turned red and he took two deep breaths to control his anger at the man. Bradford noticed, everyone noticed, that Hawk looked ready to explode. He relished the distress of this upstart detective, one that had been thrown at him only three days ago.

Hawk glanced at Marcie who looked worried. She shook her head as a signal to cool. Hawk took another breath and spoke agitatedly, "Lieutenant Bradford, we put a lot of work into these cases and there is more evidence that we should investigate. The carjacking was a cover-up for an assassination and if you give me the chance, I can prove it. The burglary was a cover-up for the murder of Julia Bowman. I believe someone wanted to kill that woman. I don't believe that either one of the two suspects on the board murdered the Bowmans."

The Lieutenant's face turned crimson. Hawk forged ahead nevertheless, "As I told Murphy, that side window was not the point of access as was first believed. There was no mud or dirt on the floor under the window. Plus, I'd like to see if Cordova's shoe size matches the size 13 shoe imprints that were so conveniently visible outside the window. More importantly, it doesn't look like a real burglary, especially by someone who burglarized before. Actually, I believe that both crimes, the carjacking and the burglary, were bad attempts to cover up premeditated murders of the Bowmans." Hawk expected to hear disapproval from the others in the room, but all remained quiet.

"If he didn't go through the window, how did he get in? Not through the door?" Jeffries asked, with much authority, his pointed nose raised high in the air. "There is an alarm, I presume?"

"Yes, there is an alarm and a motion detector that didn't trigger the alarm. And if someone had the key to the front door and went in that way, the alarm would've blared. Nor did it go off when the perp exited the house. And a garage door opener wouldn't have been much good since the garage was detached from the house. So, I assume that he came in through the front or the back door. There is a fake camera at the corner of the porch. That's why I think that whoever did this was close to the family because he knew the alarm code and perhaps had a key.”

“Yeah, yeah, Hawk. I heard this cock and bull story and I don’t want to hear anymore.” Hawk felt as though he was punched in the gut. A muscle twitched angrily in his jaw.

“But Lieutenant that makes sense,” Nora Ricci, the mysterious brunette came to Hawk’s rescue. Hawk appreciated the support. Although, not a word had been spoken between them. “I doubt that the perp would jeopardize his mom’s job and burglarize the house she worked in. Being a felon would make him a prime suspect and I’m sure he realized it. So, I don’t think it was Cordova. As for Freeman, just because we found his prints in the car, doesn’t automatically prove that he carjacked it. He might have seen the vehicle abandoned and taken it.

“Lieutenant, I would like to work with Detective Hawk on this one,” Nora said. “I think his theories have potential.” That comment surprised Hawk who wasn’t sure how he’d like having a new partner. He knew Murphy and knew he could work with him. He knew nothing of the woman, other than she was good to look at. Her request also surprised Murphy. Marcie looked surprised. She suddenly saw a competitor in her quest to land Hawk.

“Nora Ricci, you always have a soft spot for everyone, including a handsome rookie detective who knows shit,” a short broad-shouldered man that Hawk had never seen before spoke out. He had just entered the room shortly before Nora spoke. He wore a striped blue suit and a dark narrow blue tie. He looked at least ten years older than Hawk with white hairs salting his stylishly cut black hair. He stood there confidently as he screwed up his face into a wide, wry smile. He was a rugged-looking man who Hawk thought would be attractive to certain women. However, Hawk’s gut told him that he was trouble, especially with those piercing coal-black eyes—eyes that could easily kill.

Nora stared with fury at the man. Her blue eyes narrowed and her full red lips seamed into a thin line. With a cold edge in her voice, she hissed, "What the hell are you doing here? Came to make my life miserable again, did you, Devon O'Leary?"

Smiling even wider, O'Leary shot back at her. "Now love, that's no way to greet me." With a malicious laugh he sneered, "I see you're very happy to see me, but don't get too excited, I'm only here to see Lieutenant Bradford for a minute."

A red-faced Bradford turned toward his office, but before he did, he was about to say something to Nora. His index finger raised as though to admonish her. The angry Lieutenant looked around at the people gawking and kept silent. Instead, he ordered the assembled group to get back to work. As O'Leary followed Bradford into his office, he blew a kiss to Nora to aggravate her even more. Everyone in the room looked astonished, some rolled their eyes.

Hawk, his insides on edge turned to Wally, "What's that all about?"

Wally was more than happy to engage in some gossip. "From what I've heard, O'Leary and Nora worked together in a district on the West side. Rumor has it that they had a hot and steamy love affair that ended very badly. He's a real slimeball. That's why she had transferred here. Buzz has it that he was very ugly to her. Poor thing. She's certainly a good-looking addition to the room, huh?" Wally elbowed Hawk on his arm, winking. "You know what I mean? I think we'd all love to hear the full story. I bet it's a doozy."

"Detective Hawk," the Lieutenant yelled, his face protruding out the door, "Come in here." Hawk complied wondering what that was about, especially since O'Leary was still in his office. "I want you to meet Devon O'Leary. He wants to talk you into transferring to the narcotics unit on the West side. He heard about you from his friend, Lieutenant Williams, and they think you'd be a fine addition to the unit there. I think you should do it. You'd have more opportunity for advancement there."

"Yes, Detective Hawk," O'Leary said. "Our lieutenant asked me to make that offer to you." *What is this about? I only saw Williams for a few minutes, too short for him to make any kind of judgment about me. I smell a rat here. My gut says to not trust this guy. Don't do it, Hawk.*

Hawk's stubborn streak kicked in and he declined the offer explaining he liked homicide and liked it where he was. He apologized and went to his desk. Sitting down on his squeaky chair, he leaned back and thought about what had just transpired. *Something is going on here. All of a sudden, they want me out of Homicide. This is too bizarre. And those black eyes of O'Leary went icy cold when I turned him down. It gave me the shivers.* A few minutes later, O'Leary stormed out of Bradford's office, threw a hard look at Hawk, and managed to blow yet another kiss at Nora. Laughing sadistically, he passed by Marcie's desk, playfully grabbed a pen from her hand and started to walk out. At the door, he paused, "If you want the pen back, call me and I'll give it to you…. over dinner."

"Okay, people," Bradford said. "That's enough jabbering. Jeffries, as I ordered, take Orlinski and pick up Cordova and Freeman. Maybe his mother, Mrs. Cordova, herself, is involved in all of this. Hawk, I want you and Murphy in my office. Now!" *What's up with him now? He'll probably reassign me to dog complaints. Why doesn't he even want to discuss or at least hear out my reasoning? Strange. Why is that?*

Puffing hard, Wally entered the office following Hawk, who by this time had such a headache that he felt it would split open. His insides quivered and he heard the hard drumbeat of his heart. He couldn't figure out whether he was nervous or just mad. *Hold it together, Hawk. Hold it together. As Dad told me, once you lose your temper, you lose your reasoning.*

"But, Lieutenant," Wally blurted out, upset and raising the volume in his voice. "Hawk and I had worked these cases together since the beginning. Why are Jeffries and Orlinski going to pick them up? We are the ones that are working this case."

"You were and no longer are, Murphy. Besides, you only were assigned the first case only a couple of days ago. Murphy, you have a lot of experience in the department, but Hawk here has none. So, I want both of you off this case. Don't investigate the Bowman deaths any longer. Is that clear, Murphy?" Wally nodded reluctantly. Bradford drilled his deep gaze into Hawk, "Is that clear, Hawk?" Hawk didn't answer immediately, still taking some deep breaths. "I told you that you should have gone with O'Leary. Hawk, is that clear? You are to leave these cases alone."

"Yes, Lieutenant. It is clear to me what you are saying."

Bradford noticed his imprecise response but decided to ignore it. "Fine, now that we have it clear, I'm assigning you to the cold files. Since that department had been understaffed and haven't had time to work too many lately, you are to do what you can with them and who knows, maybe by some miracle, you'll solve one. Murphy, I'll give you a choice, you can work along with Hawk, or with Nora. She doesn't have a partner right now and is overwhelmed. I'm giving you this option only because you're so close to retirement and should have a choice during your last few months on the force."

Murphy thought about it for a minute. "I think I'll stay with Clint. We've only been at it a few days, but he's kind of grown on me. Besides, I think he can use my expertise." *Oh great. I'm stuck with Wally again. I'd rather work alone.*

"All right so be it," Bradford said, looking victorious. "Now hand over all your notes on the Bowman cases to Jeffries and both of you go to the records department and pull a few homicide files. Now go."

As they left Bradford's office for the Records Department, Marcie whispered to Hawk, "What happened? What's going on?"

Hawk looked around the room and saw that all eyes were on him and Murphy. He whispered back, "I'll tell you later. I've got a lot of thinking to do."

CHAPTER 18

MARCIE MADISON TURNER couldn't wait for later and ran into the hall, catching up with Hawk. Grabbing a hold of his arm, she asked, "Is everything all right? You look like you could have a coronary. You both weren't fired, were you?"

"No, Marcie. We were just reassigned to the cold case files and we're on our way to get some now. Wally decided to work with me. He had a chance to work with Nora, but the fool chose to work with me."

"Now, now, Hawk. My mama never raised no fools. I knew that if I worked with Nora, my eyes would be all over her and I couldn't concentrate."

"I never heard that, Wally," Marcie said with a shocked voice. "You're not supposed to say that."

"I know, I was just kidding, anyway. You kids talk, I'll head over to records and have them start pulling two or four of the latest unsolved cases." Wally wandered off and Marcie once again asked what happened.

Hawk looked up and down the hall. "Listen, Marcie, this is not the place to talk. Can we get together possibly for a quick dinner tonight? I'll explain everything. Something just doesn't feel right to me and I'll need to mull it over before tonight."

"Sure. I believe I'm free, but I'll check my riotously, fun-filled calendar," Marcie laughed. "Sure, just let me know where and when. I'll be there."

"What do you like to eat?"

"I like everything except for fish. Actually, if you don't mind, I'd love to have some pancakes tonight. Someone mentioned to me that they had pancakes for lunch and now I'm craving them, especially with strawberries and lots of whipped cream on top. Would you mind?"

"No, not at all. A pancake house sounds great. So, what's your address." I believe you said you live in Glendale. I can pick you up at 6:30 and we'll find a place close to your home."

"Sounds great. I'll text you my address." Marcie reached and clutched his arm and showing her usual flirtatious, mischievous smile. "Now is this a date or a business meeting?"

Hawk laughed for the first time that day. He loved that smile. "Marcie, you're funny." Without answering her question, he said, "I better go and bail Wally out of Records."

As he walked down the hall, Marcie's eyes followed him with a slight smile.

Wally didn't need to be rescued from the Records department. He was carrying on a conversation with the clerk, an older attractive Latina with short black hair wearing a police uniform with two chevrons on her sleeve. She threw her head back with laughter as Wally grinned from across the caged counter. "That must have been a doozy of a story, Wally," Hawk said.

"It sure was," said the woman. "We've known each other for years."

"Hawk, I'd like to introduce you to Cora Padilla. She's a wonderful person and we actually had a few dates. Whatever happened to us? Oh yeah, suddenly you were too busy to go out." Hawk noticed that her name tag said Espinoza and not Padilla.

"Yes, I had to take care of my sick mother, I told you."

"That's what you said, all right. But how's your mom doing now? Maybe we can still go out?"

"Wally, unfortunately, my mother has passed. And I'm sorry, but I don't think my husband would like it too much." Both Hawk and Mrs. Espinoza saw Wally's mouth tighten. "But we can still be friends, can't we? I love to listen to your stories." *Really? Wow, she is a glutton for punishment to put up with his stories,* Hawk thought.

Wally recovered from his disappointment quickly. "Yes, yes, of course, my dear. I've got a ton of tales I can tell you. For example, years ago, while I was just a young and foolish patrol officer, I went into this bar to break up a fight. There were these two hefty bruisers and I was just a skinny guy fresh out of the academy. Well, the size of those men didn't stop me, I –."

"Wally, I hate to interrupt a good story like that," Hawk put in, "but let's get to our work. Did you ask Cora to get us the files and the evidence boxes that we need?"

"Oh yeah, sorry. I was getting to that. Cora, be a dear, can you bring us the last two or three files and accompanying evidence that have been marked as 'cold cases.'"

It took Cora more than a few minutes to get them. While they waited, Wally insisted on finishing his story. Hawk turned his head away and rolled his eyes. "Well anyway. I walk into this bar on a disturbance call, expecting a lot of trouble and it was my job to break up a fight. I was ready. Those big buffoons didn't intimidate me. So, I walk in, they see how brave I look and of course, I'm in my uniform, and guess what? They both started heading toward me anyway with their huge fists ready. Well. I was ready for them; I had my fists up and then I thought why be stupid and fight them? So, I took out my gun and pointed it at them and told them that they were to stop or I'll shoot. That sure stopped them right in their tracks."

"Wally, you have more stories than anyone I know. You should write a book. I wonder what's keeping Cora." *He had better not start on another stupid tale of his. Ah, saved by the bell, here she comes.*

They thanked her and went back to their desks. Wally pulled his chair adjacent to Hawk's desk and they briefly skimmed the files. Wally said, "So how do you want to do it? You take a file and I'll take one and then talk about it? From what I can see all three cases are five to seven years old and all were rape and murder."

"Looks like it," Hawk said. He was in no mood to go through one today, still furious that he was off the Bowman cases. He knew that on the outside he seemed calm and collected, but he felt like a duck in water, on the surface calm while below the surface his feet were churning frantically. *I just need to get out of this office right now. I know something is awry. Why was I taken off the cases? Why don't they want to listen to me? Should I just let it go?* "Wally, listen, I need to run an errand. It's only twenty minutes before quitting time, but I need to leave early. I'll see you tomorrow."

"Look, buddy. I'm a great detective and I know what you're thinking. Forget it. Leave it be for your own good. I saw your face in Bradford's office and I heard your non-answer to him about staying out of the Bowman investigation. So, my friend, don't ruffle the feathers and keep your nose clean. In other words, don't be an idiot."

"Thanks for your advice, Wally. Don't worry about me."

"What does that mean? Sounds like you're going to pursue what you've been told not to. Are you crazy? You've got a good start on a terrific career with the Denver PD, so don't screw it up."

"Wally, I'm not going to break any rules. I just need to get away and sulk, okay? See you tomorrow."

Wally shook his head as he watched Hawk go down the aisle. He saw him stop at Nora's desk and speak to her. Actually, what Hawk said was, "Nora, hello, we hadn't talked before, but I want to thank you for backing me up this afternoon." Nora looked around and saw Orlinski staring at them, then she glanced towards Bradford's office.

"You're certainly welcome. Your analysis seemed logical to me. By the way, could you give me your card with your cell number on it?" Seeing that Orlinski was listening to every word as he sat at the next desk to hers, she added, "Just in case I need to get a hold of you on a case that might come up."

Hawk gave her his card, thinking nothing more of it. As he passed Marcie's desk, he whispered that he'll see her tonight. On his way home, he didn't know why at the moment, but he made a spur-of-the-moment detour to Marcus Miller's office building. The coffee shop, Coffee Aroma, was located underneath, on the first floor.

CHAPTER 19

LEAVING HIS jacket and tie in the jeep, Hawk entered the coffee house. The place wasn't overly busy. The morning and early afternoon crowd was gone and only a few tables were occupied by people typing away on their laptops, a cup of coffee placed on the side. A pleasant barista greeted Hawk as he walked up to the counter. He ordered a small cup of Americana decaf coffee and sat down to enjoy it.

Hawk didn't know why he felt it in his gut that Bowman's partner, Marcus Miller, was somehow involved in the Bowmans' murders. He had never met the man, so why did he have that strange feeling that the answer lies with him?

Maybe it was the experience that his father had with his partner in the hardware business who did everything he could to make his father miserable. That partnership fell apart soon after his father had loaned him $20,000 for back child support. Instead of paying it back as promised, the partner begged for more, after only a few months. When his father refused, the partnership, the comradery, any good working relationship all went to pot. The partner became extremely angry and aggressive. One day he even shoved his father into a storage room wall. He said it was an accident, but his father knew it was intentional. More incidents followed. The unwarranted rage intensified, and his father actually thought that his partner had become unbalanced and felt his life threatened. Eventually, the partner committed suicide. This unfortunate incident was indelibly fixed in Hawk's brain. *I bet this is what happened here.*

He had no idea whether or not he would meet Bowman's partner at the coffee shop. Chances were certainly slim; nevertheless, he hoped that he would get to see him. If not, at least he had a good cup of coffee. It really bothered Hawk that he could no longer be concerned or investigate the Bowman cases as per the explicit order of his Lieutenant. He needed to talk to Miller's receptionist and staff, Bowman's staff and most likely their neighbors. But more than anything else, an interview with Marcus Miller was crucial to satisfy his curiosity. Perhaps only then would he abandon his quest if it turned out that he was totally mistaken. Anyway, at the moment, he wasn't investigating anything, just sitting here with a cup of coffee. *That's all.*

But the more Hawk thought about what he was doing, even realizing that his career would be in danger, the more he pondered his plan of action. The more he became determined to proceed. Regardless of his orders, he could not rest and do nothing when it seemed that the investigation by his superiors was completely off base. *If he is not in this shop, then I might as well see if I can catch him in his office next door.*

Just as Hawk was ready to proceed to Miller's office, a full-bearded, heavy-set man wearing khaki pants and a coffee-colored brown polo shirt with the logo "Coffee Aroma" sauntered in. He walked behind the counter and immediately went to the registers. He opened one and grumbled something to the young woman at the counter. Not smiling, obviously upset, she raised her arms and shook her head. Hawk approached the counter, interrupted them, and asked if the man was Marcus Miller. Miller attempted a pleasant smile and answered in the affirmative. Hawk introduced himself as Detective Clint Hawk of Homicide, flashed his badge, and asked if he could answer just a few questions regarding his partner's death. Miller's smile was replaced with a look of concern. His jaw tensed and with seeming reluctance, he agreed to sit down with Hawk. Hawk even offered to buy Miller a cup of coffee and to his surprise, Miller agreed. *It's your coffee, but anything for a buck.*

At the table, Hawk said, "Mr. Miller, thank you for agreeing to talk to me."

"What's this all about? I know nothing about what happened to Jeffrey other than he was shot during a carjacking." Then he added, "We're all terribly upset about it. It's devastating." Hawk studied him carefully, looking for any peculiar mannerisms. Miller picked up the cup of coffee and slowly sipped it. Other than being tense, Miller tried to be as calm and unconcerned as he could.

"I'm actually here bothering you to get a better picture of your partner and I need your help for my report. Is that all right with you?"

"Well, I don't have much time, but I'll help you where I can. I always do try to cooperate with our men in blue. Of course, you're not in uniform." Miller relaxed after Hawk said that he just wanted his help. It was Hawk's intent to make him more at ease so that he could study him after each question. He couldn't put a finger on why but felt that he was barking up the right tree with this man. The vibe reeked with guilt. Perhaps it was his cold, hardened eyes or perhaps his thick and unsteady voice.

"I appreciate that. I guess the obvious question would be whether you knew if he had any enemies that could wish him harm."

Miller considered the question. "Again, I thought from the newspaper and watching TV news that this was a simple carjacking and unfortunately he was shot." He took another sip of coffee. His hands were steady, and he looked Hawk in the eye. Hawk felt uncomfortable when his icy glare focused on him.

"Most likely that is what occurred and nothing more than that. But we're looking at all angles to be thorough just in case." Hawk continued, "Mr. Miller, how long had you known Mr. Bowman?"

"I guess a couple of months before we formally formed this partnership with the coffee business. We'd been in business fourteen years, I believe." For the first time, Hawk smelled a faint odor of alcohol from Miller.

"How did you meet?" Hawk noticed Miller's brow furrow.

"What does that matter to you? Am I a suspect or something? I wouldn't go and try to carjack a car and murder my partner. I don't like where these questions of yours are heading. Do I need a lawyer?" Taken aback by such an inappropriate response to that simple question, Hawk saw Miller's aggravation mount. *He is nervous as hell, and he's not suppressing it very well. I need to calm him down or I'll get nowhere fast.*

"I'm sorry that I mislead you. No, you're not a suspect and you don't need a lawyer." *At least not right now.* I just need to get some background information on Mr. Bowman for my report, that's all. I just thought that the longer you knew him, the better you knew him."

"All right then. I met him at a party of a mutual friend. We got to talking and he said he was looking for a business to start. I knew the owner of a small chain of coffee houses who was desperate to sell. I would have bought them myself, but I didn't have any money. So, I suggested to Bowman that we could make a go of it and expand and even sell wholesale coffee beans from Colombia or Central America. He liked the idea, said he had money, and surprised me that he would put up the money if I would be the managing partner of the business. We'd split everything fifty-fifty. It was a godsend out of the blue. And when we needed extra cash, he made loans to the business, most of which were repaid, except for maybe a few thousand. I loved the guy. He was my bread and butter. I'm really sad that he died." Miller took a bigger gulp of coffee. His right eye twitched when he said, "I loved the guy."

"So, you got along with him really well?"

"Oh yes, he was the greatest partner and I will miss him."

"You never had any serious arguments with him?"

"No, never. He was great to work with." Miller's right eye twitched again and he took another gulp of coffee. He squeezed his coffee cup and covered his right eye with his hand.

"Were you also good friends?"

"Well, yes. The Bowmans would invite whatever wife I had at the time and me to a BBQ at least once during the summer and a Christmas party every year."

"So, you knew the house well?"

"Yeah, pretty well—," he hesitated and Hawk could see the marbles in his head spinning, thinking hard. He pushed out his full lips and looked like a fish. "Well, actually, not that well. You know, the BBQs were in the back yard and the parties were on the first floor of the house." Miller placed his index over his mouth and hooked the tip over his nose.

"I've also seen the first floor. It didn't look all that comfortable to me as opposed to modern open-floor houses. And I bet the upstairs was just as bad, small rooms, small closets, extremely uncomfortable, wouldn't you say?"

Without thinking, Miller blurted out, "Well no, the master bedroom is pretty plush. I'd find it comfortable." After he said that he hesitated. "Well, actually now that I remember, Julia gave me and my wife a tour of the house years ago." He glowered at Hawk and turned towards the counter. "Is there anything else? I need to get back to work."

"Oh, I'm sorry to hold you up. Just a few more questions, please."

"Okay but make it snappy." His tone became aggrieved.

"Now that Mr. Bowman is deceased and so is Mrs. Bowman, I suppose you'll have a new partner, probably one of the Bowmans' daughters?"

Miller suddenly looked startled upon receiving the news. "What, what are you saying, Julia is dead?" Oh my God! Can't be? Both are dead now. Where, how?" Hawk watched his performance. His arms flailed. He rubbed his hands together. He grabbed his forehead. "I just can't believe that. That's impossible." He wiped his eyes as though they had been crying, then rubbed his forehead with both hands. *What a great dramatic performance. He should get an Academy Award. Too bad it's overdone.*

"Oh, I'm sorry, I thought you knew. She was murdered during what appeared to be a burglary early this morning, probably around one or two."

"How could I possibly have known that?" I didn't watch the news, listen to the radio, or read the Denver Post this morning. His right eye twitched once again. The veins in his temple protruded and throbbed and a muscle in his jaw twitched as he swallowed hard.

"Oh, I thought that one of the heirs had called you since they will become your new partner or partners."

His brow drew downward in a frown. "No, no one let me know." Miller hesitated before he spoke again, his eyes shifting back and forth, evidently pondering whether to say it or not, "Besides, why would they since if both the Bowmans are dead, I am now the sole owner and I'm sure the daughters know that." He hesitated again. "I thought I'd let you know that since you'll probably find out anyway."

"How's that? Doesn't one-half belong to the estate of the Bowmans?"

Miller hesitated again, keeping his eyes focused on Hawk who sat still, patiently waiting for a response. Finally, in a subdued voice, he said, "That's not the case. I wanted to keep this quiet, but now that both Jeffrey and Julia are dead, I became the sole owner of the business. Now, you'll probably try to make a mountain out of a mole hill over this, but I had nothing to do with any carjacking and the death of Jeffrey." When he mentioned Mr. Bowman, his voice was rather calm. "And, of course, I had nothing to do with the death of Julia either." When he mentioned Mrs. Bowman, his voice rose a pitch higher and his right eye twitched, he once again lifted his forefinger over his mouth and hooked it over the nose. "I have a valid contract that if both the Bowmans are dead, the whole business becomes mine alone. I had a great lawyer who drafted the agreement and I don't think the Bowmans really cared because they didn't think that their daughters would be interested in the business anyway." Miller was breathing hard, his face flushed, the veins in his temples looked like they would burst.

"That's very fortunate for you, isn't it? Of course, if Mr. Bowman had sold the business, you would be out or have a new partner."

"Hey, I don't like what you're insinuating. I've never been concerned about that. Jeffrey would never have done that without my approval."

"I'll mention it in the report, but I need to clarify a few more questions. You seemed close; perhaps they might have given you a key to their house so you could check on things?"

"No. I know the maid had a key. You should speak to her and her no-good son. But don't you think that whoever killed Bowman also killed the wife? I guess they must have had some dangerous enemies." Miller looked smug, pleased with this suggestion.

"I thought of that, Mr. Miller. But right now, it looks simply like a carjacking and a burglary. Why do you mention the housekeeper? Do you know her well?"

"No, I met her once or twice at the parties. She served the food. Her criminal son helped her with the drinks."

"Criminal son?"

"Yes, I think Jeffrey told me about him. I think he was concerned that he could actually rob them."

"I see. We'll check that out. But how did you know that the housekeeper had a key to the house?"

"Oh, I don't know, I think that Jeffrey told me that as well. I really don't remember."

"You mentioned enemies of the Bowmans. Do you know who they are?'

"The only thing I know is that once I saw someone barge into Jeffrey's office and I heard some loud yelling. There were two guys, both wearing polo shirts and fancy leather jackets with matching fine Italian boots. One was big and the other average. The big guy looked like a bodyguard or something. The smaller man had his hair slicked back and looked like one of those drug dealers to me, you know the kind they like to portray on those TV crime shows? Who knows, maybe Bowman was involved in some drug deals. After all, he had to get all his money from somewhere to buy up all that real estate and restaurants." *Good job of trying to throw blame off himself,* Hawk thought.

"How long ago was this?"

"Oh, maybe a month or so ago."

"Did you hear what the loud conversation was about?"

"No, just shouting. After that, Jeffrey ran out of the office and was gone the rest of the day."

"Would you recognize them if you saw them again?"

"Only if they wore the same clothes. I'm kind of a clothes hog. I recognize clothes, not faces." Miller looked more relaxed now that he thought that he had thrown the scent off himself.

"Just another routine question that I'm sure you heard on TV many times. Where were you between two and three o'clock on Monday afternoon?"

Miller's voice rose again, "Here you go again accusing me of murder. Well, you're way off base, man, I was at a meeting in my conference room with my local buyers and some sellers from Costa Rica. Next, you're going to ask me who was there. Well, I'll save you the breath. I was with my assistant buyers, Mikey Lucas, and Hugh Atchison. Come tomorrow to the office and they will verify that." His voice was firm and confident.

"Thank you for that. Since I have such a stickler for a boss, I need to ask you where you were this morning at about one or two."

"I was at home with my new fiancé, Samantha Higby. I was in the sack having the time of my life." Miller tried to be confident, but unlike his assertiveness where he was with Mr. Bowman's death, he didn't measure up. He had that twitch in his right eye again, and a slight tremor in his jaw while rubbing his forehead. "You told me it was a burglary. So, go look for a burglar and leave me alone." He began to rise and leave.

"Mr. Miller, one thing more, for the report of course, and of course, I'll need to follow up, what is Samantha's address and phone number?'

"Listen, she lives with me and I'm not giving you her number."
As he walked off, he said within everyone's earshot, "I don't want her
to be bothered by your stupid questions or speculations." Miller's face
was flushed.

Hawk finished his coffee, cold by now. He observed Miller
behind the counter as he cleaned out a cash register. His hands
trembled. Hawk rose and as he started to walk out, approached the
counter and said, "Thank you, Mr. Miller, for your cooperation. You'll
probably hear from me again."

CHAPTER 20

IT WAS time to head over to Marcie's place and have pancakes. He was hungry and thought that you could never go wrong with pancakes under a big dab of butter and an ocean of maple syrup. The conversation he had with Marcus Miller played over in his head. He had mixed feelings about Miller and felt he was lying. Some of his answers were obvious to him, yet some were perplexing. Miller seemed at ease when they spoke of the death of Jeffrey Bowman. But Hawk was convinced that he knew more about the murder of Julia Bowman. *Why was that?* The physical characteristics that he observed, if he relied on them, indicated that Miller definitely knew of her murder. He lied at first about not being upstairs in the bedroom, then realizing what he just said, explained that he had been there years ago. *What about having a key to the house?* He fidgeted with his hands when he denied having a key, pitching the blame on the housekeeper. He was uncomfortable when explaining his whereabouts when Mrs. Bowman was killed, but not so when Mr. Bowman was killed. *No, he's involved. I just have to prove it.* Suddenly a thought came to his head. *What if Miller hadn't killed Bowman and only killed his wife? Then who killed the husband?*

It will be tough going rogue. Hawk shivered at the thought that he was blatantly disobeying Bradford's explicit order not to pursue the Bowman murders. He wondered how much of this, if anything, he should tell Marcie. His primary reason, other than just getting together with her, was to seek out her help. She's a good researcher and her assistance could be valuable.

Hawk remembered that during the interview earlier that day, Mrs. Bowman had mentioned that cops were at their house looking for her husband. He had briefly tried to search the police records of any investigations of Bowman, or any charges, files—anything. He found nothing at all. *So why did they come looking for Bowman? What's that about? And why was Bradford so anxious to get him off the case? Strange. Then out of the blue, some hotshot by the name of O'Leary comes in and offers to transfer me out of Homicide. Do I really want to involve Marcie? She could lose her job that she says she loves.* He decided to play it by ear and see how the evening goes.

Marcie lived in an upscale seven-story apartment house sporting large balconies, several with BBQ grills or bicycles stored on them. He looked toward the entrance and to his delight he saw Marcie standing at the foot of the building steps. He was six minutes early and was surprised that she was there already, and relieved that he didn't have to park and go inside. She looked radiant dressed in a yellow sleeveless summer dress brilliantly illuminated by the evening sun on its path to disappearing into the majestic Rockies that protect the front range of Colorado. The sunsets in Colorado were generally magnificent, painting the sky with orange and blue. *Denver Broncos* colors, he thought, reminding him that football season would start soon.

Hawk drove into the circular drive as Marcie waved, displaying that wonderful smile. Her lit-up face caused his heart to skip a beat. He barely had time to stop before Marcie skipped forward and grabbed the car door. "Hi, I didn't want you to go to the trouble of parking and looking for my apartment, so I waited for you."

"I hope you didn't wait long, although I'm early as it is."

"No, no, not at all, just a few minutes. Besides it's so nice out here and the rays of sun felt so good on my face. So, are pancakes, okay?"

"Oh yes, for sure. I haven't thought of anything else. Your choice, Village Inn or IHOP, they're both close by on Colorado Boulevard."

"Let's try IHOP. So how did your day go after you left the office? Were you able to go home and relax a bit? You seemed really screwed tight."

"Actually, I didn't go home. I went and talked to someone that I suspect is the murderer." *Damn, why did I tell her anything?*

"Oh, tell me about it." Suddenly Marcie's happy expression turned glum. "So, you are pursuing the Bowman cases even though you were told not to."

"Marcie, at this point, I don't know what I'm doing. I just wanted to prove to myself whether my gut is right by asking a few questions of the man I suspect."

"And, are you satisfied now and will leave the matter be?" *Boy she's pushing this a little hard. Is she that concerned for me or what?*

"Marcie, we're almost there. Let's talk about this further over dinner. But first, let's eat. I don't want anything to ruin my appetite, although that's pretty hard to do." Hawk laughed trying to bring a little levity. *Perhaps after dinner, she will lose some of her intensity about the subject. It will give me more time to decide how much I'll tell her about the conversation with Marcus Miller.*

Before the pancakes were served, Marcie blurted out. "You have such a bright future ahead of you and I think you're playing with fire if you don't listen to Bradford. I know him and he's a very vengeful man. He's a narcissist and won't allow anyone to take the limelight away from him. Sometimes, I even think that he is dangerous."

Hawk raised his eyebrow at that statement and he gulped down some water. Marcie felt that she had to explain. "I know, I know, you'll think I'm crazy, but I get this bad vibe from Bradford most of the time. Then, there is that creep O'Leary, that you met today. He comes in as though he owns the place and sashays directly into Bradford's office. They always meet behind closed doors. It's never a long meeting, just a few minutes. On the way out, he harasses Nora and me one way or another. I feel like filing a complaint with the city, but quite frankly, those cold black eyes of his give me the creeps. Promise me,

Clint, that you'll never tell anyone what I said, particularly the biggest station gossip, Wally."

"Of course, I won't and I'll ask the same of you regarding anything I tell you."

"It's a deal," Marcie said, but she looked upset and worried that perhaps she had said too much.

"I appreciate that you took me into your confidence, particularly about Bradford. Wow, that's quite a bit of news. But how is it supposed to affect me? We both have gut feelings about certain people that may be totally false. For example, did you ever see anything that Bradford had done that makes you think he is vindictive or even dangerous?"

"Vindictive, yes. I've seen him demote and embarrass poor individuals who crossed him. Take you for example. I think what he did to you by taking you off the Bowman cases is vengeful. But as far as dangerous? No, just my gut feeling, that's all."

"Well, I don't know—oh, there's our food. Let's eat and enjoy it. This conversation took a very heavy turn." They ate almost in silence except for telling each other how good it is and how bad it was for them with all the carbs and sugars.

Hawk said, "Wow, I ate too much. I'm so stuffed. I should've left half on the plate."

Marcie agreed that she also ate too much. As the server was taking away the plates and asked if they wanted dessert, both Marcie and Clint answered with a resounding "No!"

"Now, can we talk a little about the witness and what he said? You piqued my curiosity and generally, Clint," she stretched out her hand and picked up his hand that was resting on the table. "I want you to feel that you can tell me everything. I want to be your sounding board. Everyone needs one, you know." With a devastatingly irresistible smile she said in a soft voice, "And if you need input about anything, you can count on me."

Hawk decided that he could confide in her and tell her about the conversation with Miller to see what she thought. As he was about to, his cell phone rang with an unknown number. He decided to ignore it. After all, he was with a beautiful girl. The cell phone rang again. He ignored it again, but the third time the phone rang, he answered it.

"Yes."

"Hello, Clint. This is Nora from the station." Her voice hardened. "I need to talk to you as soon as possible. There is something you need to know about the Bowman murders. When can we meet? The sooner, the better."

"Nora, I'm in the middle of dinner with a friend. Can't it wait until tomorrow?"

"No. This is very important." She hesitated. "Your life may be in danger."

"Well, if you put it that way, when and how?"

"At eight-thirty tonight at the McDonalds on Colorado."

"That's pretty close to where I'm now."

"Good. Meet you soon." Nora clicked off.

"What was that about?" Marcie looked concerned. "Who was that? And why do you look shaken?"

"Marcie, that was Nora."

"Nora? From our office?" Hawk nodded. "What does she want?"

"I don't know, but it seems very urgent. I guess I must meet her. Says it's very important. Sorry, that kind of ruins the rest of the evening for us. But, it appears, I'll have to take you home."

"Oh no you don't, I'll go with you."

"No, Marcie. I think it's better that I go alone. I'll fill you in tomorrow."

"No, tonight, right after you see her, otherwise, I won't be able to sleep."

CHAPTER 21

DRIVING OUT of the parking spot, Hawk noticed a dark SUV come up behind them. Through the rearview mirror, he saw the gold emblem of a Chevrolet. He stopped at the entrance onto Colorado Boulevard, let the traffic pass, then crossed several lanes to the left turn lane. The light turned red. The SUV, now under the streetlight, was easy to recognize as a Tahoe. The driver performed the same maneuver. At the green arrow, Hawk made a U-turn on Colorado, as did the SUV. He slowed hoping the vehicle would pass him, but it stayed right on his tail.

"Why are you looking back all the time, Clint?" Marcie asked. "And why are you driving only twenty miles per hour? Is there a problem?" She turned her head, looked back, and saw the black SUV. "Wow, he's riding your bumper. What's this all about? Did you cut someone off or something?"

"No, the guy followed us from IHOP. Maybe, he's just a prankster. I'll speed up and change lanes and see what he does." He did that and still, the SUV stayed on his tail. "Well, I don't want to take you home with that idiot behind us. Any chance you can see who it is?"

Marcie once again twisted to look back and tried to see through the Tahoe's windshield. It was too dark to tell, especially with the headlights blinding her. "I can't tell, Clint," she said, her voice weak and nervous. "He has his visor lowered as well. He doesn't want us to see him, that's for sure. What does he want? This is pretty scary."

"Well, I'm not going to play games with him. I'll pull over into the Target parking lot and confront him." Hawk once again crossed three lanes to turn into the lot. The vehicle crossed the same three lanes but continued on, turned right onto Alameda Street, and disappeared. Hawk bit his lower lip, a nasty habit he developed as a teenager when he felt uneasy. He thought of Nora's words, "Your life may be in danger." *But why? Who would want to kill me? Nora must know something.*

Marcie's home was just a few minutes away. They both sat silently, each with their thoughts. Marcie finally looked at Clint intending to say something. Hawk beat her to it. "I don't know what the deal is here and who that scum bag is. It was probably some jerk trying to get his kicks tonight, and we're the ones he picked. Don't worry about it. It's a once-in-a-lifetime event, that's all."

"Okay, let's hope so. But I just have this strange feeling there's more to it than that."

"Feelings don't amount to anything most of the time."

"Well, now, Detective, you should talk. You're pursuing something that you're not supposed to because of a feeling that you have."

"No, Marcie, it's more than that. I actually see evidence that contradicts what the Lieutenant is saying. I have something to go on."

"Okay. You know my opinion." She sat silent for a moment. "Well, the evening was too short. We're here already at my little abode." She looked into his eyes. "I like being with you even though we were chased by some creep. What an adventure."

"Yes, it was great having dinner with you. Sorry about the serious talk, though."

"I must admit that the call from Nora and how concerned you looked afterward made me worry. What about exactly, I don't know. All I know is I don't like the idea of you meeting with Nora."

"You're not jealous, are you?" Hawk laughed.

Marcie punched his arm, "Oh don't flatter yourself. I'm just worried about what she said to you just now and what she'll tell you later. Watch out for her, Clint. I don't trust her. She's always watching everybody and everything in the unit. One evening I walked in and caught her looking over some papers and when she saw me, she quit immediately and made some lame excuse that she misplaced a document and was searching for it. She was going through Jeffries's files."

"That is unusual. I know nothing about her." *And keep it that way,* Marcie thought.

"Clint, I like you and want you to succeed. Remember, I'll always be glad to be your sounding board. Oh, and by the way, thanks for dinner." Hawk then detected a touch of merriment in her blue eyes and her usual smile lit up her face. "Now if this was a date, then thanks for dinner again. But if it wasn't, I owe you one." Then she laughed as she squeezed his hand that was still wrapped around the steering wheel. To his surprise, Miss Turner leaned over and kissed him on the cheek. Then she quickly flew out of the car before Hawk was able to get out and open the door for her. Sticking her head back into the car she ordered, "Now remember to call me right after your meeting with Nora. Otherwise, I'll worry my head off." Hawk waited for her to enter the building and just before she did, she turned, smiled and waved goodbye.

As Hawk was about to leave the semi-circular drive, he spotted a black Tahoe parked across the street.

CHAPTER 22

THE BLACK Tahoe sped off before Hawk had the chance to check it out. *What the hell is that about? Who is that and what does he want with me? Somehow, he followed us to Marcie's place.* His hands tightly gripped the steering wheel. His stomach turned flips and his heart raced. Someone was playing games with him. He wouldn't have thought anything of it except Nora's warning of danger kept gyrating in his mind. It became imperative to talk to Nora as soon as possible.

As he headed south on Colorado Boulevard, he continued taking deep breaths. Soon, his anxiety cooled. *What is the matter with me? I'm a policeman, a detective. I need to be strong; I have to be brave. I'm acting so paranoid right now. I can't believe it.* By habit, he glanced in the rearview mirror sure that he was just imagining the worst, but there it was. The Tahoe was prominently behind him, about five car-lengths away. His heart rate increased again. *What the hell? It must be some other SUV. I'll slow down and I bet they'll just go by me.* The vehicle slowed also. Hawk felt a tension headache. He unsnapped his holster and muzzled his weapon, prepared to use it if he had to. He looked back again and with a huge sigh of relief, he witnessed said vehicle turn into a strip mall, just a driveway or two from the McDonald's meeting place.

Hawk almost jumped out of his seat when his cell phone rang. "This is Nora. Where are you?"

"I'm almost there, but I seem to have someone following me."

"Change of plans. McDonalds is too open. Meet me at the King Soopers parking lot on Colorado. Park in the lot between cars. I'll be in a white Ford Escape in about the middle of the lot. If I'm there before you, my parking lights will be lit. I'll wait for you. Make sure you're not followed and shut off your phone."

"Nora, what's this cloak and dagger stuff? What's going on?" She hung up.

When he passed McDonald's, Hawk looked back. He saw the SUV exit the strip mall lot and again get behind him. He gunned his engine. The Tahoe picked up speed as well but still kept a distance. Five minutes later, he saw the grocery store but didn't turn into the lot. Instead, increasing speed on his Jeep, and in the center of the intersection he turned violently to the right onto Mexico Street. He heard brakes squealing behind him, but the SUV was unable to make the turn.

Relieved, Hawk drove to the end of the block and turned right again. He went down Jackson Street, a residential street, observing no headlights of vehicles following him. He needed to go right on Iowa Street to reach the meeting place, but instead, to be safe, he turned left, headed down Monroe Street back to Mexico and headed east and turned left back onto Colorado Boulevard, then left again on Exposition Street and left into the north entrance of the shopping center. King Soopers was to the right. He had no problem finding the Ford Escort, parked his car as instructed, and sprinted to the passenger side of the vehicle.

"Get in, quick," Nora said as he approached the passenger side. He was barely in and before he had a chance to put on his seatbelt, she took off. "Had any problems getting here?"

"I'm not sure. I think that whoever is in a black Chevrolet Tahoe was playing games with me."

"They didn't follow you here, did they?"

"No, I think I lost them. Nora, what's this all about?"

"Let me get onto I-25 and try to get lost in traffic just in case we're followed. They're afraid of you, Clint."

"Who's afraid of me? I'm just a rookie detective with no real experience."

"Yeah, but you have a clear mind, very analytical and they know you're not giving up on the Bowman cases. They're afraid that you'll figure out what's going on. There's too much money at stake."

CHAPTER 23

NORA PUSHED 75 in a 55-mph zone, cutting in and out of traffic. "Nora, slow down already. You're making me nervous. Nobody could follow you, so don't worry."

"All right if I'm going a little too fast for you, you wimp, I'll slow down. But before I tell you anything, I want to make sure we're not followed." *Holy crap, is she as paranoid as I am?* Nora exited I-25 onto the 6th Avenue freeway and headed west toward the mountains. Hawk couldn't believe she was going out that far and he kept wondering why. After twenty minutes from the time he got into her car, she exited onto Wadsworth Avenue, headed south and a few minutes later, Nora's Ford Escort turned left into a Walmart parking lot. Again, she parked between two cars in the busy lot.

"Okay Nora, enough of this. What in the hell is going on? Why am I being followed and why are we so far out here in Lakewood?"

Nora smiled as she opened the sunroof and switched off the engine. She turned her whole body toward Hawk, her bare tan knee peeked out of her black skirt and rested on the empty cup holder of the console. There wasn't much distance between the seats and her leaning head was just inches from Hawk as he turned to see her face. The brilliant glow of the full moon shone through the sunroof and reflected off Nora's dark hair, giving it sort of appearance of a halo. Her light olive skin glowed. Nora's sparkling sapphire eyes gazed intently at Hawk. Those sensual red lips protruded as if she was about to speak French. *What a captivating woman.* But that fleeting thought evaporated when the events of the evening crowded to the front of his brain.

In a pleasant, calm, and soft voice, she spoke almost in a whisper, as though someone could overhear, "All right, Clint, I really don't know where to begin. I guess I need to start from the beginning. You'll be the only person in the Homicide unit to know, and you have to make sure that no one else knows." Hawk sat there incredulous. *Again, more cloak and dagger stuff.* If he had not been shaken up by that black SUV earlier, he would have thought she was being too melodramatic.

"Yes, of course. Go on, please."

"I'm with Internal Affairs, assigned to the corruption task force. I guess you can say that I'm working undercover in your unit." Hawk raised his eyebrows betraying his surprise. "As you know, almost all the Denver cops are really good people who serve bravely. They're honest and would never think of taking bribes or do extortion or blackmail, deal in narcotics, deal in stolen goods. However, a cop has a lot of authority and can affect the outcome of criminal situations. To a weak or financially desperate few, it's easy to abuse that power."

"Nora, I know all that, what's that got to do with me? Here, my stomach is in knots because you said I was in danger, and you telling me stuff that I learned at the police academy. It wouldn't be so bad if I knew who and what to watch out for."

"I'll get to the point. We have a suspicion that some individual or individuals in the Homicide Unit, the Fraud and Financial unit, and the Narcotics unit take payoffs for looking the other way. People who pay these cops mostly are drug dealers and even identity theft hackers. Also, the cops themselves have a scheme to gather compromising information about prominent persons in Colorado and then blackmail them. Internal Affairs believes that four or five cops are involved who protect and cover for each other. Their operation seems to be well planned and carefully executed, much different from when a single cop occasionally digresses. Do you get my drift?”

“Yes, I assume something like that happens occasionally in every department in the country.”

“Oh no, this is not an occasional occurrence.”

“But again, Nora, how am I involved with this and why was someone harassing me tonight?”

“Well, you touched a nerve when you wanted to probe deeper into the Bowman murders.” Hawk widened his eyes in disbelief. “It looks like Bradford doesn’t believe that you’d leave the Bowman cases alone. Our concern is that the last detective that investigated Jeffrey Bowman had a bad ending. And knowing what these cops can do and very bad people they work for, we feel that you might very well be in danger.” Hawk listened carefully. “And I think that you should know so that you can act accordingly and be on the lookout. I watched Bradford’s face when you told him what you thought the evidence showed. He didn’t like it a bit and he took you off the cases immediately. If you were to take any action to investigate what happened to the Bowmans, you better keep those big eyes of yours open and be extra careful.”

Hawk felt his heart skip beats. “This is certainly like a bomb going off in my head. But why you? Why are you so careful not to be followed, Nora?”

“If we’re seen together tonight, it will blow my cover. We know that they have very sophisticated equipment that can video and pick up our conversations from a distance. That’s only one way they collect info to blackmail or exhort their victims.”

“Well, I don’t know what to say. This presents a whole new angle to this case. But what do the Bowmans have to do with any of this?”

“We have good reason to believe that Jeffrey Bowman was a conduit for the money that this group of bad cops brought in. It surprisingly is a big operation and it nets them a considerable amount of cash that they have to launder. We believe it was Bowman who invested the money in real estate and businesses in the names of various LLCs.

"To hide their identities, the cops have an interest in the properties through a series of LLCs and they probably even have some offshore accounts. We're working on tracing the money invested with the LLCs, who formed them, and who has an interest in them. It's a slow and tedious job since there are so many shell LLCs and corporations to hide the true owners. We're making progress. But with your analysis of the murders of the Bowmans, if you can pinpoint who killed one or both, we may be able to acquire proof that someone in the police department is involved. That is what we need to put them away. Bowman was probably murdered because he knew too much or maybe he simply wanted out." Nora looked at the bewildered passenger as he processed this disturbing information.

CHAPTER 24

AFTER NORA appeared to have finished, Hawk had a million questions surge through his mind. "Nora, why do you suspect Mr. and Mrs. Bowman?"

"Last year, an investigating detective, by the name of Mike Zamora, arrested a banker. However, after a few hours, the banker was suspiciously released with no charges filed. Before he was released, Zamora must have deduced something in the interrogation that pointed to Bowman. We're not sure what because the file mysteriously disappeared. But he kept good notes on his calendar which we reviewed that show that he and another detective by the name of Chris Simmons first went to Bowman's house, then to his office to question him, but were not able to find him."

"Before she was murdered, Mrs. Bowman told me that two cops came by the house looking for her husband. I tried to find out why from the records, but nothing existed. I even asked Marcie to help me find it."

"Yes, I know that you tried. And I'm sure someone else would know about your inquiry since it was on an internal police network available to all cops."

"Oh!"

"That's another reason the crooked cop mob doesn't want you to pursue the Bowman matter. They think you will anyway, and that makes them nervous. The last thing they want, with your apparent tenacity, is for you to uncover Bowman's finances or run across one of their victims who would be brave enough to talk. Or, more importantly, find out who killed Bowman."

"I wasn't even able to find out who the cops were that were investigating Bowman. No one in Records knew anything about this case. What do Zamora and Simmons say now? Oh, was one of them killed? The one you mentioned?"

"Yes, and that's why you might be in danger. Zamora had a suspicious untimely death. He was traveling Highway 7 in Adams County when supposedly a random shooter, shooting at cars, killed him." Hawk stopped breathing for a moment. "And Simmons retired and moved to Alabama and says he can't remember anything about Bowman. Doesn't even remember going out to his house and office with Zamora."

"Was anyone else shot during that incident?"

"No, Zamora was the only victim. According to State Patrol, they called it random, but privately, the investigating trooper told me that he thought it was a set-up, but no way could he prove it."

"Well, maybe I need to get the CSP report and talk to the trooper myself."

"If you do, that will seal your death warrant. Leave that one alone."

"Okay. What about Mrs. Bowman? Was she involved in any of this?"

"As far as we can tell, she wasn't. None of the LLCs in question had her name on them. I agree with you, though, that her death was more than a burglary gone bad. Clint, again, I think that it's your sharp analysis of both the Bowman murders that makes them nervous. You're in their way. Just watch. Jeffries will get a written confession one way or another out of Freeman for one or even both murders. If not, Cordova will be the patsy for killing Mrs. Bowman. And then, pronto, the Bowman case will conveniently be closed."

Hawk leaned his head back and thought a moment. He then faced Nora and asked, "Why are you afraid of being detected? I mean, hiding your car. We had to make sure no one was following you, then drive all the way out here. As you say, it's me that is in danger. I guess what I'm asking is why do you feel you're in danger as well? Because nothing is for certain."

"This is not the night to be seen together since someone was on your tail. I don't want to blow my cover. Remember no one needs to know. If they see us together now, they might think we're working together on this. Back at the unit, I shouldn't have agreed with you about Mrs. Bowman's murder. Bradford didn't like it. I hope he forgets about it."

"Nora, this whole conversation we're having is totally bizarre. It's hard to believe. First, I'm a nobody. I don't have a proven track record of solving crimes. I just don't understand their urgency to get rid of me. Everyone from Wally to Lieutenant Bradford, even Lieutenant Williams, tells me that I'm making things up. I think you and whoever you work with are making a mountain out of a molehill."

"Listen, Clint, I have a lot to say about what you said. First, don't forget the person following you. That's unusual, right?" Nora didn't wait for an answer. "Second, don't you think it's odd that everyone is saying that your analysis has no merit and doesn't want to listen to you? And third, you have to question why the men you mentioned are putting you down. Don't worry about Wally. He's your partner, about ready to retire, and he doesn't want to work. It's easy for him to go the simple route."

"Well, I agree with you there. Wally is something else." Hawk again took on a stern expression. "Can you at least tell me who the suspects are? Who am I supposed to watch out for? I sense that Bradford is the number one suspect."

"Yes. So is Williams. See why they don't like your analysis?" Hawk raised both eyebrows. "You really have to keep this under your hat, but they are our number one suspects. We believe Jeffries is one and you met that creep, O'Leary from the Narcotics Westside District.

All are involved. But we have some evidence, not enough to convict right now. Besides, Bradford may want to kill you just because you exist. I don't know if you noticed yet, but he's an egotist and he's got to be the best, no matter what. He's got to be the best dresser, be the smartest…. you get my drift? He doesn't like anyone to show him up. And guess what? You outclassed him the moment you walked in dressed in a fancy suit, looking like a million dollars. But because you were inexperienced and Wally, for the most part, is incompetent, he assigned you to the Bowman carjacking. He didn't like it at all when you said it was an assassination."

"Wow, I can't believe what I walked into. Does the Chief know about any of this?"

"Yes, he does. Why do you think he assigned you to Bradford's unit? He was looking for a bright detective who would not be intimidated, would be tenacious and not subject to corruption."

"Nora, this is too much for me to take in." Hawk chuckled with a dry and cynical sound. "My brain is tired."

"It is getting late and I threw a lot of stuff at you. But it was decided this evening that I explain to you what is going on so you can be on alert. Sorry to throw all this on you. I'm sure you didn't expect such intrigue on your first two days."

"No, I thought I'd start up slow and work into things."

"Before, we go, though, you mentioned Marcie."

"Yes, what about her?"

"I don't know whether to trust her or not. She is a real busybody. And I'm suspicious that she spends too much time in Bradford's office. I wonder what they talk about." Hawk resented that comment. *Surely, I'm not wrong about Marcie?*

"Out of curiosity, where were you when I called, Clint?"

Hawk hesitated wondering what to say. "I was at the IHOP, very close to the McDonalds we were to meet at."

"Well, good, I picked the place because I live nearby." Nora hesitated for a minute. "I know that Marcie seems to like you a lot and you two seem to hit it off. For instance, she ran out of the office after you when you went to get some cold files. Don't tell her anything about our meeting tonight. I'm not sure that I trust her."

"Well, I may have a problem then."

"What do you mean?"

"When you called, I was having pancakes with Marcie. She knows you called, and I think I told her you needed to see me right away. That it was especially important. She insisted that I call her immediately after our meeting and tell her everything."

"You mean you were on a date with her?"

"No, it wasn't a date, we just had dinner together. She wanted to make sure that I don't blow my career by not following Bradford's orders. Said she was concerned about me. We specifically said that we were not on a date, just coworkers having dinner together."

Nora exhaled deeply. "Sure, just pancakes. Okay, then." She threw her head back as though deep in thought. "Tell her that I warned you about a drug dealer who is after you because you arrested him three years ago while you were on patrol. Do you think she'll buy it?"

"She'll certainly wonder about it and she'll also wonder why I took so long to call her. We've been gone for an hour."

"You'll think of something, I'm sure. Maybe you just forgot. By the way, it looks like you're going to keep investigating the Bowman murders. We'll be working on this case together, after hours if need be. I'll be your contact person. We want you to continue in the Homicide unit and follow Bradford's instructions regarding the closed files with Wally. Whatever you do, don't tell Marcie or Wally anything more about the Bowman murders other than that you are done with them. But we expect you to work on them, on your own time, if necessary. I'll help you, though. I've already arranged for you to get double time for this, so keep track of your hours. If everyone thinks that you're leaving the Bowman cases alone, hopefully, the danger to you should disappear. But you'll still have to watch your back."

Hawk was incredulous. *I can't believe what I got myself into. How can I investigate the murders without anyone knowing about it? Did I sign up for this? And what about Marcie? I'm going to have to lie to her.* Nora, how can we work together, if no one is to know? I mean, are we going to have to meet in the Walmart lot forever?"

Nora stretched out her arm toward Hawk's face. He was surprised but didn't flinch. She grabbed the back of his neck and pulled him toward her. Then she leaned further in and gave Hawk a hard kiss. Hawk didn't protest, but he looked shocked. "What's that all about?"

"Figure it out. That's the answer to your question. In case anyone is watching us now or maybe later. That will have to be our cover. Wipe that shock off your face. It's nothing personal, just duty."

CHAPTER 25

PARK TAVERN, a neighborhood sports bar on Eleventh Street between Lincoln Park and Congress Park areas, was crowded and noisy when Lieutenant Kent Bradford walked in. The server, Janice, knew him well as he was a regular customer, usually there with his friend, Lieutenant Wesley Williams. He was at the bar earlier that evening, right after work at about 5:30 and she was surprised to see him again at ten. "Well, you're back," Janice said. "Couldn't stay away from me, could you?' She laughed heartily, her usual joking style. Customers loved her because of her pleasant, happy attitude and her casual flirtatious manner. She had learned long ago the not-so-secret path to more tips.

"No, I guess I couldn't resist your charms," Pointing to the west side of the tavern, Bradford said. "Is that secluded area behind the wall available? I'm expecting friends." Janice's face split into a wide grin. The large-bosomed forty-three-year-old with bright red hair combed into a French twist led Bradford zigzagging between tables to the isolated spot.

Bradford slid his chair in and ordered a Coors Light. He was early for the gathering. As he nursed his beer, his mind drifted to the thought of how he ever wound up mixed up in this whole affair. But he didn't worry too much about it because he could outsmart anyone when it came to getting caught. He'll soon have enough money once he cashes in his share of the funds accumulated from breaking the law and all the rules, take his measly pension, and live like a king. *A lifestyle I deserve.*

He asked Janice for another beer. Tilting back in the chair, he thought about his three broken marriages. What got into those stupid women? Always complained that he was too controlling and wouldn't give them any freedom. Didn't he allow them all the freedom they needed as long as he approved? Didn't they realize that he always knew what was best for them? Next time, he'll pick out the right woman.

Smiling to himself, he thought how smart he was for being in the right place at the right time when an unknown colleague in the police department went to the trouble to seek him out and shared a scheme to use the police department as a yellow brick road to riches. Bradford was to be that person's right-hand man. He was told that all communication would be through the dark web by using several Internet Protocol (IP) addresses yet to be set up. All the messages would be highly encrypted in a singularly complex code that Bradford alone was to master and guard from all outsiders.

It was crazy, a code within a code, worthy of Arthur Scherbius, inventor of the Enigma machine, or Alan Turing, who cracked its code. He chuckled to himself at the irony of the word "daisy" being a code for kill or eliminate. *No one else in all of Denver could have mastered this code quicker than me, Lieutenant Kent Bradford. I am the best.*

If only his domineering father, who had no confidence in him, could see what his net worth was now, approaching one million. *Too bad that he died. I can't throw my success in his fat face.* His father wasn't around long enough either to see him attain the rank of lieutenant. *Too bad.* Bradford had no doubt that he'll be the captain of the station soon and then through his superior conniving, he'll be the chief someday. *I know how to get ahead and rich just by a little twist of the arm. Put enough pressure or discover their deepest secrets and misdeeds and they're mine. Following rules is for suckers.*

Bradford's mysterious boss asked him to recruit others. He realized immediately that should the scheme be discovered he would be the one left out in the cold. But the money and the adventure would be so satisfying that he decided to take that huge gamble. On the other hand, because he was brilliant, he could outsmart anyone. *Let them try.* He was also instructed that it would be up to him to control and watch carefully the individuals that would make up his group. If they get out of line, eliminate them before they can talk or get too greedy. Once his people were in place, the shadowy person behind it all made sure that they had enough incentive by giving them a good share of the funds. That's how their loyalty would be assured. He thought it was clever of that person to take his or her fifteen percent share off the top and send it to a numbered Swiss account. He felt good about his group. He had no worries about Williams and Jeffries but was not always sure about O'Leary. O'Leary *could be a loose cannon.*

He thought about Jeffrey Bowman. Bradford didn't see it, but the person in charge began to suspect that Bowman was getting cold feet and would fold on them; especially after detectives came looking for him. It became Bradford's job to handle the problem. Bradford arranged to remove all evidence of any investigation of Bowman. He made sure that Detective Zamora would get snuffed out. The mysterious boss gave him a "thumbs up." *But who in the hell is this man, or is it a woman?*

Bradford searched high and low trying to figure it out. He needed someone good with computers to find where the messages originated. But Kent Bradford didn't want the stranger to find out, so he was and still is reluctant to delve too far with the search. The person seemed to have eyes and ears everywhere. *Hell, he could be anyone in the group. I've suspected Williams for a long time.*

Bradford suddenly looked glum when he understood once again that the person in charge had him over the barrel. The group was good at blackmail and this stranger can in turn blackmail him and everyone in the group by just informing on them to Internal Affairs. Yet, he escapes because no one knows who he or she is. *Blackmail on blackmail. It's ingenious. I hate it when someone is smarter than me. But one day, I'll find out who it is, and I'll be the one that will "daisy" him or her.* He chuckled to himself again.

The rest of the group is puzzled that someone above Bradford calls the important shots. They sit around for hours trying to figure out who it possibly could be. Jeffries mentioned that it could be Marcie since she is so good at the computer or perhaps Orlinski because he is devious enough. O'Leary thought it was someone in another division, perhaps even in another metro station. Bradford himself thought that it might be Nora. *After all, I know so little about her. She just was transferred into the unit same as Hawk did. I didn't like that she openly backed Hawk. I need to watch out for her also.*

Bradford's mind suddenly focused on Juan Rodriquez, his connection to the drug cartel. He wasn't one hundred percent sure about his loyalty. But the cartel needed the police protection that the group provided and would not do anything to upset their arrangement. It was worth millions to them and a healthy bribe to him and his group for simply warning them of any police activity against the cartel that they knew about.

Detective Hawk would be a problem. Bradford didn't like him and knew that his rookie would not break any rules, except his rule to leave the Bowman investigation alone. But for some reason, the boss didn't want to eliminate him just yet. He wanted to see if he'd drop the Bowman murder first.

Janice showed Williams and Jeffries to the table. O'Leary walked in a few minutes later. They each ordered a beer. Williams also ordered chips salsa and cheese sticks. "So, O'Leary," Bradford said. "What can you report about Hawk?"

"I followed him as you suggested. You were right. He is pursuing the Bowman murders. He went to talk to Bowman's partner, Marcus Miller."

"See, that SOB, didn't listen to me. I knew it." Bradford picked up his beer and finished off the bottle. "Janice!" He yelled out, his face turning red. "I want another damn beer, now!" Janice rushed over with a bottle, looking flushed. She wasn't smiling this time, but hung around near them, cleaning off a table. Bradford waited for her to leave, but finally lost patience. "Janice are you through there yet." Janice looked at him as though she didn't recognize him. He displayed a new personality that she hadn't encountered before. She quickly finished up and left, muttering something.

"Kent, settle down," Williams said. "You're pretty rough on her. Don't bring attention to our table."

"Don't tell me to settle down. I'm in control." Bradford turned his attention back to O'Leary. "What did they talk about? Was Bowman mentioned?"

"Oh yeah. I had my remote listening device and I could hear every word. Bowman was mentioned many times." O'Leary took a drink of his Bud.

"Well, you idiot, I'm waiting."

"I think he suspects Miller for the murders. Asked a lot of questions about their relationship. Asked where he was at the time of both murders. Found out that Miller is now the sole owner of the coffee business because if both Bowmans are gone, he inherits it all. After listening to Miller, I think that he is the one that done in the missus. Like I told you all, I didn't do it. Don't know what Hawk thinks about the mister. Maybe, he's satisfied that Miller did them both in. Now, he must prove it. I think we should let him try."

"I don't care what you think. I've been thinking we should approach Miller now that we think he might have killed the missus. We need to replace Bowman and Miller could now be our patsy. And if he doesn't want to, we'll threaten him with police harassment and we'll find the evidence one way or another that he killed the Bowmans."

"Man, Kent," Williams said. "We need to find out more about Miller before we talk to him. Maybe he didn't kill anyone and he's more honest than we think."

"Well, I know that, Wesley. I'm not a fool to do that without our homework. In the meantime, think of someone else we can use."

Bradford turned from Williams and faced O'Leary. "Where did Hawk go after that?"

"He went and picked up Marcie and went to IHOP."

"Marcie? Our Marcie from the unit? I didn't realize that they were dating already." Bradford's mouth took on an unpleasant twist. "I don't know if I like that. We'll have to watch her. What did they talk about?"

"Sorry, Lieutenant, I wasn't able to hear most of it. I don't know if there was too much interference at that center or my equipment malfunctioned."

"You screwed up, O'Leary. I don't like it a bit. Well, go on, what were you able to hear?"

O'Leary's brows knitted together, his voice rough and cool. "I heard Marcie tell him not to get involved with the Bowman murders as you ordered, to save his career. She seemed concerned. There was a lot of static and then I heard him get a call and all I heard was to meet at 8:30 at McDonalds on Colorado."

Bradford looked at Williams and Jeffries when he said, "She likes the guy and maybe he likes her. Let's keep that in mind if we need leverage against Hawk. Oh, what did you say about McDonalds?"

"They were to meet there?"

"Who was to meet there? Get your facts straight, O'Leary."

O'Leary sucked in a breath and blew it out in frustration, but he knew better than to cross Bradford. He told the group everything about what happened after he left Marcie's apartment building. He continued on by sheepishly explaining how he lost him near I-25. Bradford's cheeks filled with air, the eyes sharp and assessing. Williams shook his head, looking disgusted. Jeffries continued to remain silent. His philosophy with the vicious group was to make his opinions as scarce as possible.

"You screwed up again. You mean you lost him just like that? I don't like it. I thought you were good at tailing people. You better not mess up again like that. And you still don't know who he met with?"

O'Leary's black eyes blazed at Bradford. "No. I don't, sir. I'm sorry. He really outmaneuvered me."

"We really need to get rid of Hawk, sooner than later," Jeffries chimed in. "He will be nothing but trouble. But we need to do it right. Who knows who he met with, maybe someone from Internal Affairs?"

Williams protested, "Men, I don't think we get rid of him, not just yet. If you suspect that he met with IA, then it will look very suspicious. Killing a detective after another was killed only a year ago is too risky."

"Well, what do you suggest then?" O'Leary said, "You gonna let him discover what's going on before you do him in? I think he's just too smart."

"Boys, boys, boys," Bradford said. "You're assuming that Hawk is that good. Believe me; I'm smarter than that rookie. So, what if he thinks something is going on? He can't prove a damn thing, especially since we'll keep a tight leash on him. I'm going to keep him busy with cold cases. Let him chase the ghosts found in those dead files." Bradford laughed hoarsely and bitterly. "But if it looks like he keeps working on the Bowman cases, then we'll take care of him. I'm sure the boss will agree." No one laughed with him. They all sat silent with stoic expressions. He then hesitated, raised his head, and stared at the ceiling. "I just had another one of my brilliant ideas. We'll use Marcie to rein him in."

"I wouldn't advise it," Williams said. "Just another person in the building to wonder or know what we're up to."

Bradford didn't like to be contradicted. "I'll know how to handle it best, but I'll think about it." *That I'll need to clear with our invisible boss.*

CHAPTER 26

NORA CLOSED the sunroof as she and Hawk drove back to his car, parked in the King Sooper's parking lot. "This is what's great about Colorado, no matter how hot it may get during the day, the evenings cool off so nicely, don't they? Good sleeping weather."

Hawk didn't answer. He morosely stared at the road ahead, as though mesmerized by it. Nora turned her head toward him. "Boy. someone is in deep, Grand Canyon deep, thought. Clint, I know you have a lot to think about, but what specifically are you dwelling on? Surely, not my kissing you."

"Well, yeah. That's for sure. But I—," he hesitated, blew out a hard breath. "At the moment, I've been thinking about what I'm to tell Marcie."

"Well, for one, don't tell her about the sensual kiss," Nora laughed with glee.

Hawk was now in no mood to return the laugh. "Nora, you told me you don't trust her and not to tell her anything other than some drug dealer has it in for me. That, I certainly can do. But, as far as anything about the Bowman case, I don't see why not. I would certainly not say anything about the strong probability that Bradford and the others are corrupt cops. I would focus strictly on the fact that I think it was Bowman's partner that committed the murders."

Hawk turned to face her as she drove. "I trust Marcie. I think I'll need her to help me with the computer and camera work. I'm sure if I dig meticulously around, I'll find a video or something to tie someone to the murders. She's great at it, she's fast and she'll keep everything to herself. I know she will. She's smart and if I don't take her into my confidence, she'll figure out something is going on and she'll want to know. Of course, I'll find out why she's in Bradford's office so much and reevaluate before I tell her anything. But you can be assured that I won't tell her about you or that you're working undercover."

"You know, Clint, you really don't need her help. We have the best computer and video experts in IA. And I told you, I'll help you with anything you need. I think you're in love, that's your problem… and your mind is clouded," she said as she pointed and tapped at her temple.

Hawk snapped his head toward Nora. "I'm certainly not in love with her. I like her, but I'm not in love. We haven't even dated. I only met her a couple of days ago."

"That's exactly my point. You only met her. How in the world can you trust her already?"

"I just have this feeling in my gut that I can, that's all."

Nora chuckled; her laugh had a hard edge. "Your gut, your gut. Sometimes we rely too much on our gut."

"I feel comfortable with her and really feel that she feels the same about me. If I don't tell her more and avoid the subject of the Bowmans, she'll really get suspicious, especially after my meeting with you." Hawk hesitated as he looked at Nora. "And, of course, I feel comfortable with you and my gut feeling is to trust you as well."

"Thank you for putting me into such a lofty category," She laughed richly. "But Hawk, let's get serious then. I guess it'll probably be all right to only tell her about the drug dealer out to get you and that you still want to pursue the Bowman cases. We'll watch what she does, if anything. Take her out for coffee during a coffee break and explain what you want at that time. When she comes back, I'll be watching her. If she runs into Bradford's office that morning, that will mean something, don't you think?"

"All right. I think that's a good idea. I'll tell her tonight about the drug dealer and if she wants to hear more, I'll tell her I'll talk to her tomorrow over coffee."

Nora laughed again, "Oh yeah, don't tell her about our kiss."

Hawk finally burst into laughter, releasing his bent-up anxiety, "Rest assured, I won't."

Nora dropped Hawk alongside his Jeep. "Good luck with Marcie. Don't do anything I wouldn't do." She laughed again, showing sheer amusement.

As he exited the car, Hawk returned a low, throaty chuckle. Shaking his head, he said, "Nora, you're something else."

"I hope so." She laughed infectiously as she drove away shouting, "Be careful!" through the open window.

Hawk waited until he walked into his townhome in the Lincoln Park area before phoning Marcie. He didn't want the distraction of traffic. She answered on the first ring. "What took you so long? I've been beside myself worrying. It's way past ten and you met with that Nora woman at 8:30."

"Marcie, I'm deeply sorry. I apologize for putting you through this. You know when I drove out of your building's driveway, I saw the black Tahoe and it took off when I tried to approach it. Then it followed me, and I had to shake him."

"Oh my God! What does he want?"

"I don't know. I told Nora that I was being followed, and she suggested that we meet somewhere else."

"Oh yeah, like where?"

"We met in the King Sooper's parking lot. She seemed frightened herself and she wanted to get away from the area. So, she drove us all the way to Wadsworth in Lakewood. In the parking lot of Walmart, she explained why she thought that I was in danger."

"Well, why? That's what I want to know. Forget all these parking lots. What about the danger?" She sounded exasperated.

Hawk really hated to lie to her, but that was the agreement with Nora. And the more he thought about it, he really didn't know Marcie all that well, and who knows, maybe she can't be trusted. Maybe she is working with Bradford. "I don't think there is much there, but she heard from a reliable informant that a drug dealer that I had put away, while on patrol, was out. Now she thinks that I top his hit list. That's what she was concerned about."

"That's scary and you must be more than careful. But come on, Clint, she could have told you that over the phone. There was no reason to get you into her car and drive you to a suburb just to tell you that. There's more to it that you aren't telling me, right?"

"There is a little bit more, but nothing earth-shattering. I'm really exhausted tonight and need to get to bed. I'll fill you in over coffee tomorrow morning. Can you get away? Hopefully, I can shake Wally off for a few minutes."

"Why can't you tell me now? You want me to have a sleepless night worrying about you?"

Hawk chuckled. "There is nothing to worry about. I'll tell you tomorrow of my plans with the Bowman murders, that's all."

After saying good night, they clicked off. Hawk stretched his shoulders and neck and sat back in his black leather Lazy Boy chair, his legs raised. He turned on the television. Jimmy Fallon was on but Hawk was in no mood to watch. He thought back about the evening, his dinner with Marcie, the meeting with Nora and finally the phone conversation with Marcie. His mind swirled. Was there really a danger to him? Or was it just Nora's paranoia? He didn't know what to make of her. That kiss was totally inappropriate, although he enjoyed it. *But that's so insignificant compared to the bombshell that Bradford, Williams and others are mixed up in a crazy corruption scheme.* Clint decided that it just couldn't be. He needed to see more proof before giving credence to Nora's implausible tale. He needed to meet up with her superiors to confirm all of these accusations.

Even though Bradford really wants me off the Bowman cases.

CHAPTER 27

HAWK STRODE into the unit at 8:00 o'clock AM. Outside was gloomy with a forty percent chance of rain. The usual Colorado sunlight was covered with heavy clouds and the room looked disheartening. It really wasn't that bad, but Hawk's disposition that morning was anything but cheerful. He managed a warm, toothy smile at Marcie. She returned the smile, but it wasn't as wide as usual. Neither said a word as Hawk walked past her desk. Hawk was relieved that Nora wasn't in yet. He didn't know how to handle the uncomfortable situation between himself and the two women who seemed to be in competition over him. Marcie appeared to really care for him, at least that's how it looked. Nora seemed to want to keep him out of danger. But he had to admit that there was some chemistry between him and her.

Hawk was thankful that Wally also hadn't come in yet. He appreciated the peace and quiet as he started to go through the cold files. The first three were rape and murder cases. The investigating detective at the time for all three cases was Robert Wharton. *I'll need to find out where he is. Wally will probably know.*

Conscious of the recent publicity of crimes solved with DNA matches using genealogy sites, he went through the evidence boxes for any DNA found on the victims. There was no evidence of that, but he saw that rape kits were taken with no results noted. He made a mental plan to check with the Colorado Bureau of Investigation. Better yet, he should make a trip again to Lakewood to visit their offices on Kipling Street in person. Hopefully, Wally won't go along which would give him the opportunity to meticulously search the area where the gunman must have waited for Bowman. Perhaps there would be some overlooked physical evidence or maybe a security camera that would show something. *I'm not convinced that a thorough search of the area was made.*

A few minutes later, Nora came in. She seemed to avoid eye contact with Marcie but looked down the aisle between the desks to see if Hawk was there. They made eye contact and she smiled warmly. He returned a weak smile and nodded, but then looked away, hoping that she'd get the message that they're not on overly friendly terms. A minute later, Wally waddled in, picking his teeth. He said something to Marcie and chuckled. Then, he headed straight for Bradford's office. *What's that all about?*

He came out a minute later and walked a few steps past his desk to Hawk's. "I know how much you want to pursue the Bowman cases, so I thought I'd ask Bradford if he had changed his mind. He not only said, 'No,' but said 'hell NO.' So, I guess we have no shot at it. Sorry, Clint."

"That's okay, Wally. I'm over it. I don't care about those cases anymore. Hey, these three cold cases are interesting. We need to study every page in the file, and perhaps talk to the investigating detective at the time. By the way, do you know where Robert Wharton is?"

"Yeah, he was a detective who was transferred to a narcotics unit at a station on the West side about a year ago. We were good friends, and still get together for beer once in a while. Why?"

"He's the investigating detective on the cold cases."

"Oh, knowing him, he probably screwed up something. He was never very motivated." *Sounds familiar,* Hawk thought.

"Anyway, Wally, later this morning I might go to CBI to see if they had any results on those rape kits that never made it into the evidence boxes here."

"Sounds like a plan. I'll go with you to the Bureau, of course. I could use a ride out there."

"You don't have to, Wally. No use both of us wasting our time in traffic when you could get something accomplished here."

"Nah, we're partners. We'll go together. I don't get much accomplished these days. I'm counting my weeks and days to retirement. I can hardly wait for those beaches in Aruba." He laughed richly. "Yes sir, a view of some turquoise blue water with girls in bikinis roaming around would be fantastic, wouldn't it?" Hawk eased into a smile and nodded in agreement.

Each took a file and began reading it. Hawk was making notes, Wally couldn't sit still. He squirmed in his chair, puffed hard a few times, then he walked slowly over to the coffee bar, poured a cup of coffee, dumped three sugars in and complained to anyone listening that he couldn't find the cream. Then he shuffled over to Marcie and asked how her evening went. Hawk saw her mouth something brief, then he nodded at Nora, then Orlinski, and returned to his squeaky chair. Hawk pulled out his cell and called Marcie. "Are you ready for coffee in about five minutes? Can you get away?"

She agreed. He fiddled with the case files for a few minutes and then told Wally that he was going to take a short coffee break. "I need to discuss something that came up with Marcie."

"Oh, I can use a cup of coffee, that's for sure," Wally said. "I'll go with you."

"Wally, you have a cup sitting on your desk."

"I mean, I could use a real cup of coffee. Oh, I see you want to be alone. Well, do me a favor then. Can you bring me a latte with a piece of pastry? If you go to Thump Coffee, get me one of those blueberry muffins please."

When Hawk and Marcie walked out, every detective's eyes were on them, particularly Nora's. Both felt uncomfortable walking out together. Hawk didn't even know if they were allowed a coffee break, but Marcie assured him that everyone gets out of the building and disappears for a bit every once in a while. "There is no strict rule on that, except I suppose you can't abuse it by staying out too long. Where do you want to go that's real close?"

"Well, I've already received an order from Wally. We better go somewhere close and where they serve something sweet for Wally." They both chuckled. "Wally is funny in his own way, isn't he?"

"Yeah, but I think he's harmless," Marcie said, "But annoying at times, for sure." Suddenly her expression became grim. "So, what happened last night?"

Hawk also turned gray, matching the clouds. *Here we go. I better make this convincing.* "Well, as I told you last night Nora was concerned about that drug dealer. She said she'll keep checking on him and keep me in the loop. But then she changed the subject and like you, said she was concerned that I would pursue the Bowman murders." Hawk stopped speaking as he pulled into a spot along the street in front of Thump Coffee. They walked in toward the counter. "What would you like, Marcie?"

"Oh, I don't really care." She hesitated. "I'd like a small coffee, please. That's all. I'm not much of a coffee drinker." Hawk ordered two small coffees, a latte and a muffin.

As they waited in line, Marcie said with anticipation, "Well, go on, tell me what happened?"

"Anyway, Nora said that she noticed how angry Bradford became and she was concerned that if I pursue my investigation without his blessing, that would be the end of my career." Hawk didn't like his own explanation. It sounded phony to him and probably more so to Marcie.

"That's it? That's it? You spent an hour and a half with Nora last night and that's all you talked about?"

"Yes, Marcie. That's basically it." Hawk was irritated. After all, why did he have to explain anything to this woman? *We aren't married, going steady, or even dating. He only met her three days ago and what is her big concern? I'll just come out and tell her how the cow eats the cabbage.* "Look, Marcie, I'm going to tell you what I told her. I'm not giving up on the Bowman murders. There is something going on there and the fact that everyone is trying to dissuade me makes me more determined than ever to go for it. Justice must be done."

"Don't get angry. I'm just concerned about you."

"Marcie, why do you care so much about my career?"

Marcie gazed at Hawk in amazement. "You fool, I like you a little too much, that's why. I don't want anything bad to happen to you. If you don't want me to care about you that much, then fine." Her tone was angry disappointed, or both. She felt her heart race. "Do whatever you want. Where is that coffee? We should be getting back."

Hawk felt bad. He hadn't planned on upsetting her that much. "I'm sorry. I didn't sleep well and this whole thing with someone out to hurt or kill me, and then the stress of deciding to continue on my own with the Bowman murders, is setting me on edge. Believe me, Marcie, I like you a lot and actually I'm flattered about your concern for me."

He hesitated, but before he could say anything else the order came, he paid, and they drove off. Marcie kept silent. She looked as though she was close to tears. He took her soft, silky hand. It felt warm and a sensation of pleasure passed through him. He glanced at her. "I like you a lot also." Marcie turned her head toward him, the sparkle in her seemed to reignite. Hawk forced a smile. "But right now, I'd like two things. First, will you go on an official date with me Friday night? And second, would you be willing to secretly help me with the Bowman murders?"

"Oh, now that you upset me, you want to make it up with a date." She giggled. "Well, you're on, mister."

"Great, what about helping me? Remember, no one needs to know."

"I guess I've got to keep you out of trouble somehow. So, I suppose I will help you. Just tell me what you need."

CHAPTER 28

NORA WATCHED Hawk and Marcie return. Hawk carried a cup of coffee in his hand along with a little pastry bag. Nora and Clint shared a smile as he went by her desk. Her intense eyes followed him to Wally's desk where he set the coffee and the bag down. Wally looked up from his computer and grinned widely, reaching in his pocket to pay him only to see Hawk shake his head and wave his hand as though to mean, 'forget it.'

Nora was assigned a vehicular homicide on the East side of town, close to the Aurora border on Seventh St. A hit and run featuring a car and a young male bicyclist. There were several witnesses who identified a newer black or blue or dark gray Kia Sorento, but no one had the fortitude to remember the license number except that it was a Colorado plate. She had followed up all leads, and visited most of the body shops in the area, but so far, no luck. She was determined to find the culprit and knew that eventually she would. She went through the file again, hoping that some magic piece of evidence would pop up out of there, but as of yet, she found nothing to sink her teeth into.

She glanced over at Marcie, who was earnestly typing away and Nora could see a faint smile on her face. She historically disliked it when Marcie arrived looking happy and that seemed to have carried over to today. Whatever happened between Hawk and Marcie must have gone very well for her. Nora didn't much care for Marcie. She considered her a frivolous flirt, trying to hook a husband. According to her domineering Italian mother, Nora should be more like Marcie. Her mother was constantly needling her, often saying, "You've turned thirty-three and I still have no grand bambinos. I want to be called Nona just as my friends are. Better stop working so hard and find someone before I get too old to enjoy my grandkids."

Her mother was right. She did work too hard. She's used to it. When she was a schoolgirl all she did was study. In college, all she did was study. *I got straight A's and big deal, all I have is a certificate certifying that I am smart. Diplomas don't certify that I am happy.* With her beauty and charisma, she never had a problem attracting scores of men. Some relationships might have worked out, but she never loved any of them. The worst was Devon O'Leary. She endured two dates with him, and she felt fortunate that he didn't rape her. He bragged that he and she were a couple. She can't stand the man and is convinced that he is part of this corrupt group of cops. She looks forward with great anticipation to putting him away.

Nora's face suddenly broke into a satisfying grin when she thought of that kiss she laid on Clint. *What got into me? It was so unlike me.* Since the second he walked through that door, she hadn't ceased thinking about him. She desired to be with him. *Drat! Why did Marcie get to him first?* She envisioned bringing him home to meet her parents. Perhaps he would make a perfect husband for her. That would make her mother happy. Last night, as she dropped him off, she fought hard to suppress the urge that dwelled deep inside her to passionately kiss him again before he left the car. She bit her tongue to stop from blurting out, "Next time I'll take you to a real meal at an Italian restaurant and not for pancakes." That, she thought, might have been a little too pushy. She chuckled to herself as she thought about it. *Oh well, it's all fate, if it happens, it happens.*

The mail for the day was left, as always, on Marcie's desk who picked it up and took it to Bradford's office. Nora started timing the duration of this exchange. To drop off the mail, only took a second. To exchange a quick greeting, a few more seconds. Five minutes had passed, and Marcie was still with Bradford. Nora glanced over at Hawk. Hawk's inquisitive eyes were on her and he nodded, also aware of the situation. Another five minutes passed before Marcie walked out with an expressionless face. She looked toward Hawk before she turned the corner to her desk and sweetly smiled.

Nora called Hawk on his cell. "We need to talk," she whispered. "Meet me after work, can you?"

"Okay. Where? But I have an errand to run, how about closer to six."

She thought for a moment, then said, "How about at Charlie Brown's for a drink?"

Hawk agreed but was surprised at the location she picked. He was just there yesterday with Wally.

Fifteen minutes later, Hawk and Murphy were heading out the door to go to CBI when Bradford grabbed Murphy's arm and called them into his office. Murphy immediately took a seat at the desk, reclining comfortably, while Hawk stood, uneasy at what was to come.

In a hardened voice, Bradford asked, "What are you two doing today? Where are you going? Out to eat again, probably."

"Oh no, sir," Murphy said. We're working hard on three cold cases and are heading to CBI to check for results that might exist for those kits because there are none in the files."

"Why don't you just call them? I think you two just want to screw around."

Hawk said, "Lieutenant, we thought of that, but getting anything done over the phone with cases as old as these would be difficult and time-consuming. We're bringing the files for easier reference and think that we have a better chance of speaking to the person who might have analyzed the rape kits."

"Okay, go! Get out of my hair. Hawk, you should have taken that job with whatever O'Leary was offering you on the West side. You don't fit in around here."

"Yes, sir." Both left the office and the building.

"He doesn't like you much, does he?" Murphy said, slapping Hawk's knee in a friendly gesture as they drove down Colfax to the I-25 interchange.

"It's that obvious, is it?" Hawk laughed in a deep jovial way, masking how much it really bothered him. Murphy was pleased to return the laugh. "Wally, how long have you worked under Bradford?"

"Well, let's see. I've been in the Homicide unit after they transferred me from Narcotics about twelve years ago and Bradford was a sergeant then. So, I guess, Bradford was my boss one way or another since then."

"Was he always so, ah—," he hesitated to try to think of the proper adjective to describe Bradford.

"You mean uptight and determined?"

"Yes, I guess so."

"No, he was always arrogant and tough, but it seems he became more neurotic as time went on. He was never a pleasure to work for, but he never intimidated me. I think that he's very intelligent, a quick learner and gets what he wants. He pretty much leaves me alone. Unlike you, I'm no threat to him."

"I didn't realize I was such a threat. He barely knows me. I know he doesn't like me, but a threat?"

"Oh yeah! He must think that you're too smart or too ambitious and might undermine his authority sooner than later. Hawk, if I were you, I'd follow his orders to the letter. Think, man! He doesn't want you to pursue the Bowman cases and I sure hope you don't even consider it."

"But, why wouldn't he want me to? I just don't understand."

"He must have a reason. Maybe he doesn't want you to waste the Department's resources on a wild goose chase. Maybe he's just trying to prove a point to you."

"Well, he has done that all right. He's the boss and I must listen."

"There you go, my friend. Remember that and your life will be peaceful." Hawk didn't understand why Murphy used the word, "peaceful," but he decided not to push it any further.

"Wally, tell me about your life," Hawk asked just for idle conversation.

"Not much to tell. Got out of high school in Springfield, Illinois. Then joined the Navy. Served three years, then went to a junior college, then to the University of Illinois in Springfield under the GI bill. I barely received my degree in economics. You might be surprised at this, but I really didn't like school or to study much." *Why does that not surprise me,* Hawk thought and chuckled to himself. "Oh yeah, I got married between junior college and the U. Had a kid from that wife." He suddenly looked sad. "But hell, if I know where Mark is. Let's change the subject before I tell you about the wives I had."

"Of course, I don't mean to pry into your life. But since you want to change the subject, did it strike you that on the three cold cases, it might have been the same offender?"

"You think it might be a serial killer?"

"Maybe, let's look at it from that angle and see what it gets us."

At the counter at CBI, they were given the name of Jennifer Carlton, the person in charge of rape kits. They were told to wait, and she'd come out to see them. They waited ten minutes before Jennifer finally came to greet them. She was an older heavyset woman wearing a lab coat with safety glasses hanging from her thick neck. She seemed put out and demanded what Hawk and Murphy wanted.

"As I'm sure you've been told, we're homicide detectives with the DPD and are working on some cold cases." They both pointed to their badges, except Wally's was hard to see on his belt under his hanging stomach. "The three current cases we've looked at show that rape kits were taken from the victims, but no results were mentioned."

"Rape kits, rape kits, that's all everyone wants as of yesterday."

"But these cases are from three to five years old."

"Well, if they're that old you should have had them." She looked even more irritated. "What are they?" She looked at the files that Hawk had laid out on the table. Jennifer noted the dates and numbers writing them down, exhaling hard and frequently as if out of breath.

"Wait here. I'll go see about them." She walked out leaving them waiting again. Fifteen minutes later she returned saying, "I'm sorry, it seems those three cases slipped through the cracks. The technician handling them was fired and no one evidently followed up. We'll put a rush on them. You'll get the results in fourteen days. Leave your card and I'll call you." She mumbled a goodbye of sorts and the men left.

On the way back, Wally asked if he could buy Hawk lunch since it was his turn. Hawk declined because he intended to drive to Lafayette Street and more closely check out the Jeffery Bowman murder scene. "I'm sorry, Wally, will you take a rain check on that, maybe tomorrow, but I have to do a personal errand over lunch."

"Oh, what would that be? After all, we're partners, and I need to know everything."

Hawk wasn't expecting that. *Whoever asks what errands someone has to do? Wow, what should I tell him?* He thought quickly, "I want to retile my bathroom and I'd thought I'd drop by Home Depot and see what's available."

"Great, I love those kinds of stores. I'm handy if I can toot my own horn. I'd love to go with you. You know outside of Home Depot there's usually a hot dog or sausage cart and I'll buy you one. We can make a picnic out of it and sit on one of their park benches."

Oh geez. That backfired. Wally, that sounds great, but the more I think about it, I'll need extra time to find the perfect tile, get the matching grout and all that stuff." Feeling defeated, Hawk capitulated. "I'll tell you what. I'll take you up on your offer for lunch. You pick the place."

CHAPTER 29

THE LUNCH at a seafood restaurant on Wadsworth lasted more than the hour that they are generally allowed. They talked sports and Wally mentioned all the places around the world that he's going to go to as soon as he retired. *He must've saved a bunch of money to do that. Or is it just wishful thinking?* Wally noticed Hawk's amazed expression and as though he read his mind. He said, "I guess I can dream." Hawk had grilled trout, while Wally had a big combo plate of shrimp, fried fish, and fritters. They finished eating and, obviously, because the young waitress was so sweet and flirted with him when it came time to pay the bill, Wally paid in cash and left the waitress a hundred-dollar bill. On the way back, Wally appeared quite satisfied with himself. Like the saying, "The cat that swallowed the canary," he slouched in the seat, his head on the headrest, driving in the right lane at least ten miles under the speed limit.

Hawk was losing patience. He didn't want any further trouble with Bradford and was anxious to return quickly. Fidgeting, he glimpsed at the passenger rearview mirror and noticed a Black Tahoe slowly following them about two hundred yards back. He turned and gazed out of the rear window. *It couldn't be the same guy that followed me last night, could it?* The driver was too far back. Wally finally spoke, "You noticed him, too, I take it."

"Yes, what do you think that is all about?"

"I don't know, but I noticed him as we headed to CBI. He's certainly interested in us." '*Us?*', Hawk thought. *That has nothing to do with "us." It's me that he's following.*

Hawk again thought of Nora's warning, "That you may be in danger."

Just the thought of it and the incident the night before, made Hawk tense up. His breathing became shallow. After taking some deep breaths, he calmed down as he thought that whoever it is in that vehicle is only trying to intimidate him. Otherwise, his attempt at following wouldn't be so obvious, that even Wally noticed him.

He wondered if he should fill Wally in on what happened last night. Maybe, by some chance, he might have some insight into it. After all, he had been around a long time. But then, he thought otherwise. Wally would probably tell Bradford and then the Lieutenant would want specifics as to where he was or what he was doing. He didn't want to get both Marcie and especially Nora in trouble. *Besides, what could Wally tell him anyway?*

Again, as though Wally could read his mind, he said, "Bothers you, doesn't it? Don't worry about it. There are people who just get their kicks by threatening cops with childish behavior. Unless there's more to it than that? Do you have any idea why?"

"Nah, I don't know what's going on. I'm not worried."

"Well, you could've fooled me. You sure look upset."

Once they returned to the unit, there was Bradford standing next to Marcie's desk. Bradford interrupted his conversation with her when Hawk and Wally walked in. As usual, when he saw Hawk, he didn't look pleased. He made a point of checking his smart watch and bellowed out within everyone's earshot. "You guys goofing off again, I see. Come in whenever you want to. It doesn't take that long to go to CBI. This will go in your files."

"Lieutenant, please," Wally said, not appearing at all perturbed. "It's entirely my fault. Young Clint here wanted to come back right away, but I talked him into having lunch with me. It just took longer than I thought it would. If you want to write someone up, write me up, but Hawk doesn't deserve it."

"You two have become buddies, I see. Well, screw up again, Wally, and I'll make sure that your pension doesn't go through very smoothly. I can do that, you know."

"I know you can. I'll be good." Wally had a smirk on his face.

"The hell with you both," Bradford said and stomped away. Then he paused and turned abruptly, saying, "By the way, while both of you were screwing around, Jeffries here got a full confession out of Freeman for the murders of both Bowmans. Hawk, do you feel like a fool now with your fantasy theories?" Before Hawk could reply, Bradford turned his attention to Nora. "And you, another hotshot detective, agreed with Hawk that what he said made sense." He turned again and stomped to his office.

Hawk and Nora exchanged glances. Nora rolled her eyes. Hawk gave her a slight grin. The fact that Jeffries forced a trumped-up confession out of Freeman followed exactly the script that Nora predicted. Now more than ever, a motivated Hawk confirmed his goal to get to the truth.

CHAPTER 30

BRADFORD FINALLY left for the day as did Wally. Hawk waited for everyone else to leave the Homicide Unit, including Marcie. Before she left, Marcie looked back at Hawk and gave him a quick wave. A minute later, she returned and quickly walked up to Hawk. "Clint, I need to see you tonight. It's very important. Can you come by about nine? Ring my apartment, unit 783, and I'll buzz you in. Will that work?"

Hawk looked perplexed. "Is something wrong?"

"No. I'll tell you when you come." She didn't elaborate nor display her usual smile. Her normally sparkling eyes seemed lifeless.

Hawk's eyebrows narrowed; his voice filled with concern at the thought that something abnormal was bothering Marcie. "Of course, I'll be there. I may be a little late, but I'll be there. Marcie, you got me worried. It doesn't seem like everything is fine."

Marcie turned abruptly and started for the door. She waved her arms in the air. "I'm fine, everything is all right. I just have to make some adjustments," she said as she left. Hawk thought that she might be in tears.

The novice detective walked out of the building in a quandary over Marcie's behavior. *I guess I'll find out soon enough. In the meantime, I need to work on the Bowman cases. And then see yet another woman. I wonder what Nora's problem is.*

He drove to the northeast corner of Lafayette Street and Colfax Avenue. At that corner, across from Miller's *Coffee Aroma* stood a vacant building and a large commercial dumpster that appeared to be untouched since Bowman's murder a few days ago. Hawk parked his Jeep deep in the lot behind the structure hoping that he wouldn't draw too much attention to himself. After giving it serious thought, he determined that it must have been behind the dumpster where the gunman hid and not between the apartment buildings as the witness believed. In his mind, that would be the logical hiding place for the assassin to wait for his prey. He walked over and searched around the dumpster hoping that maybe, just maybe, he would find a clue.

On the east side, the short side, of the four-yard dumpster he stumbled across a couple of cigarette butts, including one that was smoked all the way down to the filter. The other appeared partially smoked as though the smoker was interrupted and dropped the cigarette in a hurry. *Perhaps that's when Bowman came out of the driveway and the shooter had to run toward him quickly. Too good to be true, but maybe.*

Hawk put on nitrile gloves and pulled a plastic bag out of his right coat pocket. He bent over, gingerly picked up the butts, and placed them in the bag. As he stood up, he noticed the black Tahoe stopped in his line of vision on Lafayette Street. The driver's window was opening. Facing the intense sun in the western sky, Hawk was unable to make out the driver, but something about him looked familiar. Suddenly, out of the open window, he observed a gun He quickly ducked behind the short east side of the dumpster, his heart racing. A split second later, a bullet whizzed above his head. Then another shot in quick succession hit the long south side of the receptacle. The heavy metal clanged. Crouched down low, he witnessed a wisp of dust in the back of the building where he assumed that the slug ricocheted. Pulling out his weapon, ready for a shootout, he stood up to fire, but the SUV peeled out and turned the corner onto Colfax, tires squealing and the vehicle fishtailing.

Hawk's insides shook. His knees and hands trembled. In the several years that he was a cop, this was the first time anyone tried to shoot him. He pulled himself together and decided to get out of there as fast as he could. The last thing he needed was to engage in long explanations with officers who he was sure would soon arrive. A crowd gathered, he remembered that puff of dust. He scratched the pebbly and sandy surface in the immediate area and found the slug. He threw it into another plastic bag. Then, he turned towards the people, showed his badge, and yelled out to them, "It's okay; I'm a police detective, on official business." He knew though, that 911 must have been called, but he had presence enough to know he should find the casings. He rushed over to where the Tahoe had been and effortlessly found a shell, shining brightly on the pavement, not too far from the curb. He grabbed it and placed it into the second bag with the slug. With no time to look for the other one, he ran as fast as he could back to his Jeep, flooring the gas pedal. A police siren sounded in the distance. *Oh God, I'll have a lot of explaining to do over this.*

On the way to see Nora, he wondered how his attacker always knew his whereabouts. *I bet they have a tracker on my car.* Hawk decided that he better check out his vehicle before he led the shooter to Nora. At the next intersection, he abruptly turned left, parking near the intersection of Pennsylvania and Colfax. He walked around his car, feeling underneath the chassis. On a metal strip holding up the plastic rear bumper, he found a GPS tracker. Still, with his gloves on, he grabbed it, removed the batteries and placed the unit into his last plastic bag.

His insides still shaking, and a large pit was now lodged in his stomach, as he started to stride around to the driver's side. At that moment, he noticed a homeless woman standing across the narrow street watching him. But it wasn't the woman that caught his attention so much as a shiny object. It reflected light off the beaming sun. The object protruded from the woman's packed grocery cart that she evidently commandeered from a Whole Foods grocery store. The handle looked familiar to him with its heavy double rings framing something that looked like an animal's head. He concentrated for a moment and remembered the fireplace tools in the Bowman bedroom. *Could that possibly be the missing poker? The murder weapon?* Even though he thought that would be too much of a coincidence, he approached the woman. She became agitated and began pushing her cart away from him onto Colfax Avenue.

"Please, ma'am, I'd like to buy something from you. I'm looking for a poker for a fireplace."

The woman stopped, "What did you say?"

He started explaining to the toothless, unkempt woman, with a dirty knit hat, as he slowly approached her. "I'm looking for something specific and I'd like to see if you have what I need to buy for my house."

"What do you need? I've got a lot of good stuff to sell." As a cop on the beat, Hawk knew that, in addition to begging many street people pick up items, mostly in trash receptacles and sell or trade them. He looked at the item and to his amazement it was indeed a poker—one that most likely was taken from the Bowman house, just a few blocks up the street. It had the figure of the lion between the rings on the handle that Hawk noted as he mentally inventoried what he observed at the Bowman mansion. The woman wanted ten dollars, but Hawk offered her twenty if she would show him where she found it. She readily agreed.

They walked down Colfax to an alley between Pennsylvania and Pearl Streets. Towards the end of the alley, by Fourteenth Street, were banks of dumpsters. The woman couldn't remember the exact dumpster but told Hawk that the poker had come out of one of them. After thanking her, he handed her the twenty dollars he promised. After the woman turned the corner, he studied the alley for cameras and to his delight saw several in the area. There was even a sign that read, "You're on Video Camera." He made a note to himself to come back the next day to canvass the area. *Maybe by then, I'll settle down and be able to think straight.*

CHAPTER 31

HAWK CHECKED the area around Charlie Brown's restaurant to see if it was safe. All clear! No black SUVs around. Holding the poker, he checked his pockets for the evidence with him and walked into the restaurant through the hotel entrance. Nora saw him and waved him over to the booth in the back. She greeted him with a disarming smile, her face pink with excitement. Even though Hawk didn't feel like smiling, a smile involuntarily ruffled his lips.

Nora saw the brass poker and said, "Oh, I see you carry a new weapon of choice." She started to laugh but then realized something wasn't right with him. He looked pale and dispirited. "What's wrong? Something happened, right?"

"Well, as the saying goes, I have some good news and I have some bad."

"Oh, you're going to ask what I want to hear first. Just tell me, okay?"

"Okay then, the good first." He reached into his pockets and pulled out three plastic bags and laid them on the table. At that moment, a server came by and asked if they were ready to order. Nora asked for a few more minutes. The server left, but first took a curious gaze at the bags sitting in front of Hawk, one containing bullet fragments; another held cigarette butts and the third had the small tracker device with four loose batteries.

"Well, you've been busy. Where did you get those?"

As Hawk explained how he obtained the evidence, Nora's jaw dropped in wonderment. He then slid the bags over to her and asked her to take them to the people in Internal Affairs involved in the case and run the evidence through the crime lab. "I certainly can't show up with them since I'm officially off the case and who knows, Bradford may find out."

"And what about this poker?" She pointed to the shiny, elegant brass fireplace tool.

"You wouldn't believe my luck. This may be the weapon that killed Mrs. Bowman. And I need it analyzed for blood, DNA and fingerprints."

"How in the world did you find it?" Hawk related his interaction with the homeless woman.

"Are you always this lucky? If I rub my hands on your body, maybe some of it would rub off on me." Nora laughed, as she rubbed his shoulder and arm. Suddenly she became serious. "Okay, now tell me the bad news."

After seeing and talking with Nora, the fear and anger that were knotted inside Hawk ebbed. He was again ready to fight the world. With bravado, he said, "It was no big deal really, but I was shot at by someone in the same black SUV that followed me yesterday and again today from the CBI."

First, an expression of extreme astonishment crossed Nora's beautiful face, then it turned into a sour scowl. Breathing hard, she muttered, "My dear God! Where were you?"

"I was searching for clues near where Bowman was shot, the bastard shot at me two times, one shot went over my head as I ducked behind a dumpster and the other shot ricocheted off the container. That's how I found the shell and the slug."

As Nora sat slumped in her seat, her mouth open, her deep blue eyes large as saucers, the server came back again. Too stunned to give a response, she was in no condition to think about food.

"How about some wine, Nora?" Clint asked. Nora nodded. "White or red?"

"Red will be fine," her voice faint and shaky. Hawk ordered two glasses of merlot and a plate of nachos for an appetizer. The server left and Nora stretched out her hand and gently stroked the back of his head.

"My God! Wow! We could have lost you. I knew your life might be in danger, but this is real. You are in danger. Next time they might not miss. Do you have any idea who the actual shooter was?"

"I've been thinking hard on that. It's strange, I only saw him once, but for some reason, the silhouette of the man reminded me of O'Leary. If it's him, I don't think he would be driving his own car. Maybe one that he stole or, since he's in narcotics, it might be a vehicle they seized as part of a drug raid. As he sped off, I tried to read the plate, but I think it was missing."

"Geez!" Nora breathed in shallow, quick gasps. "In open daylight like that. He could get to you anytime or anywhere he wants to. You'll have to be so, so careful, and better start acting paranoid and wear your Kevlar vest. You need a bodyguard. You need to lay low for a period while IA pursues this." Hawk couldn't believe it, for being a tough cop, Nora seemed so fragile. Not only her voice, but her whole body seemed to tremble. *She is really concerned for me.*

"Nora, please, don't take it so hard. I'll be careful and vigilant. But I'm not going to hide waiting for something to happen, waiting for another attack. As a matter of fact, I need to work faster to try to gather more evidence to put those crooked cops away."

"I see you're a stubborn boy. I'm serious about a bodyguard. And I'm the one to do it."

"Nora, that's silly. I'll be all right."

"I insist. As a matter of fact, I'll talk to my superiors tomorrow and explain that my usefulness in the homicide unit is no longer necessary. I'll see if I can transfer back to IA and get assigned to work with you. So, from now on, when you go out investigating on your own, you call me first and I'll go with you. Actually, it might be better if we transfer you out of Homicide and assign you temporarily to IA."

"Thank you for your appealing offer. But I'd be putting your life in danger and I couldn't stand it if anything happened to you. I tell you; I'll be all right. And I think I need to be in the unit a while longer to see what I hear and what evidence I might find in the office."

"All right, all right, you're going to be a tough guy who doesn't need anyone. But it isn't exactly an offer made from kindness. It's the job I've been assigned to and danger is something we live with as cops. Besides, Clint, it certainly is better if the two of us work together. Remember, two heads are better than one. What you've accomplished so far with your analysis of the murders and the evidence you found is remarkable. But we need to get to the bottom of this fast, and with two people, it will be faster." Nora seemed to have relaxed a little and forced a smile. She lightly stroked his cheek. "Besides, you tenacious man, if you put up a fight about this with me, I'll just get the chief to order it anyway." She chuckled to try to soften her tough stance. The last thing she wanted was to appear threatening.

"Very well, then, we'll work together. Actually, I'm excited to work with such a charming and attractive bodyguard by my side." *Dammit! Why did I say that? I'm not supposed to comment on how attractive she is. But I think she liked the compliment.*

"Oh, now you want me for my looks and not my brains," Nora couldn't help laughing aloud, releasing accumulated stress. "Now, let's talk about why I needed to see you. IA had a strong suspicion based on informants that a few cops were involved in shake-downs. The names of Bradford and Jeffries had popped out. IA managed to get a limited warrant to search the web, including the dark web, IP addresses, and their internet service providers (ISP). We had our talented computer geek, the best hacker in Denver, search the dark web for any communications but had not found any with the cartels, for example, or any businessmen."

"But there was a pattern of communications that ultimately, through several international IPs, started and ended in Denver. Our geek was able to decode the computer encryption or at least she thought she could because the words in the sentences in the communications made no sense and she thought she made a mistake in her math calculations. She tried again and came up with the same language. So, she determined that in addition to the computer encryption, the parties are using a code for various words. You need to have a key to know what the word stands for. Actually, it seems that they're using double encryption. The next step took her to the source of the communications. As you can imagine, it wasn't as simple to do as it seems."

"Oh, I don't think any of this is simple. It's over my head, but go on, hopefully there's light at the end of the proverbial tunnel."

"Well, yes. Listen. It turned out to be another grueling task because the IP addresses were run all over the world. That's a very tedious process to trace it back to the address of the original computer. Eventually, her efforts with the cooperation of the ISP led to an address on Monroe Street in the Cherry Creek area. Guess, what? The address belongs to an LLC. The Secretary of State site shows another LLC was the organizer, and Winston Bradford was the organizer of that second LLC. Would you believe it, he just happens to be the brother of our beloved Lieutenant Bradford?"

"Wow. Terrific, maybe we'll get those bastards. So, where are you at with that information?"

"Based just on the limited information we have, it's still a problem. We can't decipher the messages unless we can find a key or a decoder or spend the next hundred years trying to figure it out. Maybe, if we can get into Bradford's personal computer, we could find something useful."

"Or find an actual translator."

The wine and the food were served Nora had put away the bags of evidence into her purse. She offered a toast as they clinked their glasses by saying, "May you no longer be in any danger." Hawk nodded his approval and the conversation turned to how great the nachos tasted. Nora took another small sip of wine and sidled closer to Hawk. Once again stretching her hand to his shoulder, she said, "Clint, I don't want anything to happen to you. I don't think you should be going to your house tonight. I have three bedrooms and you can stay in one, at least until this blows over."

Turning squarely to face her, her sensual mouth so close to his, Hawk leaned toward those red lips. Before he knew it, he kissed her gently. Afterward, Nora licked her upper lip, her mouth curved into a satisfying smile. "Just in case someone sees us," Hawk said, with a larger smile of his own. "Our excuse for being together," repeating what Nora had told him after she kissed him in the car the last time they were together. Nora burst out laughing and Hawk joined her.

"So, what do you say? Are you going to stay in my house, at least tonight? I promise that I won't jump your bones."

"Thanks for the great invitation. It's so tempting, but I'll be all right. I'll be careful. I'll check out everything before I drive the Jeep into the garage. I'll close the garage door while I'm still in the car, and I'll avoid sitting or standing by any windows. Please don't worry." Nora looked disappointed, gently slapping his arm. "I don't think this plate of nachos is going to fill me up. What do say to actual dinner?"

"I think that's a great idea. I'm kinda hungry myself." They ordered dinner and enjoyed each other's company. They discussed politics and world history. On purpose, the Bowman cases or the few corrupt cops were not mentioned. When the bill came, Hawk insisted on paying. Nora didn't object.

"Are you going straight home now?" Nora asked, suddenly looking troubled.

"Very soon, I have an errand to run first."

"Let me guess. You have to see Marcie, don't you?"

"Why would you say that out of the blue like that?"

"I just have this feeling that she wants to see you every day if she could. Watch out for her. You saw that she went to Bradford's office supposedly to deliver the mail but spent more than ten minutes with him. What do you think that was about? I don't think it was anything good."

"That's exactly why I agreed to see her tonight. Before she left for the day, she asked me to come by. That she had something important to tell me. Maybe she'll tell me something of her conversation with Bradford."

"Well, maybe, I should go with you then." Nora chuckled, knowing that he'd never agree.

"Yeah, like she'd really open up with you there."

"Well, at least call me afterward to let me know what was so important." Hawk agreed and he walked Nora to her Escort parked in the small parking area in front. She unlocked the door and sat down. Hawk bent over and placed the poker in the space behind her seat. Before driving off, Nora looked straight at Hawk, her compelling blue eyes had the look of anguish, "Please be careful. Even with Marcie. It might be a trap."

Walking back to his vehicle, Hawk was cautious. He looked both ways, and monitored every car parked on the street. Turned and stared at any approaching vehicles. He was shaken earlier, but that pleasant time with Nora seemed to really calm him. *I'll be all right. I just must be watchful. Must be brave, not a wimp.*

Driving toward the Glendale area to Marcie's apartment, he remembered Nora's words, "It might be a trap." He briefly considered it but discounted that notion. *Marcie is not that kind of person.* She seemed genuinely kind and thoughtful. She was pleasant to be with and he liked her. However, any thoughts of Marcie were overwhelmed by Nora. He couldn't get her out of his mind. Nora, despite being a tough cop, was so gentle, so caressing, so warm, so lovely, so smart, so interesting. He couldn't help comparing the two women. Marcie was sweet and tried to be bubbly and fun. She tried to act "cool." Yet, she was somehow always reserved. Maybe because of that, he didn't always feel comfortable with her. His last girlfriend, with whom he broke up a month ago, was like Marcie, not overly exciting to be with. Not like Nora with her charisma and liveliness.

He couldn't stop thinking about Nora even though he was approaching Marcie's place. Nora understood what it took to be a cop and knew the dangers police face every time they leave the house. Marcie may say she understands, but unless you walk in the shoes of a policeman, you can't. Just like his other girlfriends who couldn't necessarily cope with him always being in danger. *What am I thinking? Do I like Nora better? Yes, and what do I tell Marcie, or do I have to tell her anything? And how awkward will it be at work with both women there?*

Thinking about the two women turned out to be good therapy for Hawk. He forgot about the danger that may be lurking around him. Suddenly, he remembered and checked the rear mirrors for anyone suspicious. This was Denver and there were always many SUVs around, but none looked like a dark Tahoe. *Of course, he might have changed vehicles.*

Hawk parked at the visitor parking of the apartment house and walked up the steps. Inside the foyer, he studied the directory and pressed number 783. A somber voice asked who it was. "I'm here, Marcie." The buzzer sounded. The door unlocked. Hawk glanced back to check for a tailgater. No one was there, only the shadows in his mind.

CHAPTER 32

MARCIE HELD her door open waiting for Hawk to exit the elevator. As he approached, she managed a nervous tentative smile. Hawk immediately noticed that she was troubled.

"Come in, Clint. Thanks, so much for coming."

"What's wrong, Marcie?" he gently asked.

"It's that's obvious, is it?"

"Well, I wouldn't be a detective if I couldn't see it. What is it?"

Marcie invited him to sit on the floral sofa. Hawk declined the drink that she had offered him. She sat next to him but at a distance. A muscle quivered at her jaw. Her fake smile quickly faded away. Hawk looked at her and repeated his last question.

Hesitating, she took in a deep breath. "I don't know where to begin. I like being with you and I thought that, hopefully, we'd see more of each other. But I'm moving back to California. My dad and mom insist on it. Dad found a terrific job for me as an engineer with a good salary. I told you before that my father thinks that after all the money he spent educating me, I'm wasting my time working for the police department. I really don't want to go, especially since I met you, but maybe it's for the best."

"Oh, Marcie, I'd hate to see you leave. Could you reconsider?" *Why am I talking her out of it? It may be best for both of us. She probably wants me to make some commitment to her. One that, after knowing her for such a short time, I could never make.*

"No, I've made up my mind. That's what I need to do. Clint, don't look so upset. I think it's best and I'll tell you why. First, that incident when someone followed us, really upset me. You were in danger and by association, I was in danger too. I didn't like the feeling at all. I don't know how you policemen can handle it." Hawk wanted to say that that was an isolated incident and he started to speak. But she raised her hand to stop him.

"Second, there is this thing with Nora. She really likes you. I can see it. I see her watching you when you're at your desk. I see her eyes follow you as you walk by. And I see her sneer when we're together. I don't want to compete with her for your attention." Again, Hawk was about to say something and, again, she stopped him.

"Now the third point, and it's probably the most important to me. Yesterday, when I delivered Bradford's mail, he asked me to sit down. In the past, he always liked to talk to me because I flattered him. He's an egotist who loves praise and I laid it on. This time, he asked me how tight I'm with you and whether I had been out with you. I admitted that we had those pancakes together but didn't tell him about the time I went with you when they found Bowman's Cadillac. Well, he asked, but it almost sounded like an order, that I must encourage a relationship with you and report to him what we discuss and what you're doing." Hawk's eyes widened with anger.

"Why, that no good bastard wanted to use you as a spy."

"Well, you don't like it and I like it even less. Clint, he's out to get you. I saw blood in his eyes when he mentioned your name. You must be extra careful. Don't walk around any dark alleys, he probably has thugs that can beat you to a pulp."

"Marcie, I'm so sorry that because of me you have to go through this."

"Now you can see that these three reasons, actually four with the pressure from my parents, are why I've decided to leave."

"Marcie, I don't know what to say. This is quite a shock. I'm certainly sad to see you go."

"Clint, I like you a lot. My biggest regret is that we didn't have a chance to know each other better. Maybe we could've gone out on some actual dates." Marcie almost broke into a wide smile. "But I don't think that you're the marrying kind, Clint. If you were, you probably would be married by now. I just can't seem to find the right person yet and maybe you haven't either. I'll miss you." A few tears rolled down her cheeks. In a trembling voice, she continued, "But even if we were to become serious, I don't have the disposition to sit at home waiting for your call telling me that you are safe and you're coming home. That incident with the SUV really shook me up. I'm not as strong as you."

"I understand how difficult it would be for a girlfriend or wife to live with a cop. But almost every policeman has a family. Getting injured is just part of the job and the families learn to live with it."

"No, I could never." She hesitated. "I have no idea whether we would've hit it off, but it's best if I settle down with someone who isn't in danger all the time. Clint, I've made up my mind for the sake of my own sanity."

"What are you going to do then? I mean about your job here."

"I'm going to take a personal day or two. In the meantime, I'll quit officially through HR and then come by to say goodbye to everyone. I really like detectives Nancy Salazar and her partner, Jim Withers. They are some of the most hard-working people in the police force. They do everything by the book and are highly successful in solving cases. I also like Harry Ling and his partner, Darrell Higgins. They are great to work with. Orlinski is okay. His work habits are a little strange, but he gets the job done. And of course, how can I forget the lovable Wally Murphy? I'll miss them all, except for Jeffries, who I think is not always honest and then there is Lieutenant Bradford. I never trusted him but played along."

"Yes, I agree, almost all of those people you mentioned introduced themselves and offered help when I needed it. They seem to be a competent group of detectives and I'm pleased to work with them."

Marcie seemed to settle down. She suddenly flashed her sunny smile. "I'll be all right, I'm sure. I'll call before I come to say goodbye to everyone to make sure you're there. And please be careful. Remember that Bradford is out to get you."

There was nothing more to be said by either of them. Hawk rose to leave. She was determined to return to California, and he was in no position to offer her anything that would tempt her to stay. As he stood Marcie stood as well. She gazed at Hawk with her soft eyes and moved close to give him a bear hug. As she kissed his cheek, her lips slid toward his mouth for a first and last kiss.

CHAPTER 33

AS USUAL, Janice seated Lieutenant Bradford at one of the two tables directly behind the narrow wall that hid its occupants from patrons at the semi-circular bar of Park Tavern. It was a secluded area that only held a few tables and two rarely used coin-operated pool tables. Usually, he strolled in and expected that particular area to be unoccupied. On the few occasions when that part of the business was crowded, he acted annoyed. Janice would try to accommodate him with some other fairly secluded table but noticed that his tips were ten percent rather than the usual fifteen when he was seated where he wanted. He was yet to leave her twenty percent as the other members of his group did. She suggested on many occasions that he call in advance and she'd try to keep that area clear for him. This time, he followed her advice.

Wearing beige leisure pants, white sneakers, and a blue polo shirt, Bradford arrived a few minutes early and, as always, ordered his Coors Light. He made a point to arrive earlier than the others so that he could think quietly for a few moments. On this evening, his thoughts were disturbing. *I don't know why I feel so lousy about where all this is going. We're still doing great, making money, but why do I feel that it'll come to an end soon?* Dreaded nightmares the last two nights had jolted him awake. His hands and forehead would be covered with sweat. He saw himself banging on a locked metal door, yelling "Let me out! Let me out!"

He saw the mean, fat, and ugly guard's mug staring through the tiny glass window, laughing sadistically. "You'll never see the light of day in solitary, you freaking criminal!"

Just three nights ago, yet another nightmare jolted him awake. He saw himself hanged from the gallows as spectators applauded. He was at the end of the noose, his legs flaying and body contorting until no more. He took these nightmares seriously. He began to doubt himself, convinced that the dreams were bad omens. *Could it be that I'm not as smart as I think I am?*

Polishing off his beer, he yelled out to Janice for another one, then changed his mind. "No, actually I need something stronger. Get me a double whiskey straight." The customers at the surrounding tables turned their heads to see who the loudmouth was. He saw them but didn't care. Mentally, he'd accepted that someday he would go down along with the others. *All of us except for the mysterious boss. He or she is the real smart one. We do the nasty work and he or she gets paid. We'll end up in jail and the boss gets away scot-free. How in the hell did I get into this mess? Greed, greed, greed, that's all. I didn't need the money. Why in the hell did I agree to any of this? At the time I thought it would be a great challenge, that's why.*

Damn that Clint Hawk. Ever since he came into my life, I've been plagued by these nightmares and thoughts. Bradford couldn't put a finger on exactly why Hawk bothered him so much. He was just a rookie and didn't know anything about being a detective. He never displayed any malice toward Bradford, so why was he so worried? In reality, though, Hawk's quick analysis of the crime scene frightened him. He could see that if Hawk continued to dig into the Bowman murders, he would be capable of following evidence that would lead to O'Leary and Jeffries and then to himself. O'Leary tended to be sloppy. Jeffries was too arrogant. Sloppy people and arrogant people make mistakes. *Who knows what evidence they left behind for someone like Hawk to find?*

I feel it in my gut that Clint Hawk suspects me somehow and he's tenacious enough to get to the bottom of this. I made a huge mistake when I insisted that his spot-on analysis of the cases was simply a fantasy. That just raised his suspicions, I'm sure. I could've handled it better.

He made a quick start on the drink Janice placed in front of him. After swallowing half the glass, he began to mellow. A feeling of bravado washed over him. With the help of the alcohol, he convinced himself again that he was smart enough to solve any problem and things would remain fine. *It's all in my mind and there is no impending doom. My damn dreams keep me rattled. And if it's Clint Hawk that's the problem, we just get rid of him now.*

Bradford emptied his glass, creating a long list of scenarios to get rid of Hawk. First was the clever way to plant drugs and a dumpload of cash in his house. He discounted that because it would take too long through the legal process. He needed to get rid of him instantly. He couldn't understand why the boss was opposed to doing it now.

The boss said to wait, but he felt he had no choice. Regardless of what the boss wants, Clint Hawk had to be eliminated by the next day for sure. At that moment, his plans were interrupted as Williams and Jeffries, also dressed leisurely, joined him at the table. O'Leary showed up a minute later.

After exchanging greetings, they ordered drinks. His voice weak and tremulous, O'Leary said, "Men, I screwed up." The rest of the group immediately twisted their necks in his direction.

"What did you do, now, O'Leary?" The Lieutenant kept his voice low even though he wanted to yell at the fool.

Speaking in almost a whisper, O'Leary meekly answered, "I took a couple shots at Hawk around six o'clock. I missed him."

"What the hell!" Williams yelled out.

"Will you keep your voice down," Bradford said. "I know it's noisy in here, but someone might hear us so keep it low volume."

Williams, still angry, glaring hard at O'Leary said, "We didn't give you permission to out Hawk!"

At that instance, the server was at the table. "Janice, what do you want? Bradford barked,

"Sorry sir, I just came up to see if you would like some appetizers."

"I'm sorry for snapping at you, but we're busy here. We'll call you when we're ready to order. Go away!"

Janice left shaking her head. "Do you think she heard anything?" Jeffries asked, face pale with concern.

"Nah, even if she heard something, she wouldn't know what we're talking about," O'Leary said.

"Oh, you think so, O'Leary," Bradford said sarcastically, disgusted with the man. "Well, go on. Tell us what happened and why?"

"As we discussed before, I put a tracker on his Jeep. I left the westside earlier planning to follow him after he left the building for the night. I was too late to catch him leaving, but the GPS indicated that he wasn't too far away. I couldn't believe it, but he went back to the Bowman murder scene, parked in the lot by the dumpster where I had waited for Bowman. As I drove up, I saw him bend down, pick something up, and place it in a plastic bag. I suddenly remembered the cigarette butts I tossed before I rushed up to Bowman. When I saw that, I panicked and I took two shots at him. I swear he bent down just as I aimed for his head and the slug went over him. I saw him stick his head out on the side of the container and I aimed for that, but in a panic, I missed him again. I didn't wait around for him to shoot back or let anyone see me through the tinted car windows. After I settled down a little, I tried the tracker again, but the stupid piece of crap no longer worked."

Bradford's head pounded. "You're the biggest freaking idiot! Did he see you?"

"No, I don't think so. I was in that Tahoe I took away from a drug dealer. You know, the one I never turned in as confiscated property. It has those tinted windows. I only rolled down the window for a few seconds to shoot. He was too busy dodging bullets to notice."

"What did you do with the SUV?"

"Nothing yet. I hid it in my garage for now till I figure out what to do with it. I'll probably burn it."

"Lieutenants," Jeffries said. "The timing and the method were wrong. But O'Leary was right in trying to get rid of him. We need to get rid of him tonight. He didn't have time to hand anything over to forensics yet. So, now is the night to stage a burglary in his house, make sure he's dead, and take whatever evidence he might have found. He's the type of guy who'd go to Internal Affairs if he suspected us. As usual, O'Leary and I will take care of it."

"Good." Bradford agreed, still fuming. "The sooner the better. And you better not botch it this time."

Williams said, "Shouldn't you run this past the boss first? It may set off a chain reaction that we'd not be prepared to handle."

"Dammit, Williams. What's gotten into you? I've decided that we do it. We'll do it now, understand!? And you better play along."

Wesley Williams walked back to his Nissan Pathfinder parked a block away from the bar. He was in no hurry. The shear mention of Internal Affairs by Jeffries knotted his stomach, bile crept up to the throat. He didn't like any of it. He realized that no matter what he said, he could never dissuade the tyrant, Bradford, from whatever he decided to do. Williams deplored the idea of the group killing yet again. The longer he stayed with the group, the more his conscience began to eat at him. He couldn't object. For his safety, he had to show that he's in sync with Bradford and his 'den of thieves,' as he called the men at the table. He hated being around those killers. He hated Bradford and what he was doing and more importantly, he feared O'Leary, the trigger-happy psycho. Jeffries seemed to be not as evil, but not by much. All three men showed no remorse for taking a person's life. *None of those bastards, including Bradford, have a conscience.*

In his gut, Williams knew that they'd all be discovered and put away sooner than later. He'd be dragged into it, even though he didn't have any control of what they were doing. But he participated and accepted money. He wanted out but knew that if he tried, Bradford would never allow that. He'd receive a bullet to the head or he'd use the threat of death to his family to keep him in line. *Oh God! What have I done?* He no longer cared about the money that Bradford had originally enticed him with, although what came in saved him from bankruptcy. But with the ill-gotten money, he now has sleepless nights and never-ending arguments with his wife because he is so uptight and irritable. He understood that his marriage was on the rocks, but he didn't know how to save it.

As Williams approached his vehicle, out of anger and frustration, he kicked the back tire hard, abhorring the day that he met that arrogant narcissist. As he slid into the driver's seat, he leaned his head against the headrest, and as he shut his narrow blue eyes, he thought about the past and where he went wrong. After receiving his accounting degree from Arizona State University, he thought that he'd be set for life as a CPA. He hated it. Police work suddenly intrigued him and at the age of twenty-six, still unmarried with no family, he entered the police academy.

That's where he met Kent Bradford. They became occasional friends. Since then, they remained friendly, even though he began to understand Bradford's controlling and reckless personality. Both attained the rank of sergeant at about the same time, then both became detectives in separate divisions and units—Williams in the Fraud and Financial Unit due to his CPA background. Nine years ago, Bradford was promoted to lieutenant, and Williams attained the same rank six months later.

Two years ago, Bradford called him out of the blue and asked him to lunch. He approached Williams just at the right moment. At that time, Williams was swimming in debt with no hope of paying it off on his lieutenant's salary. His youngest daughter was diagnosed with severe heart issues that caused the poor girl to go in and out of the hospital numerous times. The medical bills that were not covered by insurance were staggering. He was desperate for money at that time. Bradford promised him he'd have all the funds he would need to pay off the hospital bills in short order if he went along with his proposal. And now he was stuck.

A shiver ran down William's spine as he leaned forward and started the engine. His head pounded as he drove home, Internal

Affairs on his mind. *Should I contact them before they come for me? Maybe, they'll give me a break and give me protection. But first, I'll need to build up my courage to discuss this with Debbie. My wife has no idea. What a shock it will be to her when I tell her what I'm involved with and what I plan to do.*

CHAPTER 34

INSTEAD OF immediately heading home, Hawk decided to stop at the Safeway on Sixth Avenue for bananas and some berries. Afterward, he took Downing Street up to East Eleventh toward his house. On the Eleventh, he made a left turn and proceeded west. As he approached Park Tavern on his right, he witnessed Bradford, Williams, Jeffries, and O'Leary come out of the place. He immediately turned left onto Ogden Street, parked as quickly as he could, jumped out of his vehicle, and took several photos of the group discussing something. For several minutes, Bradford continuously stabbed a finger into O'Leary's chest. He watched them leave separately, expecting to catch sight of one of the detectives driving away in a black Tahoe. He didn't. O'Leary drove off in a gray Ram pickup, Jeffries in a white Ford Explorer. He couldn't see what the other two men were driving.

As he turned onto Tenth Street, still thinking about what he saw, his cell rang. It was Nora. He answered on the second ring. "Nora, hi, you wouldn't believe who I just saw together?"

"Who?"

"Bradford, Williams, Jeffries, and O'Leary standing outside Park Tavern in the middle of a heated discussion. I'll tell you about it when I get home. But I bet you a donut and a coffee that they were discussing me."

"I bet you're right. That's why I'm calling you now. How close are you to your place?"

"Just a few minutes away."

"Good. Run in, get your toothbrush, your PJs, and a change of clothes and hurry over to my house. Don't fight me on this. I have this woman's intuition that something bad is going to happen to you, especially if O'Leary saw you collect some evidence. They're going to try to nail you tonight. I know it. Now, hurry over here. We'll hide your Jeep in my garage just in case they know about us."

"Nora, I'll be watchful. If I don't stay in my house, they'll ransack the whole place."

"That's exactly why I fear for your life. Now, don't argue, don't be such a macho man, and get over here. My woman's intuition is seldom wrong. Now hurry."

Hawk thought for a moment. He didn't want any surprise confrontations in the dead of night. Besides, an evening with Nora would be an experience to be savored. "Okay Nora, you win. Text me your address."

His neighborhood and home seemed peaceful, as always. *I can't imagine that such a peaceful night and peaceful neighborhood could be violated by an attempt on my life. Nora just wants me with her tonight, that's all.* The thought of Nora made him smile. But he also had the feeling deep down in his gut that there could be danger yet to come.

He looked around the place trying to spot a possible entry into his house. The end unit townhome had windows in front, side, and back. Despite having double pane glass, any one of them could be used to break in. The most logical entry point is a basement window. If someone entered through one of them, Clint most likely would not hear the breaking of the glass in his second-floor bedroom. More likely, the front door would be kicked in to mimic a home invasion. Sleeping on the couch with a gun nearby would give him all the advantage he might need. *But why take a chance? I better get my things together and head out.*

Before he walked out, he looked around the house. He worried that a break-in would cause a lot of damage to his place, and possibly some of the valuables would be stolen. *What would be best? If I leave the lights off as normal, they'll assume that I'm home, asleep, and try to get in. Maybe the whole place lit up would scare them away thinking that I'm expecting them.* He left the porch lights on and switched on every light in the house, lighting it up from the basement to the second floor and leaving the shades partially open. *Of course, there probably isn't anyone out there trying to get me tonight. Nora and her intuition.*

Nora welcomed him with a hug, kissing his cheek. "I'm so glad you listened to reason and came." She showed him to the guest room of her small three-bedroom home. The place was tastefully decorated with Scandinavian-type furniture. Portraits of family members were prominently displayed on one of the walls. The other walls had an eclectic collection of fine artworks. A bronze bust of George Washington stood in the corner on a black marble stand. From the outside, the house appeared small, but Nora's decorative touch gave it an airy, pleasant feel.

The guest room was tiny, just large enough for a double bed, a nightstand, and a dresser. Hawk threw his change of clothes and his shaving kit on the bed and returned to the living room. Nora had coffee and some Italian pastries set on a table in the small dining portion of the L-shaped living room. "Please sit down," pointing to the table, "And perhaps you'd like some decaf coffee with some cannoli that my grandmother made from scratch. And while we enjoy them you can tell me what Marcie wanted."

Hawk took a small sip of coffee and a big bite out of the cannoli. "Molto Buona. My compliments to your nonna."

Laughing, Nora said, "Grazie. I didn't know you spoke Italian, Clint."

"I don't. That's about all the Italian I know." He chuckled.

"So, what about Marcie?"

Hawk laughed. "Well, it appears that you scared off Marcie."

"Stop joking, you knucklehead, what do you mean?"

"She can't take the competition from you and wants to leave Denver."

"What competition? Will you tell me what's going on?"

"Competition over me, of course," Hawk laughed again, obviously enjoying Nora's consternation.

"Shut up! Who wants you anyway?" Now Nora laughed, finally ditching her overly serious tone.

Hawk proceeded to fill Nora in on the conversation with Marcie, including her four reasons for leaving Colorado. He knew that Marcie's conversation about Bradford would bring a response from Nora. "So, she actually said that Bradford asked her to spy on you? That's unbelievable! Why would he expose himself like that to her? That should have raised all kinds of alarms in her mind."

"Well, it obviously did since she told me basically to watch out for him. That he had blood in his eyes when he talked about me. And I frankly think that the conversation with Bradford was the last straw on the camel's back that pushed her into leaving Denver. She didn't want to be in the position to put up with all that crap."

"I'm so glad you're here, Clint. I think that we need to get to the bottom of this fast because, from what I see, they're going to start closing in on you."

"I can't believe that I'm such a big threat to them. However, let's talk about the four men that I saw earlier tonight."

"Yes, tell me about that. Where were you when you saw those men?"

"As I headed home on Eleventh Avenue and approached the Park Tavern bar, I saw Bradford, Williams, Jeffries, and O'Leary walking out together. I parked at the closest intersection and walked around the corner to take some photos." Hawk pulled out his phone to show Nora the photos.

"All right, so you saw them. Why do you think that was significant? After all, friends were at a bar for a drink."

"I think it's worth investigating. I frequent the place for dinner since it's so close to my townhome. I know one of the servers fairly well, actually. Everyone that goes to that place knows Janice. She's just one of those people who is overly friendly and knows everything about everyone."

"So, you want to talk to her?"

"Yes. Would it be possible for you and me to get together for a late lunch there tomorrow? Let's say at about one-thirty? Hopefully, I can get away."

"Sure. I'm not coming in tomorrow to the station. I'll call Bradford and tell him I'm taking a personal day. Instead, I'll be at headquarters on Cherokee Street talking to IA about getting me transferred back there so I can work covertly on the case with you."

"Okay, then. We got a date tomorrow."

"Oh, if it's a date, I better wear something special." Nora burst out laughing. "Here, let me refill your cup." As she walked past Hawk, she massaged his neck and stroked the back of his head, still chuckling. "By the way, what do you like for breakfast?"

CHAPTER 35

ALTHOUGH HAWK had a restless night, he had a wonderful breakfast with Nora. His first thought while driving was of Nora. That morning she had looked radiant as the eastern sun beamed through the kitchen window lighting her face. Her shimmering hair was tied into a ponytail. She wore a snug light pink blouse together with a short dark blue skirt. She looked young and ravishing. He didn't want to leave.

Just the idea that he could snuggle up to her in her bed, was the only good thought that came of this sleepless night. Although, he wasn't sure if either of them was ready for this next step. *That's too much of a commitment.* He also thought of Marcie and actually felt relief that she'll soon be out of the picture. He agreed with Nora that there was more to Marcie than met the eye. Was she in cahoots with Bradford and decided that she had finally had enough? At night, all sorts of thoughts come to a person's mind whether they're accurate or not. And Hawk realized that. But the main source of his tossing and turning was the fear of being ambushed at any moment.

One of the first to arrive at the unit, he proceeded to his desk and tried to figure out how to contact one of the DNA sites that dealt with genealogy. He heard about other jurisdictions that were successful in following this line of investigation. That method could be used to find relatives of the perpetrators, or if not, the perpetrator himself who was involved in the three closed cases. Harry Ling and Darrell Higgins beat him to the unit and they gave Hawk a friendly greeting while exchanging comments on how hot the weather would be. Bradford came in a few minutes later and gave Hawk a cold glare before he turned to his office. Next, Jeffries entered and sent an annihilating look in Hawk's direction. Hawk nodded as if to say hello, but Jeffries ignored him as he sat down at his desk.

Orlinski was next to come in. He dropped his stuff on his desk and walked over to Hawk. "Say, Clint, I'm missing a page from a file. I didn't leave it on your desk by chance?" Hawk looked in the drawers and replied in the negative. "Well, if you find something, please bring it over. So, how do you like working in this unit?"

Hawk wanted to tell him exactly how he felt about two of the group as bad cops. He also wanted to tell him that he has a huge pit in the bottom of his stomach worrying that today or tomorrow may well be his last day on earth. "Thanks for asking. You know, I only heard you referred to as Orlinski. What is your first name?"

"Orlinski is fine. But if you have to know, it's Stan. You know, I think you'll make a great addition to our unit here. I sure would like to know you better. Let's have lunch soon."

Hawk readily agreed and after Stan Orlinski walked on, he went back to his research. The door opened wide, and good ol' Wally rolled in. Again, he hit his elbow on the door frame and cursed loudly. "Stupid door. Always does that to me." Hawk looked at the others and saw their smirks. Wally didn't pay attention and slowly proceeded to his desk next to Hawk's. He greeted Hawk and sat down on the chair which let out a loud groan and squeak. This time laughter erupted in the room. Wally took it well and laughed along. "I'll have to save this poor, pathetic chair from more torture and get me something stronger," still chuckling to himself.

Looking at Hawk, Wally asked, "So, where are we going to lunch today? I know this great place on Seventh Avenue where we can sit outside under an umbrella."

"Sorry, Wally, not today. I have an appointment I need to take care of. Maybe tomorrow, how's that?"

"Oh yeah. Sounds interesting, anyone I know? It isn't Marcie again, is it? By the way, where is she? She's not at her desk. Is she with Bradford?"

"No, it isn't Marcie and I don't know where she is." Hawk wanted to stay out of Marcie's resignation. It was up to her to tell the people, not him.

"So, who is it?"

"It's an old girlfriend and I want to see if there are any sparks left between us." Hawk lied hoping to get Wally off his back. "Wally, we're kind of stuck on these cases until we get the DNA results. Would you mind seeing that clerk you like so much and get a couple more for us to look at?"

"I don't mind if I do." Hawk watched Wally start to leave the room. But before he could, Bradford walked out of his office and told everyone that he had an announcement to make. Wally stopped to listen.

Bradford's announcement was short, "People, Marcie has resigned and will be moving back to California. If you had any projects that she was helping you with, they're on her desk and you need to pick them up and work on them yourselves or get help from other units until we get a tech replacement. Nora has been suddenly transferred to another station and I'm assigning her cases to Salazar and Withers. That's all. Get to work. I want results, people. A general grunt of disgust arose from the group, especially Salazar and Withers. Hawk was surprised that no cases were assigned to him and Wally. They were the ones with little to do. *I bet he doesn't think that I'll be around much longer.*

After forty-five minutes, Wally returned with two more files. He took one and gave Hawk the other. Both files were of gang members in the Montebello area. At noon, most of the detectives left for lunch. Only Jeffries, Higgins, and Hawk stayed behind. Hawk waited until one-fifteen and left for his rendezvous with Nora. He noticed Jeffries follow him out, but kept his distance. Bradford watched them both through his open blinds.

Hawk stopped in the first-floor lobby and waited for Jeffries to pass him, but Jeffries lagged behind. Stalling for time, Hawk fiddled with his phone until finally, Jeffries walked past him with an unfriendly nod. He watched as Jeffries proceeded past the building and beyond the chain-link gate to the parking lot. Hawk knew that he would be followed if he used his car with probably another tracker attached to the chassis. He called an Uber and had the driver drop him off a block away from Park Tavern.

Nora waited outside the bar in her car. She watched Hawk as he jogged up to the tavern, then joined him. "Sorry, I'm late. But was sure I would be followed so I waited for Jeffries to leave and took an Uber. I'm pretty certain that was his intent as he waited for me to leave first."

"Figures. I understand."

They walked through the door and Janice immediately recognized Hawk. "Clint, you're back. It's been a few weeks. And who is this lovely lady?" Janice said, looking at Nora. "Is she your new girlfriend?"

Hawk stumbled with an answer, but Nora saved him by intervening, "We're just working partners, both in the Denver Police Department." *I wish I were his girlfriend, though. That'll satisfy my mother.*

"Well, you make a nice couple, too bad. Let me seat you. Where do you want to sit? The outdoor patio is open and as you can see the lunch rush is pretty much over. Or are you on official business and don't want to eat?"

"No, no, actually we're starving," Hawk said, rubbing his stomach. "Could we sit at the bar here, we would like to ask you for some help?"

"I knew there was more to it. But sure, the bar is fine. Just let me grab a salad for the couple at table four and I'll be right with you to take your order."

Nora and Hawk sat down and stared at the menu. Nora turned to Hawk, giggled, and said, "So, I'm the NEW girlfriend. How many girlfriends did you bring to this place?"

Hawk laughed heartily. "Just a zillion, why?"

"A zillion, huh? I figured. Can't you just stay with one?"

"Actually, Nora, with my hours on patrol and the amount of night shifts, I haven't had a lot of girlfriends. Maybe half a dozen or so."

Nora lightly slapped him on his arm. "What, you couldn't pick one or what?"

"I guess I just couldn't find the right one then."

What did he mean by "then?" Did he find one now? "We'll have to see about that. Maybe I can find one for you." Nora chuckled infectiously causing Hawk to smile back. "Anyway, now getting down to business. To fill you in quickly, the poker did have blood on it. The lab people are trying to match it with Mrs. Bowman this afternoon. Should know the results tomorrow morning. They also promised me the results of the DNA test on the cigarette butts as quickly as they could possibly do it. Three days most likely."

"We're making progress at least. What about the slug and shell?"

"Not very encouraging. The shell has a partial print and they're still working—." Nora stopped talking when Janice came back to take their orders—Nora ordered a Cobb salad and Hawk a cheeseburger. After placing the order in the kitchen, she returned to them and asked, "What can I help you with?"

"I saw Lieutenant Bradford and three other police detectives walking out of here last night. Do you know Lieutenant Bradford?"

Nora took out a small notebook and started to write. Janice said, "Oh, yeah. I sure do. He's in here almost daily after work, sometimes alone, other times with the man named Jeffries, or sometimes with Lieutenant Williams. After work, they seem like nice guys. They're very courteous to me. But then, almost once or twice a week they come in late, around nine. Now, Lieutenant Bradford, he's something else. He runs hot and cold. Do you know what I mean?"

"It could mean many things," Nora said, displaying a pleasant smile. "What do you mean by that?"

"Let me tell you, honey. One day, he could be the nicest guy, very pleasant, and talk about how smart he is and how good of a policeman he is. Asks me about my family and so forth. Other times, he acts like a tyrant. Yells at me to bring him his order immediately, regardless of how busy I am. Last night, for instance, he came in before the others and just sat at the table behind the wall there," pointing to her right, "staring at the tabletop. It almost looked like he was talking to himself."

"Is that unusual?" Hawk asked.

"Well, yes. It was the first time I had seen him so down. As a matter of fact, he even ordered a double whiskey instead of a second beer. He has never done that before. But that must have done it because he seemed to snap out of his funk and actually became very boisterous when the other men joined him. He even yelled at me when I came to their table to see if they needed anything else. I tell you, I've watched that group here, and as far as I'm concerned, they're up to no good."

"What do you mean by that, Janice?" Nora asked.

"Oh, I don't know. I just got this feeling that they're always plotting something that is secretive. Generally, as soon as I walk up, they shut their mouths."

Hawk asked, "Have you ever overheard what they're saying?"

"My ex-husband always used to say that I've got big ears. So, I guess to answer your question, Clint, yes, I hear something once in a while."

"Like what?"

"Well, like last night." Janice hesitated and looked at Hawk with anxiety. "I'm sure they mentioned your name and not in a good way. I think I heard Bradford say, 'To out you.' Does that mean what I think it means?" She lifted her hands and palmed her face. "Does that mean that they want to kill you?"

"Yeah, I'm a little worried about that. Yesterday someone tried to use me for target practice."

"If it was one of them, I'm sure it was that creepy O'Leary. He's got the eyes of a killer if I ever saw one."

"Did you hear O'Leary say anything?" Nora asked, looking worried.

"Only thing I heard him say, after I took their orders and started walking back, was something about really messing up. I looked back and noticed how red in the face Bradford got. He looked like he was ready to kill O'Leary."

Nora again asked, "But you didn't know what O'Leary meant by that?"

"No, I was too far from them by that time. Even my big ears couldn't hear." Janice chuckled. "But, Clint, what are you going to do about the threat to you?"

"What can I do without more proof? By the way, Janice, had you ever heard them say the name of Bowman?"

She thought for a moment. "No, I don't think so."

Nora asked, "By any chance did you hear anything about the Mexican cartel discussed or about any people not paying like they should?"

"You know, your salad and your cheeseburger are ready. The Cook is getting annoyed. I better go get them."

Nora and Hawk exchanged glances. Neither said the words, but were quite surprised with what they heard.

Janice came back with the orders, but neither of the detectives started eating, waiting for more information from the talkative server. "Now what was your question? By the way, are you sure that you're just partners? You're sitting too close together, touching shoulders to be just partners. I read body language. Kiddies, you're fooling yourselves. So, Nora, you need to make sure that our darling boy here stays safe."

"Oh, I certainly will. But what about any discussion on Mexican Cartels? Have you heard any mention of payoffs by anyone?"

Janice thought long and deep. No, I really didn't. All I know is that bunch were up to no good. I could just tell. Is there anything else? I need to go take care of business."

"No, Janice, thank you so much," Hawk said. "You were absolutely wonderful. Please don't tell them that we were asking questions."

"Of course not. I don't want to get in trouble with a lot like them."

Nora said, "One more thing. If I put together an affidavit or just a statement from you about what you overheard, would you sign it?"

"I don't like that. That's a mean group." She thought for a moment. "Well since it's for Clint, at least let me look at it and I'll decide then."

They thanked her again and she hugged them before they left. Out in the parking lot, Nora offered to take Hawk back to work, but he asked that she drop him off a block away. They had only a few moments to discuss the case. "Do you think we have enough for a warrant to get Bradford's computer?" Hawk asked.

"Let me run it by the IA captain. But, Clint, what are we going to do with the threat against you? You better stay with me tonight, as well."

"Nora, I went back for a quick look around my place this morning and I was so relieved that everything looked intact. But tonight, I think I better sleep there. I'm just too worried about my home being ransacked. I'll be extra careful. Don't worry. I just have to outsmart the bad guy." Clint laughed. Nora didn't.

"All right, then, I'll come over to your place. Surely, you have an extra room?"

"That's so nice of you to offer, but I don't want to risk your life or expose that we're working together. Listen, I really need to get back to work. Let's talk about it later."

"Would you at least call me every couple of hours to let me know that you're alright?"

"I'll be in the station working on cold cases. What could happen there?"

CHAPTER 36

WALKING BACK on Washington Street, Hawk kept glancing all around him, even behind him, to make sure no one was lurking to get him. He eyed every vehicle that went by, carefully watching to see if any stopped or slowed as they went past him. *This is crazy. I can't live my life this way. I need to get over it somehow.* As he approached the police building on the corner of Colfax and Washington, he was reminded how much he loved his job as a cop. He felt proud to be one and he thought he would love his job as a detective as well. *I've had a hell of a start with these dirty cops. Who would have thought that my first experience as a detective would land me in such a pitfall? Somehow, I have to get to the bottom of this so that my life can return to normal.*

Hawk walked back into the homicide unit barely sixty minutes after he had left. Wally looked up from the cold files open on his desk. "Well, you sure took your time. How was the old girlfriend?

"She was nice to talk to. It had been a while."

"It wasn't Marcie, was it?" Wally cackled. By the way, I heard the announcement that Marcie quit and is moving back to California. Too bad, I always thought that both of you were sweet on each other. What happened?"

"Nothing happened. There was nothing between us and she decided to leave, that's all."

"I think that you scared her away. Oh well, at least she won't be snooping around here anymore."

"Oh, I didn't know she did that? Why do you think that?"

"I think nothing of it, just curious probably. And then that Nora is not in either. You know, Clint, I think she is sweet on you as well. What did you do to those women that they've disappeared from the scene?" Wally chuckled again, his shoulders rising with every chuckle and his stomach shaking.

At that moment, Bradford and Jeffries marched out of Bradford's office. Jeffries sat down at his desk while Bradford approached Clint. "Hawk, I've been thinking that maybe there is some merit in your evaluation of the Bowman murders. We have a possible witness that may shed some light on this. I want you and Jeffries to partner up and go see this guy."

"But Lieutenant, I'm Hawk's partner," Wally protested. "I should be going with him."

"You're no longer partners. He and Jeffries will work together. And until I find something else for you to do, continue working on those cold cases. Is that understood, Wally?"

Wally turned red, and taking a deep breath, "Yes sir."

Hawk didn't like the notion of partnering with the person who might want to kill him. *Is Jeffries going to be the one to do me in? Well, not if I can help it.* As he took his gray jacket from the back of the chair and walked toward Jeffries, Wally mumbled, "Be careful out there."

Hawk and Jeffries headed to the parking lot. Neither man said a word. Hawk followed a few steps behind and set his phone to record. When Jeffries approached his vehicle, he threw the key to Hawk, "Why don't you drive, I've got too much of a headache." Hawk caught the unexpected key and got behind the wheel.

"Okay, boss, where to?"

"The witness lives several miles from here, near Bennett," Jeffries said, slumping into the seat. Hawk noticed a smirk on his face. "It'll be a nice long ride. Takes us away from the office." *Yeah, and it takes us to an open, isolated prairie.* "Take Leetsdale Drive to Parker Road. Then all the way to Quincy Avenue and head East. I'll give you directions after that."

"So, who is this witness we're to see? Did he actually see the carjacking and murder of Bowman?"

"Yeah, yeah, something like that. We'll find out, won't we?" Jeffries's sadistic grin made Hawk's gut twist into a knot. His answer about the witness was too vague. *Is this a ploy to get me alone? Take me to a desolate area where ranch houses are far apart with little traffic on the farm roads.*

"That's a hell of a long way to go if you're not sure about the guy," Hawk said. "Have you talked to him about the case?"

"Nah, I think it's best to surprise him. He might be a hostile witness and who knows, maybe he's the killer."

"I thought you got Freeman to confess to all of this. Why do we need to talk to anyone else, especially someone you don't know much about?'

"Because, you bastard, you got Bradford thinking that there might be someone else, that's why. Now don't ask so many questions. Just drive. I told you I have a headache. Leave me alone." Jeffries shut his eyes and leaned against the headrest of the unmarked overused Ford Crown Victoria. Hawk quietly unsnapped his holster.

CHAPTER 37

A TRIP to his death. That's how Hawk saw it. A shiver ran down his spine. At that moment, no hummingbird's heart ever beat faster than his did.

The weather in Denver was hot and he imagined it would be hotter yet on the Eastern plains, especially with a cloudless turquoise blue sky. *If I must die today, it's not a bad day to die; however, I'm not going to die. There's a plan somewhere in this brain.*

Working intensely, his brain hurt from searching for that plan. He thought of faking sudden illness and returning to the station. Or simply stop, turn around, tell Jeffries that he doesn't feel right about the suspect, and refuse to go any further. Hawk decided that was the best option. He needed to do it now, while he was still surrounded by people on sidewalks and in cars in all directions. He'll deal with Bradford later.

He slowed as they headed south on Parker Road, and got into the left lane to turn onto the major intersection of Iliff Avenue in Aurora. Jeffries's eyes flashed open. "What in the hell are you doing? You have to go straight ahead. Now get out of this lane and go straight."

"Hey, Jeffries, you're not my boss. I decided to return. I feel this is a wild goose chase and it isn't worth the time. I know what happened at the carjacking."

"Oh, you do, do you? It doesn't matter much what you think, you know. Bradford wants us to see that guy and you and I are going to go. Now straighten this damn car and go."

"I don't think so, Jeffries. There is no one there that we need to talk to, is there?"

Jeffries didn't hesitate to sit straight up, pull out his weapon and point it at Hawk. "You're right, there is no witness out there, but someone is anxiously waiting for you. Now hand over your gun." Hawk's heart seemed to jump out of his chest. He never imagined that Jeffries would pull a gun on him here, in the busy metro area. He reluctantly complied, handing over his gun. "I didn't plan on this. But it doesn't much matter if you're killed here or out in the prairie. Now get back on Parker and drive or I'll shoot you here now." *If I force his hand now, he's crazy enough to pull that trigger. I might as well do what he says, it'll give me more time to figure out how to get away.*

"How are you going to explain that?"

"Simple. Cops get shot all the time."

"No one would believe you."

"Sure, they would. With Bradford backing me up, *no problema.*"

Trying to calm his voice, Hawk asked, "Why are you doing this, Jeffries? Did you kill Bowman?"

"I didn't actually, but I was in the SUV that delayed Bowman for a minute or two. You're a real curious SOB, aren't you? But since you're going to die anyway, I'll brag about it to you."

"And it was O'Leary that actually shot him?"

"Boy, you know that, do you? No wonder Bradford is worried about you."

"Did Bradford know about it?"

"Of course. He's the boss. Well, I thought he was the big boss, but it appears that there is someone above him that organized our whole operation."

"A main boss? Do you know who it is?"

"Nah, Bradford has been trying to find out for the two years we've been doing this. He thinks it's someone in our unit or maybe in William's or O'Leary's station."

"How can he not know who it is?"

"I guess whoever it is, is very smart and knows how to give orders yet avoid detection."

"Does Bradford suspect who it could be?"

"I don't know why I'm telling you anything. But you'll never be around to tell anyone. In our unit, he thinks it's Orlinski or maybe Marcie."

"So, why was it necessary to get rid of Bowman? What did he do to you?"

"Hey, shut up. I don't want to talk about it anymore. Just drive."

"Okay, but since I'm a dead man, why don't you tell me? Satisfy my curiosity. I'm fascinated by how clever you all must be for doing whatever you do and get away with it. I think that you're probably the big boss." Hawk worried that his iPhone had enough juice left in its battery to record this conversation. He couldn't believe that Jeffries was telling him anything at all. *But like he said, he wants to brag about it.* Besides, it has always been Hawk's style to make the person he was interrogating feel as relaxed as possible and keep talking. Under the circumstances, it was extremely difficult for him to stay relaxed enough to form the questions he needed to ask. He felt more confident now since he had come up with a plan to save himself and capture Jeffries. He just prayed that his plan would work—that he could calm himself enough even though his body was as tight as a drum.

"Are you crazy? I'm just the grunt. If you knew the stuff we're able to pull off and make a ton of money, you would be really impressed."

"I'm thinking that you guys are involved in the drug trade. Probably with the drug cartel."

"No, we don't get our hands dirty with that, we just get paid for keeping quiet and when there's a raid against them, we warn them. Just try to keep them out of trouble with the law."

"That doesn't sound like you can make enough off that to share between you and Bradford."

"Oh, we make plenty from the cartel. And then there is always blackmail or extortion from wealthy businessmen and aspiring politicians. You should see all the electronic surveillance equipment we use to gather the dirt on those guys. And it isn't just the two of us, Williams and O'Leary are involved as well."

"And that doesn't bother you? I mean, you're a policeman, sworn to uphold the law."

"Well, frankly, it did at first. But the money was so good that I don't think about that anymore. Actually, I surprised myself that I could do that and live with my conscience. I tell you; my grasping wife sure enjoys the luxury of our lifestyle on vacations."

"She knows what you're up to?"

"No. She doesn't even ask as long as the luxuries are there."

"Surely, she suspects something?"

"Maybe, but like I said, she never asks."

"Did you guys kill Julia Bowman also?"

"Nope. Don't know who did, but they did us a favor getting rid of her. She probably knew what her husband was up to?"

"Like what?"

"He was our money launderer, man. He invested the money into real estate and had contacts with offshore bank accounts. We all got a good chunk of it, except the big boss got fifteen percent right off the top."

"So, how does the big boss communicate if you don't know who it is?"

"Only with Bradford in some kind of crazy code. Bradford told me he had to memorize certain words for regular words."

"Like what?"

"Well, like for example, the victim is perfume, kill is daisy, cash is daffodil. That's all Bradford told us."

Hawk said, "All flower names or related to flowers like perfume."

"That's why Bradford thinks it's a woman."

"So, who's going to shoot me? You? Once we get there?"

"No, O'Leary is happy to do it."

"How are you going to get away with it?"

"Another punk that hates cops. Lured us out so he could shoot us. You'll take the first shot in the head, the second shot will miss me and hit the side window. Then O'Leary will take off. At least it'll be quick for you."

Hawk suddenly accelerated. "Hey, what in the hell are you doing? You're going too fast. Slow down, you bastard. Slow down! You're going to miss the turnoff half a mile up."

Hawk didn't slow, he got the Crown Vic up to eighty miles per hour since the road ahead was clear of traffic. At a point where the embankment of the adjacent ditch was the tallest, he quickly and deliberately turned the wheel ninety degrees. He assumed that the airbag would deploy with the collision. To avoid more serious injuries, he attempted to relax his body beforehand as much as feasible under the circumstances. Clint threw his arms in front of his face, particularly to save his nose.

As expected, the crash at East Quincy Avenue, near Highway 129 was severe.

CHAPTER 38

THE AIRBAGS deployed when the Ford sedan smashed violently into the ditch. Hawk felt the full force of the airbag slamming into his arms as he held them up to protect his face. His head whiplashed forward, then backward, immediately causing a strain in his neck. Part of the dashboard smashed into his leg and knee. His chest felt like a ton of bricks were stacked on top of it from the snug seatbelt that managed to hold him in place. His head felt as though a vise closed around it which kept twisting tighter and tighter, almost squeezing his brains out.

Hawk waved away the chalk dust left by the bags and glanced at Jeffries. The right side of his forehead was bleeding from striking the passenger window. Jeffries appeared to be knocked out after taking the brunt of the collision. The Glock 9mm pistol was still in his hand, and Hawk's Sig Sauer lay on the floor. Even though stiff and sore, Hawk unbuckled his belt, took out his phone, and took a photo of Jeffries holding the gun. He knew someone would have called 911 by now as a group of people were beginning to gather around the scene, staring through the windows, looking for life inside. One of them opened the driver's door. Hawk thought he heard him say, "Are you all right, buddy? An ambulance is on the way. Geez, what's that guy doing with a gun?"

Before managing to get out, Hawk gingerly pulled Jeffries's gun from his hand. He had to be careful because Jeffries's finger was still dangerously wrapped around the trigger. With great pain, he reached for his weapon and placed it back in his holster. Jeffries opened his eyes. After exiting the vehicle, Hawk tried to stretch and move his stiff neck back and forth and side to side to loosen it. He felt wobbly. A stranger took his arm to keep him steady. "We better not move that guy in there until an ambulance comes," he heard someone say.

"I'm a Denver police detective and that man in there is my prisoner," Hawk told the people standing around. After saying those words, he sat back down on the seat of the car sideways, his feet on the ground. He felt safe enough to do that because Jeffries seemed barely conscious and immobile. He heard the ambulance or firetruck or both with their sirens wailing in the distance. He took out his phone and prayed that he was able to record the valuable admissions made by Jeffries. Hawk played part of the recording back and with an enormous sigh of relief, he heard his voice. He next clicked on Nora's cell number.

"Hello, Nora."

"Hi, Clint. I'm glad you called. I was about to tell you that we have some good news. The DNA came back, and as you suspected it was O'Leary's."

"Nora, wait before you go on. To save my life, I just now caused an accident on purpose. Jeffries is hurt and will most likely go to a hospital by ambulance. I'll try to accompany him in the ambulance and will call you to let you know what hospital they'll take us to. Take someone with you from IA and meet me there. I see the Arapahoe County Sheriff approaching me now. I've got a lot of explaining to do."

"What!? Oh my God! Are you alright?" Nora's heart raced; she could only take in shallow breaths.

"I'll be fine, a little sore and stiff now, that's all. Listen. I have to go now. I'll call you."

The sheriff's deputy approached with authority. He looked angry, probably just part of his nature, Hawk thought. "You the driver here? Is this a police car?"

"Yes, I was the forced driver and my name is Clint Hawk, Denver PD."

"So, what the hell were you doing out here? You have no jurisdiction here."

"It's a long story. But that person in there is my prisoner and I'd like to borrow one of your evidence bags so that I can bag this weapon." Jeffries was coming around. He realized what occurred and began to moan loudly.

"Don't believe him," Jeffries tried to yell out, but his voice sounded very muted because of his pain. "He's lying, that bastard. I'm a Denver Police detective." At that moment, the paramedics rushed to his side of the car. They tried unsuccessfully to open the jammed passenger door. The right front wheel was buckled; the bumper was pushed up as the right fender crumpled. The brunt of the collision was mostly on Jeffries's side, just as Hawk had planned.

The firemen brought out their "Jaws of Life" and Hawk was on his feet next to the deputy. The fireman went through the driver's side and unbuckled Jeffries from the seat belt, then pulled him gently away from the glass of the door. Jeffries cried out from the pain. Another fireman carefully knocked out the safety glass in the door and then applied the tool to the door. The tool was able to crumple the metal from the frame and then separate the hinges from the body of the car. Next, they placed a neck brace on Jeffries and carefully pulled him out and onto a gurney.

"I'm going with him in the ambulance," Hawk told the deputy. I suggest you follow us to the hospital. He needs help now and I need to be checked over as well." The deputy didn't like being bossed around. He grunted and mumbled, but complied. Hawk had a little trouble convincing the EMTs to allow him to ride along in the same ambulance. But he showed them his credentials and told them, "That's how it's got to be."

The ambulance took them to the Medical Center of Aurora, a distance of twenty miles from downtown Denver. It took Nora and Captain Norton from IA over half an hour, with lights and sirens blaring to get there. By this time, due to his injuries, Jeffries was admitted to a hospital room. Hawk insisted that he be allowed to handcuff him to his bed. The deputy reluctantly agreed, still not sure if Hawk was telling the truth. In any event, he followed Hawk to make sure that he stayed in his sight. Hawk was also examined thoroughly. His blood pressure and other vitals were noted, neurological tests were given and X-rays were taken. He was diagnosed with a sprain-strain injury to his neck and lower back with scrapes and bruises on his knees and legs. Hawk's headache subsided somewhat, but his neck, shoulders, and upper arms hurt like hell and his lower back spasmed.

The Arapahoe County deputy called in his sheriff for advice about what to do with the strange accident. The sheriff told him to give the driver a ticket for careless driving causing bodily injury and let the judge figure it out. Hawk was issued a summons with the first smile he had seen on the deputy, who obviously took great relish in handing him the ticket. After that, he left Hawk holding the ticket with a parting statement, "Next time stay on your own turf." *You jerk, I explained to you that it wasn't my choice. Either I had to crash the car or be killed by a bullet. At least with the collision, I had a chance to survive. Thank you, my guardian angel, for protecting me again.*

At that moment Nora rushed into the emergency room with Captain Norton following. They found Hawk sitting in one of the reception chairs, his elbows on his knees, his face cupped by his hands. "Clint, Clint," Nora rushed up to him. She wanted to hug him tight and kiss him, but she restrained herself because her supervisor watched. "What happened? You didn't tell me anything. We were so worried. This is my boss, Captain Norton of Internal Affairs." Hawk acknowledged him with a slight nod. It hurt his stiff neck to move it.

Explaining everything from the beginning, Hawk took his time. His speech was still somewhat sluggish. The excruciating headache he suffered from earlier returned with a vengeance. Nora and Norton listened carefully; their faces showed astonishment. After he finished, he produced his cell phone, showed them the picture of Jeffries holding a gun in his hand, and asked them to listen to the recording. Some of it could have been better, but mostly everything was audible. "Captain, please play the recording again onto your voicemail, if possible, so that you have a record of it. We need, though, to have it transcribed." He also handed his traffic ticket to Norton and asked if he could get it dismissed somehow. His third request was for a guard to be posted outside of Jeffries's room. "He could try to escape, or more likely, his gang doesn't know about the recording and may want to get rid of him before he says anything that would implicate them."

Norton took the phone and the ticket. He replayed the conversation again onto his voicemail. "Detective Hawk, please send me that photo of Jeffries with the gun. Nora will provide you with my number. What you accomplished is quite remarkable. Thank you and thanks from all the dedicated cops for what you did. You took quite a chance with that accident, it could have ended badly, but in reality, it saved your life. Don't worry about the ticket, I know the sheriff well, I'll get it dismissed and also ask Aurora PD to post an officer outside Jeffries's door. If they're not willing, and I doubt they would object, I'll get our own officers to do it. Now, let's go see Jeffries. Lead the way."

Jeffries was awake, his head bandaged, a brace on his neck. As the three of them walked in, his eyes widened upon seeing Nora and a high-ranking officer with Hawk. "Sir, I'm glad you're here. Get these damn handcuffs off me. Hawk is setting me up. He thought I was going to kill him. You don't believe that lying scum, do you?" He pointed to Hawk. "He's telling lies. He crashed the car on purpose to kill me. Arrest him and I want these cuffs off of me."

Norton said, "Daniel Jeffries, you're under arrest. You have the right to remain silent, you have the right to an attorney——."

"I know the Miranda rights. I don't need to hear them after all the years I put in at the DPD. Why is a captain here to arrest me anyway? And what am I being arrested for?"

"I'm with Internal Affairs, Detective. For now, the charge is attempted murder."

"You can't be serious. I can't understand how you would believe a cock and bull-story that a rookie made up about me. It's personal. He never liked me from the start. Call Lieutenant Bradford, he'll vouch for me. I swear that Hawk is a big liar. He's trying to set me up. I know for a fact that he's a dirty cop. You should be arresting him, not me, I've done nothing wrong."

"As soon as you're released, you'll be taken to jail," Norton said, with an expression of great pleasure on his round face. "So, rest up, Detective Jeffries." With that said, Hawk, Nora, and Norton walked out of the room. On the way to the lobby of the hospital, Norton told Hawk that he and Nora would take him back to his car at the station. "Oh, we should've taken his room phone from him so he doesn't call Bradford. I want to surprise him with an arrest warrant and a search warrant for his phone and computers."

"I already took the phone from the room while Jeffries was out for x-rays and left it at the nurses' station with instructions not to give it to him," Hawk said. "I also bagged his gun and his cell phone, but the deputy took the bags at the scene of the accident, placed them in his cruiser, and wouldn't let me have them."

"We'll get them," Norton said. "Again, good work, Detective." Hawk glanced at Nora, who gave him a beaming smile. She winked at Hawk and he smiled back.

"Captain, I think I should stay here guarding Jeffries until an officer comes. O'Leary was out there somewhere. I'm sure he heard the commotion of the accident and drove by to see what happened. It won't take him long to figure out what occurred and find this hospital. He probably already apprised Bradford of what transpired."

"I think that's a good idea," Nora said. "I'll stay with him. Detective Hawk is too weak to be here by himself.

CHAPTER 39

O'LEARY SAT waiting in a confiscated tan GMC Sierra pickup in a ravine on an infrequently used dirt farm road, about half a mile from Quincy. He and Jeffries picked this location specifically because the pickup could not be seen from Quincy or from the scattered farmhouses around. The minutes passed, and still no Jeffries and Hawk. He began to worry. *What could be the problem? We had a perfect plan.* Suddenly, he heard sirens along Quincy. *It has to do with Hawk, I bet.* Since it appeared that Hawk and Jeffries were a no-show, he decided to investigate.

On his right, as he headed towards Quincy, he saw a lot of commotion that looked like a sensational accident involving Jeffries's assigned Crown Victoria. Damn! The accident ruined their plans to get rid of Hawk. He parked the pickup a quarter of a mile away and walked to the scene. He wore worn cowboy boots, dirty blue jeans, and a loose black T-shirt with faded writing, "Born to Love," stenciled in dark red. To be unrecognizable, he wore a black baseball cap down low to his ears and large dark sunglasses that covered his eyes and a good portion of his face. As a further precaution, he attached a fake curly black beard and mustache that he previously used when he killed Bowman.

What he viewed was devastating and O'Leary relished the sight in front of him. From his distance, he believed that no one could have survived such a crash. If he were right, that would be the best scenario. Hawk would be dead and with Jeffries gone also, one less person would know what they're doing. More importantly, his share would now be greater. He briefly wondered how the accident happened, but if both were dead, it didn't matter to him.

He waited in the background with several other gawkers. To his chagrin, he saw Hawk stand up from the vehicle and join the deputy sheriff. A few minutes later, Jeffries was pulled out of the wreckage and placed in an ambulance. Hawk followed him in. *I can't believe it. They're alive. Gives me the chance to kill both of them now.* He returned to the farm road and called Bradford. Pleased that the Lieutenant ordered him to make sure both were dead; he followed the ambulance to the hospital.

To O'Leary, killing gave him a thrill, a stimulation that he needed. It all began when he was a boy of ten. He found it exciting to capture and mutilate animals. He laughed when they whimpered before they lost their last breath. He got away with it because he knew how to avoid severe punishment. As he became older, he learned how to talk his way out of trouble using superficial charm, manipulation, and lying.

When he graduated from Metropolitan State University with a Criminal Justice degree, his dream was to become a policeman in order to exert power and control over both his fellow officers and criminals and to get away with all kinds of scams. O'Leary applied to the police department. He hid his true personality and had the talent and smarts to pass the rigorous detective exam. It was his second nature to fool so many people. He lobbied to be assigned to the drug unit where a dirty cop had the opportunity to steal drugs, confiscate money, guns, or anything else of value. When Bradford offered O'Leary the opportunity to make a lot of money, he jumped at the chance.

O'Leary wasn't married and he didn't care whether he was or not. He had no feelings for any human being. He also presented the personality that he thought would please whomever he interacted with. It was never love that attracted him to women, but occasional sex, whether voluntary or involuntary, didn't matter to him. After every date ended, most women were lucky to have escaped him. Nora was beautiful and he wanted her. But when she didn't want anything to do with him, he thought seriously of killing her.

Always conniving on how to "skirt the law," he learned how to cover his tracks and stay out of trouble. He's not worried this time either. He'll take care of both Hawk and Jeffries and no one will suspect him.

Once at the hospital, O'Leary found a parking spot close to the emergency entrance so that it was visible to him and sat in the pickup for over an hour. Soon, a heavy-built, bald-headed black man with a gun holstered on his side, walked in with a dark-haired woman. He assumed that the man was a cop. From a distance, the woman looked so much like Nora. *It can't be, what would she be doing here?* He waited in his vehicle for the cop to leave. He was losing patience and thought that he might as well go in. The cop, if he was a cop, might have nothing to do with Jeffries or Hawk. Seven o'clock Visitor's Hour started and he decided that he could wait no longer. He hoped with more visitors coming and going, nobody would notice him.

It was hot. He checked the mirror to make sure his makeup was intact. Even though he had the windows open, he sweated under the fake beard and mustache. He applied a brown cream to the exposed part of his face. *Perfect. I'm such a clever guy.* As he began to exit the pickup, the bald, black man who he thought was a cop came out, busy on his cell. O'Leary watched him walk to a Ford Explorer and get in. With the spotlight on the driver's side and the typical cheap hubcaps, he knew it was a cop car. *Good, he's gone, I won't have to worry about him.*

In the foyer, he ambled to the information counter and asked for the room that Daniel Jeffries was in. Having seen the condition of Jeffries's vehicle, he assumed Jeffries would be out of the ER and admitted to a room. The volunteer, a pleasant girl of about twenty, directed him to a room on the fourth floor. Taking the elevator to that floor, he exited, read the room directory, and proceeded down the hall.

At that very moment, Nora sprinted down the hall as she carried a paper tray with two lukewarm coffees and a couple of cafeteria ham sandwiches. A casual glance toward the person ahead of her and his familiar gait put her on alert. She focused harder on his gait. He stepped with a peculiar toe-heel pattern as opposed to the normal heel-toe. He barely put any weight on his heels. She studied him more closely as she neared him. *Oh my God! That's O'Leary. No one else walks like him. I should know since I watched his walk for weeks when I worked with him. That's him, I know it, with his broad shoulders and narrow hips, no butt.* She considered the back of his cowboy boots. They were the same battered boots that he had occasionally worn around the station, particularly when assigned undercover work. She remembered that the boots had a horseshoe-shaped silver ornament attached to the top of the heels. *Yes, yes, yes. Those are the same ones.*

Nora had to do something quick. She imagined that as soon as O'Leary rounded the corner, he would take Hawk by surprise, and shoot him on sight before her partner could react. It would be a breeze for him to kill Jeffries as well before the stunned staff could respond to the sound of the gun. O'Leary could easily run down the stairs and out of the building. "O'LEARY!!!," she yelled out loud enough for the whole floor to hear. She especially hoped that Hawk heard her scream. By reflex O'Leary responded, "What," and abruptly spun around grabbing his gun from his belted waist.

Standing near him, Nora threw the coffee in his face, stunning him for a few seconds. She didn't waste time; she sprang high and kicked him in the chest. O'Leary stumbled backward but didn't fall. Nora twisted around as she was taught during many years of Taekwondo training and kicked him in the head. He fell to the floor and lifted his gun toward her, but in a fast sweep of her leg and foot, Nora stuck his wrist, knocking the pistol out of his hand, which slid along the highly polished floor. O'Leary stretched out to retrieve it, his hand almost on the weapon when Hawk's large shoe stepped on his wrist. At the same time, Nora dazed O'Leary with a swift kick to his head, and he fell on his right shoulder.

Turning the dirty cop on his stomach, Hawk yelled, "Nora, do the honors. Cuff him." After the foul-mouthed O'Leary was secured, they rolled him over. Hawk took out his phone and took a picture of the captive's face. Next, he took off his sunglasses and took another picture. Then he ripped off the moustache and beard causing O'Leary to yell and swear. Nevertheless, Hawk took another photo of him without the disguise. His face had two tones—dark brown on his upper cheeks and his natural suntanned color where the beard was glued on. "Voila," Hawk said.

"And now we have the one and only O'Leary." Nora snickered.

A crowd had gathered around Nora and Hawk. Two hospital security guards were seen running down the hall. "Police were called, they should be here soon," said one of the nurses.

"We are police," Nora said as she flashed her credentials to the crowd. "This man is under arrest by the Denver PD." At that moment, a young-looking man with an Aurora Police Department uniform skidded in, seemingly confused by the scene he saw.

Hawk explained what happened. The Aurora officer told him that he was assigned by his sergeant to guard a prisoner by the name of Daniel Jeffries. Pleased to see him, Hawk escorted him to Jeffries 'room and asked him to make sure no one other than hospital personnel with ID badges displaying matching photos of their face was able to enter. He pointed to the chair outside the room in the hallway and said, "You shouldn't have a problem, officer. I think we got the man we were most afraid of harming Jeffries. But you never know. Someone else might be sent out. He should probably be discharged in the morning and we'll have our officers take him away. Will you have replacements through the night?"

"I don't know. I assume the sergeant would send someone to relieve me later."

Hawk thanked him for his service and wished him, "Good luck. Be careful."

In the meantime, Nora called Captain Norton and described the turn of events. He told her that more officers should arrive in 30 minutes to pick up O'Leary. "We have no choice but to wait until

Jeffries is released. I don't like it at all, him lying around in the hospital. Anyway, hang in there until they come. Good work, Nora."

Soon, three Aurora Police officers arrived in answer to the nurse's call. Nora explained what transpired and advised them that the man sitting on the floor was a DPD prisoner someone would pick him up soon. Nora thought that they were relieved that they didn't have to handle the situation, but yet the Aurora officers mumbled something about their turf as they left.

"Our coffee and sandwiches are all over the floor." Nora laughed in sheer joy at the release of her tension in the capture of O'Leary. "Are you awfully hungry? I guess we better get something else to eat."

Hawk's smile deepened into laughter as well. "Sure, but I can wait. Forget the crummy sandwiches, let's find a fancy place to eat and celebrate over wine."

"Sure, sure, you bastards," O'Leary said with a malicious tone. "Laugh and celebrate all you want now, but neither of you is going to be around much longer. You think I'm alone? Well, I'm not."

"What do you mean," Hawk asked. "Who else is there?"

"You SOB! You'll never be safe until you're dead, even if I'm locked up."

Nora looked concerned. Out of the prisoner's earshot, she said, "Norton told me that Bradford and Williams had been arrested based on your recording, and their computers in the office and homes had been picked up for analysis. O'Leary is here and in custody and so is Jeffries."

"The only one left is the big boss that calls the shots. I doubt that he or she would take any action at this point. Since no one knows who that person is, why would the big boss risk exposure? Anyway, we'll find him or her, don't worry."

CHAPTER 40

THE GREEK restaurant on Chambers Road in Aurora delighted Nora and Hawk. Both starved, their meals tasted extra good. Nora mentioned how skillfully the owners transformed a drab old Pizza Hut into a pleasant blue-and-white Mediterranean restaurant reminiscent of modern Greece. They laughed and dined in merriment until they found themselves the last couple in the restaurant. During the evening Hawk tried to mask his pain after the accident the best that he could, but Nora noticed him squirming in his seat, squeezing his nape of the neck, massaging his right shoulder, and an occasional tightening of his jaw and squinting his eyes caused by severe pain. She sidled up to him to massage his neck and shoulders. As she softly stroked the back of his head, she suggested several times that he should rest at home. He repeatedly responded that he enjoyed her company too much to leave just yet.

Hawk stood once again to walk and stretch. The need to blow his nose in the restroom provided him an excuse to get up and move around. Feeling so sorry for him, Nora said, "Oh, wait, I just remembered that I have aspirin in my purse. Let me get it." She looked around for her handbag, then slapped her forehead. "Geez, I forgot to take my bag. I was in such a big hurry to see you that I left it at my desk. It's a good thing I always carry my police ID on my person, otherwise, I could have had an issue back at the hospital."

"That's all right. Thank you. I'll be fine."

Nora knew better, so she stopped a waitress as the woman walked by. "Miss, would the restaurant by chance have any aspirin?" The server nodded and went towards the kitchen. A minute later, the pleasant agile-looking woman in her fifties introduced herself as the owner and gave Nora a bottle of Advil.

"Take what you need. I know how terrible it is to be in pain."

"It's not for me, it's for my—" she hesitated a moment. "It's for my boyfriend," she said smiling, surprising Hawk. *Wow, how did I attain that status already? Should I correct her? Who knows, maybe it's all right.*

During the evening, they purposely gave no further thought to O'Leary's threat, setting it aside as "sour grapes," or no more than a man who relished making dire threats. Nora once again invited Clint to stay the night. "I give the world's best full body massage. My dad always said that I was the only masseuse that eased his disc pain."

Hawk declined, though reluctantly, "I'd love to, but frankly, my bed is calling me." Nora insisted on paying the bill and they walked out into the parking lot. While waiting outside for their Uber rides to their police stations, Nora gently pulled Hawk toward her, and her lips pressed against his. Hawk gave her a bright smile even though he was struggling with pain.

The next morning, still stiff, sore, and in pain from the collision, Hawk slowly shuffled into the Homicide unit. It didn't feel the same. Marcie's sparkling smile and greeting were absent. Nora was gone. Orlinski's desk stood empty as did Jeffries's. Detectives Salazar, Withers, Ling, and Higgins greeted him warmly. "Walking a little slow, Clint," Nancy Salazar said. "Are you alright?"

"It's a long story. I'll tell you all about it later. "Let's just say that I had a good day and a bad day yesterday."

"Now, you've really got my curiosity up." At that instance, Nancy had to take a call. As Hawk painfully proceeded to his desk, he glanced toward Bradford's office. The shades were open and he saw Orlinski sitting at the desk, scratching his head. Orlinski motioned him in.

"Hawk, I was brought up to date on what you did." Orlinski invited him to take a chair opposite from him. It's absolutely remarkable. Because of you, I'm sitting in this room. Bradford was arrested last night. They tell me I'll be in charge for maybe a week. Lieutenant Perez will be the interim head of this unit. I heard he's strictly no-nonsense. Everything by the book."

"I'm glad you're here, even though it's only for a while. The last time I saw Bradford, he wanted me to work on the Bowman cases. Of course, that was a ruse to do away with me."

Orlinski shook his head back and forth. He said, "That is so unbelievable and terrible. It's a good thing you were clever enough to tape the conversation with Jeffries, otherwise no one would believe it."

"You know about that already?"

"Yes, actually, the Division Chief called me late last night to tell me what happened. I'd like to hear more from you about it. Let's plan on a quick lunch next week."

"Sure, great. Anyway, getting back to the Bowman case, I think I know who killed Mrs. Bowman. I just have to prove it. Will you assign me to that case again?"

"Sure, go for it. Do you need some help? You can continue working with Murphy."

"No thanks. I can manage on my own."

As Hawk ambled to his desk, Murphy was already seated at his. "Clint, my buddy, what were you doing with Orlinski in Bradford's office? And what was he doing sitting in the boss's chair? And where the hell is Marcie, Nora, and Jeffries?"

Wow, all those questions at once. Hawk wondered how often he would have to repeat yesterday's chain of events. He hurriedly told Wally what transpired and told him what Jeffries said about a mystery boss. "He or she evidently set up the whole blackmailing and extortion scheme that the dirty cops were involved with. That person actually called the shots and communicated with Bradford using some sort of a computer encrypted system and a word code."

"Did Jeffries mention who it was?" Wally asked casually.

"No, no one seems to know. Bradford thought it might be someone in this unit. Can you believe that?"

"No, impossible to believe. What made him think that?"

"You know, I never asked that question of Jeffries. But if I had to guess it was probably because whoever was in contact with Bradford, knew too much of what was going on in the unit."

"If that's the case, then my money is on Marcie."

"Marcie? I don't think so," Hawk said. "I didn't know her all that well, but she didn't seem to be a ruthless type, just the opposite, in fact."

"Yeah, sure. You don't want to believe it, but those are the people you gotta watch out for. Her outside, which I grant you is very nice, may not be what's inside her, my friend. Besides, I could tell you were head over heels for her. She may be pulling wool over your eyes."

"Nah. Let's get to work, shall we."

"No, wait, from what you told me, it had to be someone who really knew computers. She certainly was terrific at it. And isn't it suspicious that she suddenly left? She must have thought you were getting too close and would figure it out, mister know-it-all.

"Well, maybe. It's hard for me to believe it though."

"So, who all were arrested because of you?"

"As far as I know, Bradford, Williams, Jeffries, and O'Leary are in jail facing multiple charges."

"Oh well, sometimes you win and sometimes you lose. I'd hate to be in their shoes. He chuckled and quickly changed the subject, "Okay Clint, could we have lunch today? I'd like to take you to a great spaghetti place in Highlands. You wouldn't believe the large portions they serve."

"Sure, Wally. Let's plan on it. Let me know when you're ready."

"You shouldn't ask me that question. I'm always ready to eat." Laughing, he patted his protruding belly. "I better wait though. How about noon?"

Hawk just sat down in his squeaky chair when his cell's ringtone blared out the *Bad to the Bone* melody. It was Nora. "Hi there, Clint. How are you feeling? I've been so worried about you."

"Nora, I'm fine. Just moving a little slow, but I'm fine."

"You're not at work, are you?"

"Yes. I'm fine. I'm thinking about Julia Bowman's case and the discrepancy of the shoe size thirteen we noted outside the window and Miller's actual size, which I estimate to be a nine and a half or a ten."

"It's perplexing, all right. So how are we going to solve that?"

"We!"

"Yes, we. I told you we'll be working together. Don't you remember? I've been assigned to you. And as you know, I'm still your bodyguard." Nora laughed infectiously.

"I don't need a bodyguard. The danger is over. No one is after me now."

"Actually, you still may be in danger. There's still someone out there, the main boss as you call him or her, that has a lot at stake to lose, especially, if he or she thinks you're getting too close for comfort. We all have confidence that you're the one to solve the puzzle."

"Who's 'we,' Nora?"

"Me, of course, and Captain Norton."

"You give me too much credit. I've just been lucky so far, that's all." Hawk pondered the possibility that the mystery boss may want to kill him but discounted it since he had no clue who it might be.

"So it's settled. I'll help you with Julia Bowman's case, but don't you investigate anything without me. Call me first. I'll meet you in front of the building and we'll go together. Just give me a few minutes to get there. Are you going out now?"

"No, I'll be here trying to figure out the discrepancy in shoe sizes and maybe how I can flush out the boss. If the person is in the unit, he already knows that Bradford and his gang are in jail. I'll call you."

"Okay, but this evening you need to come by my place. I'll make us the best Chicken Scallopine that you ever tasted. My grandmother brought the recipe from Sicily all the way to Pueblo, Colorado. You should know that Pueblo has the best Italian food. And afterward, I'll give you that massage that I promised. Just watch, tomorrow, you'll be as good as new."

"Sounds terrific. Your background is intriguing and I'd like to hear more about it. My ancestors came from Tennessee. Actually, fought Santa Ana under Sam Houston in the battle of San Jacinto in 1836."

"You must be proud of your colorful background as well. I want to hear more. I love history."

After promising to call her before leaving the station and saying his goodbyes, Hawk sat back in his chair, struggling in vain to lift his arms behind his head. He thought about Nora. It was obvious to him that she wanted him. *She's pushy, all right. But I like being with her. I guess I'll just have to wait and see what happens. But I'm not about to let her push me around, at least not all the time.*

Quickly Hawk devised a possible scenario for the different shoe size dilemma. *What if Miller wore the large sneakers over his regular shoes? He wouldn't have kept them. He would've thrown them away, with the poker from the Bowman house. I doubt that they are still in a dumpster.* He recalled the words of the crime scene investigator, Chet Watkins, "Soles of Adidas shoes with much mileage on them." To Hawk, that meant that the shoes were old. They wouldn't have been Miller's because his feet were smaller. Where would he get them? *A thrift store, of course.*

Hawk looked up the home address of Marcus Miller using White Pages on his computer. Several men in the Denver metro area shared that name, but only one was about his age. Miller lived in the area of North Monaco Parkway near East Seventeenth Avenue. A search on Yelp for the closest thrift stores to Miller's home listed the Goodwill on East Thirty-Sixth, less than two miles away. Next was an Arc Thrift Store on Iliff, also less than two miles away. Assistance League on Evans was slightly over two miles. Hawk jotted down the addresses.

Next, he searched the closest stores to Miller's business on Colfax and Lafayette. From that location, ARC Thrift was slightly over one mile on Colfax. The next closest was the Goodwill on Broadway, three and a half miles away. Hawk again jotted the addresses and phone numbers and called the managers of each. After giving them his name and identifying himself as a detective with the Denver PD, he asked if they had video equipment in the store and if he could see or take the tapes of the last two weeks. They all answered in the affirmative.

Hawk called Nora. "How would you like to go thrift store shopping with me?"

"Oh, I love those kinds of stores. You can find some real treasures," Nora laughed.

"Good. So, if you want to go, let's go now. I have a lunch date and need to be back by noon."

"What did you say? A date? With whom?" Nora seemed really perturbed and Hawk had to laugh.

"You're not jealous, are you?"

"Well, no. Well, maybe. I don't think I like you going out with another woman."

"Well, my date is big and cuddly." Hawk could hear her silence.

"Nora, I'm just teasing you. For two days, Wally had asked me to join him for lunch. Had you going, didn't I?"

"You jerk. I'll be over in about fifteen. But you better have a good reason why we're going to thrift stores now."

Exactly fifteen minutes later, Nora called. Hawk looked around his desk for some paper so he could take notes, but couldn't find any. As he walked past Wally's empty desk, he saw a few notepads, the type that printing companies give away as freebies. These had the name of Egan Printing. He grabbed one thinking that Wally probably would never miss it.

Out by the door, Nora gave Hawk a pleasant smile. "Your chauffeur is at your service. I hope this is business not pleasure." Hawk explained the need to visit the thrift stores. Nora raised her finely tweezed dark brown eyebrows. "You've got to be kidding. The stuff that your mind comes up with."

"What?"

"It's interesting. Okay, let's go for it."

The manager of Goodwill had expected Hawk and took them to his back office. They quickly reviewed the tapes. "Aren't you going a little fast?" Nora said. "How can you tell who's who?"

"Believe me, I'll recognize Miller, if he's there." But the tapes were a bust. The detectives went on to the Assistance League store. That also disappointed them. The third store was an ARC Thrift Store and after twenty minutes of reviewing tapes, Hawk said, "Stop. Please rewind it a few people back and go slow." The manager complied. "Geez Louise!" Hawk exclaimed. "Wow! I think that is Marcus Miller checking out. Could you zoom in on his purchase there?"

The manager zoomed in. A pair of shoes. "Can you go a little closer in?"

"No, that's the best I can do with this equipment."

"In that case, could we borrow it?" Nora asked. "We have technicians that will show a mosquito on that shoe." The manager agreed but asked for a receipt and a verbal agreement that Hawk would return it. Elated at the find, Hawk would have agreed to anything.

"I told you, Clint. You're just a lucky guy. Things are falling into place."

"Don't jinx it, Nora. We still need to check out video cameras in that alley where the poker was found. Hopefully, Miller's mug will stick out prominently. And we still have to figure out who the hell the big boss is. Let's hope my luck still holds."

CHAPTER 41

NORA DROPPED Hawk at the station and went back to headquarters on Cherokee Street. She reminded him that tonight he was in for the best Italian dinner he had ever eaten. Still smiling, Hawk walked back to the unit thinking of Nora and her funny ways of keeping him in line. He likes living alone but has to admit that at times he wouldn't mind having an interesting girlfriend. Wally spied his cat-that-swallowed-the-canary face. "Well, lookie here. You must've had a good morning. I bet you saw Marcie, didn't you?"

"Actually, it was Nora."

"Nora! You're kidding. Are you sweet on her now?"

"Who knows…maybe. Nora is with Internal Affairs now. She insisted in helping me out with Mrs. Bowman's murder and also tracking down the elusive mastermind behind the now-jailed cops."

"How did you ever arrange for someone from IA to work with you?"

"Oh, I don't know. Possibly because I was involved with the arrests of four bad cops."

Wally didn't comment further on the subject, but he quickly said, "Hey, it's a little past eleven thirty. Are you hungry yet? I love the food at the Italian restaurant on Thirty-Second Street and Spear. Since it's a relatively cool day, lunching outside sounds good to me."

"Sure. But give me a few minutes. I need to look something up."

Even though it was July, a gentle cool breeze swathed over the cozy patio of the restaurant. They were seated by the barrier under an umbrella. "That's what I love about Colorado weather," Hawk said. "Yesterday was a scorcher at ninety-five and the rest of the week it's going to be in the upper seventies and lower eighties. It's just as the saying goes, 'If you don't like the weather, wait fifteen minutes.' Colorado weather is never boring."

The waitress appeared to take their drink orders. Hawk ordered his usual water and Wally ordered a double martini. "You know, my friend, that this close to retirement, I decided to live it up a little. A martini or two never hurt anyone. And soon I plan to have a lot more in retirement."

"That sounds terrific. So, what's good here?"

"Everything is great. I particularly like their spaghetti with sausage. You should order their lasagna."

"No, I think that may be too heavy and, besides, Nora invited me for an Italian dinner tonight."

"Wow, you guys aren't letting any grass grow under your feet. Good job, Clint."

"I guess so."

"Guess so? With someone as hot as Nora, you should be dancing all the way there tonight."

The waitress came back, brought them their drinks, and asked what they'd like to eat. Wally ordered the spaghetti and asked for an extra Italian sausage. Hawk ordered their specialty of the house salad with a side order of two meatballs. "You'll love their meatballs, good choice," Wally said chuckling, his stomach bouncing. Soon Wally focused on the Colorado Rockies. "You know," Wally insisted. "The reason they haven't won the World Series yet is that the best pitchers don't want to play in this high altitude. It ruins their stats."

"Oh, why is that, Wally?"

"It's because the baseballs fly higher and further and they have to cope with too many home runs."

"You really think so? After all, there is a good pitcher now and they've had good enough pitchers to go to the playoffs."

"I know so. A baseball player told me about it. By the way, I was thinking about Marcie. You said that Bradford thought that she might be his boss. It really makes a lot of sense. Look at it this way, the messages were in code using the names of flowers. That's really feminine. And if he thought it was someone in our unit, and as I said before with her computer skills, she's perfect for it. We need to really check it out. Again, I'll repeat, the fact that she is gone today, makes it look very suspicious."

Hawk remained silent for almost a minute. "Clint, did you hear me? I think Marcie should be thoroughly investigated. I'll help you with it."

Hawk forced a smile. "Wally, I really appreciate your offer and I'll relay it to Nora. We'll give your theory a try. Sounds feasible."

At that moment, Hawk's cell rang. "Sorry Wally, speaking of the devil, it's Nora. Let me take this since we're supposed to go search for videos this afternoon." A second later, the food was served and Wally plunged into the spaghetti, rapidly twisting the noodles around in a spoon.

"Clint," Nora said over the phone. "A lot had happened so far. Bradford is on suicide watch. Williams is singing like a canary. He insists that he knew he made a big mistake when he let Bradford talk him into joining the group. He tried to get out of it, but Bradford threatened him and his family with bodily injury or even death if he quit. Jeffries was just released from the hospital, still cussing up a storm. O'Leary wants to make a deal to talk."

"That's quite a rundown. Thanks."

"Oh, there's more," Nora went on, "Our computer techs are getting closer to cracking the word code, and in a few more days they say they'll be able to track down the source of the transmissions. They were, however, able to decipher numbers and they came up with what looks like a bank account."

Across the table, Wally took a breather from stuffing the food into his mouth. He wiped his mouth, annoyed that Hawk was taking too long. Hawk, saw what he thought was his impatience and lifted his index finger to indicate that he needed another minute. "That's interesting. Why don't you give the numbers to me? It might help with researching it from this end." He grabbed the notepad that he took from Wally's desk and carefully wrote down the numbers. He knew that Wally, a curious gossip, was listening and watching everything.

"One more thing, Clint," Nora said. "To make life easier for you since you're stiff and sore, I looked up the owners and businesses of the buildings of the cameras in the alley overlooking the dumpsters. We can hit some of them this afternoon."

"Actually, let's skip that for this afternoon. I have to do some research. I'll meet you at your house at five thirty." Wally looked up from his platter again and pointed to Hawk's salad.

"Okay. What restaurant are you at?"

"We're at an Italian restaurant—" Nora interrupted.

"What! You're eating Italian when you know that I'm having Italian for dinner?!"

"No, Nora. I ordered a salad."

"Good. I feel better now. But don't eat anything Italian. Okay, see ya."

Hawk was finally free to eat his salad and the meatballs. Wally was more than halfway through his spaghetti. His three sausages had already disappeared. "I tell you, that Nora reminds me of my first wife, Virginia. She also had a knack for getting her own way. No nonsense type of woman." *He must have heard our conversation and I didn't even have the speaker on.*

"Yeah, Wally, I understand. But don't most women have a knack for that? What happened to you and Virginia?"

"I guess we fought constantly from the time we dated. I should've known better when I asked her to marry me." Wally chuckled. Marinara sauce stuck to the corner of his mouth. "Actually, I'm not sure now who asked whom to marry. It might have been her and I just went along." *That better not happen to me,* Hawk thought of Nora.

"What about your second wife?"

"Oh, Joanna was a peach. I really loved her. Sweet, a little pushy, but not bad. But my job got in the way. She became a nervous wreck after my shoot out on West Colfax with some gangbangers. The straw that broke the camel's back came when I was thrown to the ground by an uncooperative witness. I hurt my back and hit my head really hard. She filed for divorce and eventually married an accountant. I actually miss her a lot. She had a store and I enjoyed helping her out in it. Hey, I miss her shop more than I miss her."

My last wife, Penny, just worked all the time. I never saw her. Even when she took a vacation, do you think that she wanted to take me along? No, not me. She had a group of girlfriends and they did everything together. It was a good day when we got that divorce decree."

"What kind of business was Joanna in?" Hawk asked out of curiosity, as he felt a spasm in his lower back. His neck pain was much worse than in the morning. He would give anything to go home and climb into bed.

Wally hesitated, taking the last forkful of spaghetti. I guess you could call it a gift shop. Oh, here is our bill. Is it your turn or mine?"

"It's mine. I got it." Hawk finished up his second spicy meatball and quickly forked down his salad. He slipped his credit card in the folder.

"Oooh, that was good. I really enjoyed it. Thanks for lunch. I'll get it next time."

The two men walked back to Wally's Crown Vic and he drove off in a hurry. "Why are you driving like a bat out of hell, Wally?"

"Oh, I'll slow down. I guess I have too much adrenaline flowing through my veins. Can't stop wondering why Marcie disappeared. Let's dig into her background."

CHAPTER 42

AT THE Sixth District station, as both Wally and Hawk made it back to their desks, Wally offered, "I heard from your phone conversation that you're going to be doing some research. I assume it's about Marcie. Let me help you."

"I appreciate that. But you've got your own work to do. First, I'll see what more I can find about Mrs. Bowman's killer. Actually, Wally, I'm not up to par right now. My injuries from the accident have been much worse since yesterday. I think I'll take Nancy up on her offer of some aspirin and sit here for a bit and try to relax my muscles. She also offered to help with the Bowman case. Maybe I'll play around on the internet to see what I can find on Marcus Miller."

"Okay, you got it, bud. I'll be right here if you need me."

Hawk's cell rang again. "Hi, how are you feeling? They say the second day is worse than the first."

"Hi back, Nora. I guess whoever 'they' are knows what they're talking about. I took some aspirin and I hope it'll kick in soon. But my Texas grandpappy would tell me to 'Take your lumps and don't complain like a baby.'"

"Oh, tough guy, are you? Well, anyway, I have more news. To save you from the pain of getting in and out of the car, I got the owners to send us footage from their alley videos. The tech and I analyzed it carefully. We viewed a man in black wearing a black baseball cap with the bill low over his forehead. He dumped a pair of sneakers similar to the ones we saw Miller buy. He also flung the poker you found into the dumpster. We couldn't get a good view of his face, though. The only part that stood out the best was his left ear. In the background, a car with a partial bumper, fender, and headlights was poorly seen. Our car-nut tech believes that they are off a BMW X5 SUV. I should've waited for you to look at the video feed first. With your luck, his whole face would've been visible."

Hawk ignored the comment on his luck. *She's going to jinx it.* "Was any part of the plate visible on the bumper?"

"No, unfortunately."

"Did you by chance find out what car Marcus Miller drives?"

"No, not yet. I asked one of the officers to look up all vehicles that Miller or his business owns." Nora hesitated a minute. "Wait, he actually handed me a list, including delivery vans. Wow. Coffee Aroma, LLC has a BMW X5 registered to it. That's good news. If only we had a view of his face."

"Just an ear, huh?" Nora confirmed and Hawk thought a moment. "This is bizarre, and don't laugh. I remember watching one of those TV crime shows where they said that every ear is unique. No human has an ear identical to anyone else. It's almost like fingerprints. I wonder if Chet Watkins, our CSI man, can shed any light on that. Or maybe, Janeel, the medical examiner, can as well. So, blow up the ear and get a photo of it."

"I will. Look, you try to rest. I'll give them a call and if they confirm or even not, I think we have enough to bring him in and interrogate him. After all, the shoes in the video look like the ones in the ARC video. The bumper of the car is from a BMW that his company owns, and maybe with your idea of an ear match if there is one, it will be enough to turn it over to the DA. And don't forget the motive. It's powerful. With the Bowmans gone, he inherits the entire business, including the real estate connected with it, according to what he told you. Let's go pick him up. Are you able?"

"Yes, I'm able." Hawk hated the idea that Nora felt sorry for him or didn't think that he could do the job. He would prove that he could do it, no matter how much it hurt. "Why don't you let Wally and me go pick him up? He was in on this case with me from the start. I think he'd like that."

"Okay. Good luck and don't forget dinner tonight."

"Okay, okay, Nora. I remember. I'll be there ready to chow down."

Before telling Wally of his plans, Hawk anxiously began looking up whatever information he could find on the person who could be the mysterious boss of the dirty cops. He didn't like it a bit to even believe that someone he grew to like could've done this treacherous act. He needed more proof, something that would tie that person to Bradford. He searched government documents, Facebook, Twitter, Instagram, and any other sources he could think of. He wanted to share his conclusions with Nora but decided to run it past her after dinner.

Ninety minutes later, Wally sidled up to Clint's desk stealing a glance at the screen, "Hey sport, what are you working on so diligently?" Hawk quickly switched from the internet to Word.

"Wally, I'm glad you're here. We have enough evidence on Marcus Miller to arrest him for Mrs. Bowman's murder. Do you want the honor of picking the murderer up?"

"Sure. I'm a little bored, anyway."

"Good. I'll tell Orlinski what we're doing and if he agrees, we'll be off."

Orlinski looked surprised at Hawk's conclusion. After hearing all the evidence against Miller, he agreed to the arrest.

During the drive, Hawk had a lot on his mind. Then he noticed that Wally was very quiet the few blocks that it took to drive to Miller's place of business. He appeared deep in thought, not at all his usual jovial self. "Wally, are you alright? You look a little flushed."

"Oh, it's nothing. It's hot and I have a touch of indigestion, that's all."

CHAPTER 43

MILLER'S ARREST did not go well. When he heard that they were there to take him in, his face turned crimson red, fingers clenched into fists. His chest puffed out like a gorilla's and he pulled his arm back threatening to take a swing at Hawk. Miller glared at him with burning eyes, daring him to touch him with any cuffs. *Oh man, all I need now is a fistfight with this fool.*

Wally stood behind Miller, his hands turning into fists as well. Glaring at the man, Wally raised his voice, "Look, Miller, don't be stupid. You're charged with a very serious crime, that of murder. You can get mad all you like, but you're going to be arrested. It's your choice how you want it done. We can do it the hard way where the three of us get hurt, mostly you. Or we can do it the easy way, where you come with us peacefully. This way you won't have to worry about additional serious charges, like resisting arrest and assaulting police officers. Simmer down. Take a deep breath. Put your arms behind your back."

The swearing was ferocious, but Miller grudgingly complied. Wally cuffed him and read him his rights.

Hawk's cell rang as they drove back to the station. "Hi again, Clint. Did you pick up Miller?"

"Yes. We're heading back now."

"Good. Take a picture of his ear. You were right. Both Janeel and Chet verify that ears are the new fingerprints. Send the picture to me and we'll compare it here in the lab."

Once in the interrogation room, Hawk and Wally were hopeful to get a confession. Miller remained silent. Not a word escaped him until he asked for a lawyer. Before he was taken to a jail cell, Hawk called the traffic division and asked one of the officers to come up with a good camera. When the picture was taken, Miller's anger returned, yelling that his rights were violated and he was going to sue everyone he could. The interrogation ended with a promise to Miller that it would continue tomorrow morning. Before Hawk and Wally walked out, Wally hissed at Miller, "We got you good, you bastard. You'd better 'fess up now because tomorrow will not be pleasant." He looked hard at Miller to see if the stern warning had any effect. Miller did not budge.

On the way back to their desks, Wally asked, "Hawk, are you sure you have enough evidence on him? Or is it some of your wishful thinking that since you zeroed in on him from the beginning, you needed to arrest him?"

"Don't worry, Wally. We have enough on him to put him away. And he'll probably admit to it once the DA offers a deal, if not before."

Just as they sat down at their desks, Marcie walked through the door. Hawk's heart skipped a beat when he saw her. She looked stunning in her flowery pink blouse and dark pink skirt. Her high-heeled shoes made her look tall and erect like a model, her long shiny blonde hair styled to perfection.

Everyone in the room stopped whatever they were working on and gave her a warm welcome. Marcie greeted each one individually with a hug and explained that she had come to say, "goodbye," because she was leaving Denver in a couple of weeks.

Marcie glanced at Bradford's office and saw Orlinski behind the desk. She went in and Hawk saw her say something to him, then hug him before she walked out. Hawk had to smile to himself when he saw how awkward the embrace was for Orlinski, who kept his arms open, not touching her back. Finally, making it to the room where Hawk and Wally worked, Marcie gave each of them a beaming smile, mostly directed at Hawk, though. She gave Wally a quick hug, but it was obvious to everyone that she reserved the biggest and most heartfelt embrace for Clint.

Surprised that it felt so right to be near her, Hawk's heart beat fast and furious as he returned her hug. It felt so good to be with her. *Can it really be that she is the boss of the dirty cops? How devastating if it turned out that way.* At that moment, Orlinski strode over to them in his typical nervous gait. "Hawk, I rummaged in Bradford's drawers, and at the very back of the lower one I saw a book called *Beware the Wolves.* It looked interesting so I thumbed through it and I found this three-by-five card with names of flowers and words next to each. Check it out." Orlinski gave Hawk the card and pointed to the names and words. "And on the back is some kind of code for numbers. I figure you'll know what this is about?"

Hawk couldn't believe his luck again. He quickly glanced at Wally and Marcie. Wally took a good look at the card, leaning his body toward it, as did Marcie. Marcie said, "That's interesting, a list of flowers." She said nothing else. Orlinski turned and went back to his temporary office. Hawk took the card and stuck it into the inside pocket of his dark gray suit coat intending to give it to Nora that evening. Marcie sidled closer to him and almost in a whisper, she asked, "Clint, could you get away for a few minutes? Come with me to Thump Coffee on Downing. You know, the place we went to before."

Hawk readily agreed and as they began walking out, Wally yelled out to him, "Say Clint, don't forget your dinner with Nora at her house tonight." He laughed hoarsely. "And remember what I told you. Be careful." *Now why did he do that? What a jerk!* Marcie took a quick glance at Clint and frowned.

"Shall we take your car or mine?" Marcie asked. Hawk's been down that road before and he didn't want to drive just in case, Marcie had other plans. *It can't be. I'm so paranoid now. No way she'd pull out a gun on me like Jeffries did. But just in case.*

"Marcie, let's take your car. I've been in a bad accident and I'm still not one hundred percent yet."

"I thought that you seemed rather stiff. You don't have your usual quick step about you.

Sure, I'll drive if you tell me what happened." Hawk explained as quickly as he could what happened to him, about Jeffries, O'Leary, and the others. "That's a horrible story and it confirms what I need to talk to you about. Here we are. And don't argue, I'm buying."

They sat down at the most secluded table they could find. Marcie ordered a Chai and Hawk had his usual, a small decaf with cream. "Clint, I'm leaving in a week or two. But I have this huge hole in my stomach about leaving you. I hope you feel something for me like I feel for you. I think about you all the time. I see us together." How could he explain to her that they just met, but deep down he felt something for her? When he opened his mouth to speak, Marcie raised her index finger and placed it on his lips. "No, please let me get this out. It's so hard on me. I know what I feel for you is love. And I want us to be together. Let's run away together. Let's go to some island where no one can find us and dwell in each other's embraces for the rest of our lives."

Not expecting anything like this to come out of her mouth, Hawk's eyes flashed wide. "Marcie, even though it sounds wonderful and romantic, it's impossible. First, I love my job. I've worked hard to get here. And second, I have maybe five thousand dollars in savings. How are we to survive with no money? You know the old saying, 'When poverty walks through the door, love flies out the window.'"

"Don't worry about money. I have a trust fund that pays me whatever I need. You don't need to worry about money ever again. But how can you say, now, after almost being killed twice in two days that you love your job? A life should not be defined by work. We'll go off somewhere and we'll be safe. Even if we go to California, we'd be safer than here." She paused. With an intense gaze, she continued, sniffling, "I guess, you'll never love anyone more than your job it seems and I can't compete with that." Marcie hesitated; her face changed from one of pleading to one of anger. "Or are you in love already with someone else? It's Nora, isn't it? She's a fast worker. She already has you coming over for dinner at her house, no less."

Suddenly, Marcie leaped up from her chair, tears rimmed her eyes, then spilled down her cheeks. "I can't compete with two loves, your job, and Nora. Clint, I need to leave now. I need to cool off. Find your own way back." She rushed out into the parking lot and opened her car door.

Hawk ran behind her, his back spasming. "Marcie, wait. Wait, Marcie. Let's talk. Let me explain." But she slammed the door to her Mini just as he reached it. She hastily pushed the electronic start button and rammed the transmission into reverse. Her foot hit the accelerator pedal with such force that her back tires squealed. Hawk stood in the middle of the parking lot watching her tantrum unfold. He shook his head. *Imagine living with that anger, especially on some island in the middle of nowhere.* Abruptly, Marcie stopped, opened her window and yelled out, "See you, sucker! Your job is going to kill you!"

CHAPTER 44

THE FOUR-block walk back to the Sixth District was slow and painful. His back and neck relentlessly spasmed. Hawk's mind dwelt more on Marcie's unexpected behavior than his pain. It was almost like another person with a temper took over her psyche. *She always appeared sweet, even vulnerable. Did she want me so much that my rejection would cause her such anguish? What else is she capable of?*

It was close to five and the office was nearly empty. Higgins stopped Clint on his way in and asked if he could take a quick look at a file open on Higgins' desk. "I'm stumped. It's the murder of a store owner, shot during a robbery. We're working with the Robbery unit on this. They only got away with the few dollars in the cash register, according to his wife. Based on MO of previous robberies, Harry and I think we know who the culprits are, but we can't find any evidence that we can use to convict."

"Sure, Darrell, I'll be glad to look at it. Could I do it tomorrow, though? I want to look up something first, then I have a dinner engagement."

"Oh yeah, with Nora. What a guy!"

"Boy, what a small office. Everyone knows everything."

"We also know that you're looking for the main person who led Bradford and his gang. Any leads?"

"Yeah. I'm pretty sure I know who it is. I hope I'm wrong, though."

"Well, the consensus around here is that there was no other person in charge. Bradford made all this up to take the monkey off his back. And if there was someone else, even though we like Marcie, we think she'd be the logical one if that person is in this unit."

"We'll see if my gut is correct."

Hawk spent another hour combing through the file. He came to a definite conclusion about the mysterious boss. He had a sinking feeling in his chest and hoped he was wrong. It actually pained him to suspect that person was the instigator of this band of thieves and murderers.

As he walked up the path to Nora's house, she greeted him with a wide smile and rushed to embrace him. "Ouch, not too hard."

"Oh, is my sweety too tender?" Her infectious laugh made Hawk laugh along. First, laugh he'd had all day. He really enjoyed Nora's liveliness. She had a habit of sparking his mood. "Let me have your coat. You can also take off your tie and your shoes," with a coy smile she added, "And anything else you want to as well." She laughed again.

"All right I'll do that," Hawk laughed.

"Why don't you lay down on the couch and make yourself comfy? Remember, mi casa, su casa. We're almost ready to eat. Get some rest while I'm running back and forth from the kitchen. And help yourself to the appetizers on the coffee table."

Hawk thought lying down was a splendid idea and he complied. Before him, on a glass top table with a marble base, were crackers, an assortment of cheeses, and olives. The table in the L-shaped dining room was beautifully set with fine china, silverware, gold cloth napkins, and wine and water glasses on a white tablecloth. He picked up one of the small cocktail plates from the table and helped himself. "What would you like to drink?" Nora asked, still smiling broadly. "I have wine, beer, sodas, and, of course, water. With dinner, we'll have red wine, if that's all right."

Hawk took a beer and couldn't keep his eyes off Nora as she glided smoothly from the table to the kitchen. She wore a snug light blue sleeveless dress, her sandals had numerous straps, each a different color. With her dark hair pulled back, she looked absolutely sexy. All he wanted at the moment was for her to jump on top of him.

Nora noticed him eyeing her. It pleased her. "What are you thinking about, Clint."

"You, of course. Who else?" Nora came over to the couch, leaned down, and kissed him. He returned the kiss.

"I better get back to the dinner. It's almost ready to come out of the oven." Hawk stared at her backside as she went into the kitchen.

"Come to the table, Clint."

She placed a salad in front of them. "Looks delicious," Hawk said. "I really like the pears and walnuts."

"Thanks. I hope you like the chicken scallopine also. I always keep my fingers crossed when I make it. It never seems to come out as good as my grandmother's."

"I'll love it, I'm sure."

"Are you going to tell me now who you think is the boss?"

"Let's wait until after dinner because I'll need to go through why I think who it is. But I may be wrong. On the way here, I was thinking about Darrell Higgins and what he told me."

"What, you weren't thinking about me?" Nora giggled.

"Sure, I thought about you, but I can think of other things at the same time. Maybe I have one of those multitasking minds," Hawk laughed at his silly statement.

"Oh sure, you're so talented," Nora laughed gently. "So, what did Darrell tell you?"

"He told me something that I never considered. Evidently, some people in the unit do not believe that Bradford had a boss at all. It was all a ruse. Think of it. It makes sense. He could keep his gang in line by blaming someone else for the orders he gave out. The gang members couldn't give him much grief for decisions they didn't like because they weren't his decisions but some unknown person's. And then, how better to take another share of the money coming in?"

"Wow. That would be genius. But what about all the messages back and forth between him and this boss?"

"Probably easy to do. I bet some of the messages didn't come right after the other. He could use two separate computers at different locations that he routed all over the world. Or he could have used his brother to act as a boss."

"You know, I wouldn't put it past him. But, for my money, my bet is on Marcie. There is something about that girl. I think she's as phony as a three-dollar bill. Come on, Clint. Don't keep me in suspense. Who do you suspect?"

"Alright, I'll tell you. And I think I have it right. It's—." Suddenly, the doorknob turned and the front door swung open.

"You should keep your front door locked," the steel-voiced intruder said, as the person made their way into the house, then slammed the door shut, vibrating the whole front wall.

From sudden shock, Nora dropped her fork onto the plate. "What the hell? What are you doing here?" Her voice sounded high and jumpy. "Oh my God! What's with the gun?"

CHAPTER 45

WIDE EYES, Hawk and Nora propelled themselves out of their seats, suddenly suffocated by a sense of dread as they stared at the gun pointing at them. "I know you figured out who the person behind Bradford was, Clint. I needed one more week to leave town and find a good life on an island somewhere far from here. I know you know and I bet Nora knows. I don't think you two told anyone else yet. Sorry, but both of you now need to go. He smirked and glanced at the coffee table. "I see your Sig on the coffee table. Just what I need. Too bad that you shot Nora and then yourself. At least that's what they'll think."

Wally slowly inched his way to the coffee table, his gun still pointed at the couple. Nora moved around the dining table, close to Hawk. "Stay put! Don't move! It doesn't matter to me how you die." Wally squatted, grabbed the holstered gun from the coffee table, slid it out of the holster, and pointed it at them. He returned his own Glock 19 to the holster on the side of his belt.

Out of his jacket pocket, he removed a MODX 45 noise suppressor. "You see, Clint, I studied up on your Sig 380. I even bought one and practiced attaching a silencer within a second or two, so don't try anything heroic." With the gun still pointing at them, Wally quickly attached the silencer. "Just to make sure no noisy neighbors hear anything," he said, cracking a sadistic smile, so unlike anything that Hawk or Nora ever witnessed.

"After you're dead, I'll just happen to come by and visit you folks and to my horror, find your bodies. Nobody would believe that I shot you. I hate to do it, I really liked you, Clint; unfortunately, you'll have to pay for me messing up at the restaurant."

Hawk's heart thumped. Barely able to get the words out, he asked, "What in the hell are you talking about? What mess? Have you gone totally nuts?"

"What's this about, Clint?" Nora asked, her eyes wide as the dinner plates on the table, her voice shaky. "What's going on? Don't tell me Wally is the one?"

"Tell her, Clint," his eyes were intent on their faces. "I want her to hear it from you, the great detective. Tell her of my blunder."

"Wally, be reasonable. Please put the gun down. We can talk about this civilly."

"What blunder are you talking about?" Nora said, her voice still trembling, her temples throbbing.

"I told Clint that because the code used the names of flowers, I concluded that the brains behind the corrupt cops must be Marcie. After all, flowers are associated with females, more than males. Or something to that effect. Clint, I noticed the expression on your face change, but you kept silent. You knew that you had never mentioned to me that the code involved the names of flowers. I knew you caught the blunder."

"Wally, that wasn't enough to suspect you."

"Oh yes, it was. I made another blunder when I told you the names of my wives. You asked me what business Joana was in and I blew it. I hesitated and said a gift shop. I know you must have googled it and found out she had a flower shop and I had told you that I liked working with her at the store. Then, I happened to glance at your monitor and noticed a document from the Navy before you so suspiciously switched programs. You remembered that I was in the

Navy and you must have found out that I was in communications dealing with codes and decoding. Am I right, so far?"

Breathing hard, his knees weak, Hawk said, "Yes, yes. You're right. I didn't want to believe it, Wally. I still can't believe this nightmare."

A line of sweat snaked down Wally's round face. "Tell me what else you discovered. Tell me about that notepad that you took from my desk. Nora called you with some numbers. And when you were writing the numbers down, I noticed your eyes focusing on something on the paper. What was it?"

"When I was writing the numbers down, I noticed some impressions of a few similar numbers that were imprinted from the sheet above on the paper. Evidently, when you wrote them down, with a heavy hand, they imprinted themselves on the page below, the one I used. I took a lead pencil and rubbed it across the imprint and I was very disappointed to see that they matched with the numbers that Nora gave me," Hawk explained.

"Pretty clever, all right. Where is the paper now?" Wally asked.

"I turned it over to IA yesterday," Hawk lied. In reality, it was in his coat pocket. "And what about the decoder that Orlinski handed you? Where is it?"

"It's at the same place." Hawk lied again; the decoder was in his coat pocket as well.

Recovering slightly from the shock, Nora decided that it was time to act. She cocked her head toward Hawk. "What! You moron! You have evidence like that and didn't even tell me about it? I can't believe it! I thought we were working together." She screamed. "You idiot!"

Hawk understood her diversion. "Don't call me a moron, you jerk. I didn't have a chance to do it yet. I was going to tell you over dinner. And don't yell at me like that. I didn't have time to tell you." He raised his voice as well.

Wally didn't buy it. "Shut up! I know what you're up to and it won't work. Trying to get me distracted, you fools. I'm not falling for an old trick you see in the movies." With a stark malicious expression he said, "Okay, it's time to set up the scene." He held Hawk's Sig with the attached silencer a little higher and pointed it at Nora. "Go sit in that chair there," pointing to one of the four matching chairs nearest to her.

"No, I'm not going to budge. Why should I do what you tell me to do? You're going to shoot me anyway? Go ahead, shoot."

Wally Murphy's face turned crimson. Hawk saw his hands begin to tremble, the shaky index finger wrapping tighter around the trigger. *Do something fast.* He had no choice but to take this chance to pounce on him and go for the gun. At that instant, an Amber alert blared on Nora's cell, in her purse on the table near Wally. The gunman jumped at the noise, jerking his head and gun arm slightly to the right almost at the same moment that Hawk had started for the gun. Both hands wrapped around Wally's gun hand, pushing the weapon upwards. The gun went off, the bullet struck the ceiling above the table, littering it with plaster and debris.

Nora leaped into action. With the ferocity of a tiger protecting her young, using both her legs and feet, she attacked Wally. With Taekwondo precision, she struck him in the groin. He screamed and started to lean forward. Instantly, Nora slammed him in the back of his knee. He began leaning to the side. She twisted around and kicked him in the back of the other knee. Wally tumbled backward, releasing his grip on the gun as Hawk shoved him down with his right shoulder.

Hawk helped Nora turn over Murphy, who weighed close to 250 pounds. Together they managed to bring out his arms to cuff him. They helped him up and seated him in the same chair that he wanted Nora to die in.

Nora, breathing hard and fast, called Captain Norton and asked for someone to pick up Wally Murphy. As they waited, Nora advised Wally of his Miranda rights. He didn't respond, but sat in the chair, elbows on his knees, his sad eyes fixed on his feet. Hawk and Nora glanced at each other; their faces subdued as well. Each tried desperately to shake off the fear and shock of the last three minutes. Nora collapsed into the nearest chair, still unable to control her breathing. Her heart pounded irregularity, as though with each beat, it might escape her chest. Hawk just stood over Wally; his insides felt twisted.

"Why? Why did you do this, Wally?"

Wally didn't respond for a minute. Finally, he said, "I told you about my wives. All three thought I was a loser. They all wanted something more in life than I could give them." He hesitated, sniffled, and swallowed hard. "I just wanted to prove to myself that I could do something big and shove their noses in all the money that I was able to acquire. Sure, it wasn't legal. But how many men actually become filthy rich by playing by the rules? I guess it got a little out of hand. I never intended for anyone to get killed. I was too smart for my own good. But as I said, if I had a week more, I'd be out of the country."

Wally slowly lifted his head and looked straight at Hawk with his defeated-looking eyes. "I liked you, Clint. Even though Bradford suggested many times, in his messages, that I should get rid of you. I didn't want to do it. At first, I guess I never thought that you were that much of a threat unlike Bradford, who was concerned from the very beginning. Actually, I believed that no one would discover me. A bungling old fool on his way out to pasture with a lousy pension. Of all the rotten luck!"

After pausing, he shook his head and attempted a grin, "You, a rookie detective with no more experience at solving crimes than a rookie patrolman, discovered me. You have a knack for this work. Deep down inside, I'm relieved that it was you who brought me down. And I'm more relieved that I didn't have to kill you both. I was fooling myself. I would never have been able to enjoy the millions that I had accumulated."

Murphy turned his face toward Nora. "Sorry, Nora. I'm a fool." He lowered his head again. A few moments later, he said, "Sorry, Clint. I never expected that I could want to hurt you." The three sat in silence, each with their own thoughts. Nora looked absolutely drained. Hawk felt the same.

Finally, Norton with two other IA detectives arrived. He shook his head in disgust as they led Wally to the car for booking at the main station. "Good job. I spoke to the Chief and it looks like you'll both be getting awards." He left, leaving Nora and Hawk behind.

Nora stared at the plaster dust on the table, some of it on the partially eaten salads and some floating in water glasses. "Are you still hungry?" Nora joked.

"No. Not at all. That's not what I need right now."

Nora stood up and walked to where Clint Hawk sat. "I need a hug. I need to be held."

Hawk stood and embraced her, their cheeks side by side. Not a word was said, but they remained in that position for a full minute or so. Afterward, Clint followed Nora and also fell onto the couch. Nora removed her sandals, leaned back, and extended her still trembling legs onto the coffee table. Hawk placed his feet on it as well. Sitting together, their heads leaning back and staring at the ceiling with their shoulders touching, Nora exhaled with force and said almost in a whisper, "That was so, so lucky. It was so close. I thought for sure that we were goners. I can't count all the prayers that went through my mind. I still shudder to think how many times, in just the first few days on a new job, your life was in jeopardy. Four attempts on your life! It must be some kind of a record. Good thing you're so damn lucky. You must have a terrific guardian angel, that's all I can say."

Hawk turned his head to face her. He took her hand and squeezed it. "It's all over now. We're cops and it's what we do." Nora looked at him and stroked his face. A smile began to break through her deep frown. The smile deepened into an uncontrollable laugh. "Did anyone ever tell you that you have a funny face?" Clint Hawk couldn't help laughing as well.

EPILOGUE

HAWK CAME in late for work the next day. For the first time in days, he slept like a log. He was both mentally and physically exhausted from the series of ordeals that he encountered in less than one week. Word of Murphy's arrest had already spread throughout the building. Uniformed officers stopped him on the way upstairs to his unit. They showered him with 'high fives' and congratulations. In the unit, everyone stood and shook his hand. He felt embarrassed by all the attention. He commented, "Any one of you would've done the same." Hawk firmly believed it, because, in his mind, he didn't do anything heroic, just his job. He sat down at his desk, looked at his computer, and didn't feel like opening it. He was still raw from the experience and not motivated to work. He wondered what case he would be assigned next. The closed case files still lay on his desk. It appeared that Wally, taking a hard swallow at the thought of him, didn't do anything with them.

Suddenly, Nora walked through the door, carrying a box. Every individual on the floor gave her a heartfelt round of applause. She smiled at the detectives and threw a silent kiss with her lips as she glanced at Hawk. Hawk gave her a huge smile. As people in the unit watched, she walked over to Wally's old desk and placed her cardboard box on top. She looked back at her fellow detectives and announced, "Hello everyone. I'm so pleased to let you know that I've been reassigned at my request to the Homicide unit. She smiled even more broadly when her fellow detectives applauded her once again.

The door opened, and a man, also carrying a large cardboard box, entered the room. He was tall, slim as a rail, and stooped. He wore dark brown pants, a light-green striped coat, a white shirt, and a navy blue and gray bow tie. His graying black hair was ruffled and Hawk immediately noticed his suspenders that matched his bow tie. "Excuse me," the man said. I've been assigned to the Homicide unit. Who is in charge, please?" As he finished speaking, he lowered his head and his red-rimmed glasses slipped down his long-pointed nose. Hawk felt like bursting out laughing at the comical figure. He also spotted Nancy place her hand over her mouth to suppress a giggle.

Orlinski strode out of his office. "People, I'd like you to meet Mortimer Holiday. He recently transferred from the Tampa Police Department and he'll replace Murphy." Orlinski escorted him to Nora's old desk. At that moment Hawk was pleased to realize that Nora would now be his partner. Orlinski then turned and faced the group. "First of all," he said. "Your new superior, Lieutenant Earnest Perez will be here tomorrow. He's transferring in from the District 3, Homicide unit. But right now, Hawk and Ricci, I want you to see about a woman found dead in her garage in the Cheesman Park area."

The Murdered Wife

The author invites you to take a SNEAK PEAK of part of the first chapter of the second book of the Clint Hawk and Nora Ricci murder mystery series:

CHAPTER 1

Present day, Denver, Colorado.

AMANDA ELLIS had an awfully bad day. First, it was with her husband, Steven, then it escalated to severe conflicts with her employers. The problems piled on early. It was evident to her that her husband was having yet another affair. Because of his roving eye for women, their three-year marriage was once again in jeopardy. Forgiving him on at least two previous occasions, she again knew he was involved in another fling. This time with a sexy assistant in the office, Tina Dionisio. She noticed on a few occasions how the two flirted with each other, just like two high school kids. And she realized that Tina would love to take her place as Steven's wife.

He came home at 11:30 the night before from a supposed urgent business meeting. She smelled the faint odor of perfume on his clothes. She had noticed that same fragrance for the past two weeks as he sheepishly wandered home at all hours of the night. The perfume reminded her of a particular brand that she sampled numerous times at Nordstrom—that of Versace Yellow Diamond, the same brand that Tina wore at an office party and then at a BBQ in their backyard.

Amanda confronted Steven with her suspicion of the affair with Tina. He did not deny it, instead, he belligerently told her to, "Mind your own business, you bitch." With that said, he stormed off and bedded for the night in the guest room. She cried, tossed, and turned all night long. The fight that next morning turned out to be a doozy of a shouting match. At first, he denied having an affair, but then he admitted it. "Just live with it. That's the way I am, and you can't change me since I can't change you, it seems."

"It's with Tina, isn't it?" His cheeks puffed out and his face turned red. "Well, isn't it?" He remained silent for a few minutes. He took a deep breath and calmed himself. Finally, he admitted it and apologized, but seemed to lack sincerity. "You bastard, you no good SOB. I've had it with you. I'm finally filing for divorce," she screamed in rage, "I'm going to ruin you. I'll take everything you got, you bastard. You won't have a pot to pee in after I'm through with you." Steven's eyes blazed with anger as he took two steps toward her. His fingers were balled into a fist. He raised his arm as if to strike her, but then, quickly thinking better of it, he lowered his fist.

For a minute, he stared at Amanda with his blazing blue eyes, then, turned and stomped out of the kitchen. The spring door to the backyard slammed shut. He strode to the detached garages in the back, raised the garage door and out of anger struck the hood of the Lexus LX SUV with his fist, hurting his hand and leaving a slight dent on his car. The tires squealed as he hit the accelerator pedal, almost striking the curb on the other side of the street. Luckily, there were no other cars or pedestrians walking to the adjacent park at the time.

Later as Amanda walked to the garage, she saw the open garage door left unattended by Steven. She shut it and then opened the door to her Mercedes S-Class convertible. Still trembling from the fight, she headed for work in the Cherry Creek area of Denver. Deeply regretting what came out of her mouth when she yelled at her husband, she knew she made a huge mistake. That was the first time she ever threatened him with a divorce. She knew Steven's faults, bit the bullet, and lived with them. She did not want a divorce. As an investment banker Steven averaged a million dollars a year in income and she, herself, did not do too badly as an architect in a large international construction firm with a salary of a quarter of a million. They lived a good lifestyle, traveled extensively, stayed at the best hotels, ate at the most prestigious restaurants, had three homes, and belonged to two country clubs. She really did not want to give all of that up. She would have to make it all right again with her husband when she got home. *If, of course, he'll be there.* She thought. *I'll have to make it work.* Not waiting for later, she touched his name on the phone, but after several rings, it went to voicemail.

With a massive pit in her stomach, Amanda exited the elevator on the ninth floor and walked into the architectural department of Jonas, Wentworth and Briggs International Contractors, better known as JWB Contractors. Too riled up to work, she dragged herself to her cubicle, sat down at her desk, and stuffed her brown Gucci leather bag in the desk drawer. Leaning with her elbows on the highly polished wooden desk, she cupped her face in her hands. She sat there like that for at least five minutes before she decided that she needed to work. The deadline for her part of the project in Dubai was only a few days away.

Standing up to her drafting table, she noticed a sheet of new material requirements for her project. Amanda felt the veins in her temples throb as she reviewed the new specifications. *Oh my God!* She thought. *They want me to replace the material in the project. Less rebar, inferior grade steel panels and they'll probably mix more sand than cement in the mortar. That's just blatant fraud. I suspected they did this for years, but now I'm involved with it and I'm the one that'll have to sign off on it.* She searched her desk looking for the original specs she was given, but they were no longer there. *They took them off my desk! Wow! I must do something, or I'll be in trouble when the hot weather and winds in Dubai deteriorate the breezeway affecting the floors above.* She understood immediately that with just that adjustment to the project of lesser and inferior materials, the company would make a bigger profit. *And that's just my project, what about the rest of the building?* At that moment she was determined that she had to protect herself and somehow let the Dubai people know about it. *I never thought I'd ever become a whistle-blower.*

The file room was on the eighth floor. Amanda scampered there using the stairs, hoping to find a copy of the original plans and specifications of the project. Being an employee of five years, they trusted her enough with the key. She entered the large room stacked with five-drawer filing cabinets along the walls and in the center, turned on the humming fluorescent lights, and shut the door behind her. Fortunately, the projects were well-indexed. Finding the thick file, she quickly gazed through it looking for her assignment within the numerous plans and papers. She noticed the cost estimate of the entire project was more than two billion dollars and running her index finger down to the breezeway that she worked on, it showed a figure of three and a quarter million. She whistled to herself out of surprise at what they were charging. At the end of the quote, she saw the signatures of the developers executing the agreement. She quickly pulled out her iPhone and shot a photo of the names. Then she went back and took another photo of the cost of her project. Thumbing further, she found the specifications that she originally received for the breezeway, quickly took a photo, and placed her phone into the back pocket of her tan pants.

Suddenly, the door opened. A security guard entered...